Forgiving
August

Dudley J. Delffs

P.O. Box 35007, Colorado Springs, CO 80935

Library of Congress Catalog Card Number:
    93-11938
ISBN 08910-97473

Cover illustration: Mary GrandPré

The stories and characters in this book are fictitious. Any
resemblance to people living or dead is coincidental.

Delffs, Dudley J.
    Forgiving August / Dudley J. Delffs.
        p.   cm.
    ISBN 0-89109-747-3
    1. Fathers and sons—Tennessee—Fiction. 2. Young
men—Tennessee—Fiction. 3. Family—Tennessee—
Fiction. I. Title.
PS3554.E4423F67   1993
813′.54—dc20   93-11938
                                                          CIP

Printed in the United States of America

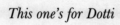

This one's for Dotti

Acknowledgments

I would like to thank Lisa Reagan for her connections, in one sense the way this began. I want to thank Karen Lee-Thorp for her input and support, along with Nancy Burke and all the fine staff at Piñon Press.

My thanks to Traci Mullins, not only for great editing, but for support and encouragement in believing in this story as much as I do. This manuscript would not be the way it is now without the editing suggestions and honest feedback provided by Gloria Chisholm. Thanks, Gloria.

Thanks to all my dear friends and family in Tennessee and Colorado for providing such a rich relational community. Also I'm indebted to Dr. Larry Crabb and Dr. Dan Allender and their colleagues for teaching me a thing or two about forgiveness.

Finally, my wife, Dotti, sustained me with gifts of time, sensitivity, and deep encouragement, which enabled me to say what I had to say. My thanks and love to her go beyond all the Augusts in both our lives.

-1-

I was eighteen years old before I ever defied my father. Sure, I'd defied him silently, the way most children do—occasional white lies, broken curfews, the forbidden first beer. But it wasn't until the summer after I graduated from high school, when my will shifted, changed focal points, that I came to defy both him and my mother in ways that could not help but change us all.

Looking back, it seems as momentous now as it did then, because once I made my first adult-feeling decision, to act on this spirit of defiance, the rest of the summer collapsed upon itself, causing a domino chain of events that still affects me. That summer is forever crystallized in my memory. One moment rock candy, the next a shard of glass. If it sounds extreme, it was—one of the few times in my life when change seemed as tangible as a blade, whittling away at all I had known and expected.

When I think of it now, it seems remarkable that it fit so well into the confines of one summer. Only my life goes on and the consequences continue to carve deep places inside all of us, my father, my mother, and me.

During the summer after I graduated from Crescent County High School, each of us tried to reinvent ourselves, tried to freeze the inevitable. My mother, with her sad, passive beauty and longing for control, let go and became unpredictable. She cut her hair, returned to Weight Watchers, and began listening to jazz. She learned things she didn't want to know about her husband and son, and ultimately about herself as well. My father, the unbelievable used car salesman, on the other hand, burned into supernova, becoming more of who he'd been all along.

And me, well, I came to terms with myself, with what it meant to fight for who I wanted to be, to break free from the desperate embrace of my parents' control. Once I decided to defy my father, I discovered a new, independent perception of the only world I'd known until that time. And with my new adult perception of my family, I discovered a pattern, a visual illusion betraying itself. I had discarded the pattern as cliché—alcoholic father, neurotic mother, sensitive son—but I realized that summer that you can't reduce life to that, especially when it's your own.

My senior English teacher, Mrs. Hartsel, said that clichés are like pockets: At one time they served a purpose, but now they're so chock-full of holes that whatever you put in them just slips right through. Change slides down to your ankles, maybe into your shoe. But that summer the pocket was sewn up, at least for a while. It gave me a chance to count my change, to jingle-jangle the music of my upbringing one last time.

———

The music I remember first is the double ring of the service bell at Ray's Shell Station downtown—if there is such a thing in so small a place as Clearfield. I like the smell of gasoline, and Ray's was a magic place for me. I grew up there, waiting in the cab of Daddy's pickup while he pumped in the hi-test, fumes rising in the heat, a smell like fire, burned sugar maple, sweet and acrid. It's one of my eternal memories. Ray would bring out a six-ounce Coke—with peanuts in it—for me, or maybe bubble gum. Standing there on June 3 of my eighteenth year, I half-expected Ray to emerge, treat in hand.

Ray was probably about sixty, but he'd looked perpetually tired and suntanned as long as I could remember. He had deep-set eyes and yellowed false teeth, which clicked when he talked. I stood there like a photographer, taking it all in, Ray in his gunmetal-colored work shirt, the graveyard of tires visible over his shoulder, the smell of gas, the hum of the pump.

"Hey, Bounty! Wake up!" Ray had yelled, and I thought he would lose his teeth.

My daydream cost me, as my favorite octane spewed out the full tank, dribbling down the gray fender of the big Mercury, spotting my khakis and loafers.

"Watcha thinkin' on so hard that you'd forget how to pump gas? And what's with ya Sunday best?" He offered the chamois rag from his hip pocket.

"How you been, Ray? Guess I was daydreamin'." I had decided to rehearse the confidence I would need to tell my father about the first link of my defiance chain. "I'm on my way to the bank. Got an interview for a summer job. Figure I better look like a banker."

"No more grease monkeyin' at the car lot, huh?" He paused and spit over his shoulder, toward the mound of tires. "Smart as you is, Bount, they'd be fools not to hire ya. Remember ol' Ray when you givin' out loans. Here's the key."

He handed me the men's room key baited on the end of a bent clothes hanger as I handed the chamois back.

"Thanks, Ray, I won't forget you. . . ."

"Good thing, to better yourself. Ol' Jimbo can't hold you down in that car lot the rest of your life, you a high school graduate and all. Go after what you want." He spit again. "Nobody else gonna do it for ya." Ray smiled big and his gums popped.

I decided I still liked the smell of gas as I turned the corner and unlocked the paint-peeling door reading ME. I had to wonder, though, about the way my luck ran. I could hear Judy Tate's voice from Personnel: "I'm sorry, Mr. McGraw, we don't hire boys who wear gasoline as aftershave." I didn't have time to go home and change; I was already late. I squirted some pink soap-o-matic and washed my face and hands as best I could. The stains on my pants grew bigger, focused right around my crotch, of course. Clark Heraldson, vice-president of Crescent County National Bank, would have to hire me, gas smell and all.

I paid Ray and swung the big Merc back on the highway, cruised past the Qwik-n-Grab and the city limits sign. My father's business, J & R Motors, sits about three miles outside of Clearfield, halfway between it and Crescent, the county seat, dominating its stretch of highway and farmers' fields. You drive along with nothing but acres of tobacco and corn, then suddenly rows of used, one-owner Ford sedans and Chevy pickups pop up, like metallic crops from some alien world. It looks and feels so secluded that I'm always amazed when people stop to window-sticker shop or go for a test drive. It was a place, I realized pulling into the lot, that confined me.

I'd wanted to quit for some time, had grown tired of summer after summer of oil changes and wax jobs, the tedium of starting cars that were never driven. So that spring I tried to dismiss my restlessness as the usual wanderlust, but it wouldn't leave me. Instead it gathered momentum with each graduation present I received, with the Baccalaureate speech and prayer in the gym from Pastor Powell (our first black speaker at such an event). By the time graduation itself arrived, I wanted to rush across the stage, grab my diploma, gather my Cross pen sets and inspirational books, and go as far as the hundred dollar bill from my Aunt Rebecca and Uncle Lake would take me.

But it wasn't until I woke up the morning after graduation and headed out to the car lot that it peaked, adrenaline coursing like a geyser. "You could be here the rest of your life," flashed through the sky of my mind. *The rest of my life.* There would no longer be the usual fall reprieve thanks to school. If I was going to make a run for my future, a place far away from small town

Tennessee, a future populated with exotic peoples and sights I'd only read about, then quitting couldn't be postponed.

It was in this frame of mind that I dropped off the J & R Motors' bank deposit at Crescent County National that day. And that's where I found the job application, on the little oak desk with the calendar and blank deposit slips. A blank form, as blank as my future, only one left, stared up at me, and I took it as the first course of action in my new campaign. A job away from the car lot would be the first dent in my father's hold on my future. It wasn't that I wanted to be a banker, as much as I no longer wanted to be the son of a used car salesman.

But in that moment, checking my watch and wishing I'd told my father this morning, I could be nothing else. At breakfast he was already in a lousy mood about a trade-in deal that fell through the day before; I knew better than to compound his disposition. So, as far as Daddy knew, I would be there for the rest of the afternoon, changing the oil on some old lady's Buick LeSabre. I would simply tell him now and get it over with. Getting out of the car I saw the big oil spots on the pavement that always reminded me of a black snowman and realized my father's Jeep was missing.

⟨⟨⟨⟩⟩⟩

Ricky, the "R" of J & R Motors, a paint-and-body man who listened to country music and spit sunflower seeds, came out to greet me.

"Get them duds mighty dirty if you're gonna do that oil job," he said.

"Where's Daddy?" I asked. My palms felt sweaty though it was only leftover gasoline.

"Pikeville Parts Salvage. Need a front bumper for that ol' GMC I'm workin' on. What're you dressed up for? Somethin' wrong?"

If I told Ricky, he'd be sure to tell my father before I could. Daddy would then have ample time to build his case, to think of dozens of reasons he needed me down at the car lot. I shrugged my shoulders. "Nothin's wrong. Just need to talk to him's all."

Then again, if I told Ricky, maybe he'd be on my side, could help convince my dad that I wasn't needed at the company, that he and Jody, the other gofer, could handle it. After all, most summers were slow.

"Rick, do you think Daddy'd mind if I didn't work here this summer?"

"What d'ya mean?" Ricky leaned back into the shadow of the office building, a former service station, and folded his arms across his chest. "You're all dressed up 'cause you got another job, don't you?"

"What if I have? Summer's always slow. It's time I got a real job, started thinkin' about my future, you know?" Maybe it was a mistake to think he'd help.

"Not sure I do, Bounty. I know your dad sure as hell won't understand. You haven't told him?"

"No, I haven't got the job yet. On my way to the interview now. When he comes back, cover for me till I can tell him tonight at supper."

"I don't know. . . . He's gonna go ballistic when he finds out. What if he don't let you quit? Maybe you should talk to him first." Rick studied me as if I were a traitor.

"He'd just say no. I gotta get the job, then there'll be nothin' he can do. Just cover for me, Rick." I tugged at my collar. I didn't feel like discussing this with Ricky anymore. It was too hot.

"I'll do what I can. But he's gonna be ticked, Bounty. You know how he is when things don't go his way."

"Yeah, I do," I said, getting back in the Mercury. "If anybody knows, I do."

Coming into Crescent, only two more miles—a total of five from Clearfield—I noticed my mom's Cutlass parked in the lot next to Imperial Insurance Agency, where she worked. She'd have to be convinced, but she'd want me to keep the job if I got it. Then she could persuade my father that this was an important opportunity for me, something she seemed to do with more and more frequency.

As I sped down the Boulevard, newly changed from Crescent Boulevard to Patsy Cline Boulevard because she once lived there for a few months in the fifties, I realized that Crescent was changing before my eyes. Like my own discontent, it was no longer satisfied to model small town charm with a courthouse square and Dairy Queen, but had become "updated"—one of the mayor's words—to attract industry and interstate tourists from Nashville (over an hour away). Crescent now boasted a Hardee's, Pizza Hut, Shoney's, McDonald's, with rumor of a Taco Bell by summer's end. I wondered if Terry's Steak and Shake would be able to survive. Real estate was still going up, an aftereffect of the new Saturn plant to the north in Spring Hill.

The most telling, and most disturbing, change was the renovation of the courthouse. Dating from the late 1790s, with red brick colonial features, it was a state landmark. When a new elevator had to be installed for handicapped accessibility—a good cause in itself—the courthouse added a mirrored facade at its west end to enclose the new elevator for its three stories. The mayor and county commissioner fed lines like "A blend of past and future" to the local paper. The statue of Wilfred T. Haynes, the judge who withdrew Crescent County from Tennessee and tried to join Alabama so we could enter the War Between the States sooner, was moved to the west end to accentuate the "blend." Daddy said Wilfred T. was liable to come to life and secede again unless that monstrosity was removed. As much as I shared his opinion, I liked the sharp clash for the progressive hope it offered me.

As I pulled into a metered space in front of Moon's Discount Store, I checked my neat rep tie, my soon-to-be-banker's tie. Inside the antebellum bank building, I adjusted to the cool, carpeted lushness. I caught my reflection in a beveled glass column and checked my features for hints of the nervous fear that clawed inside. I scowled at the baby face looking back. I'd been thinking about growing a moustache my entire senior year, but the one time I tried—over Christmas—my parents shamed me into shaving after a few days of clumpy fuzz. Maybe by the end of the summer.

"Mr. McGraw? Bounty?" Judy Tate's voice sounded a shrill alarm. I must've been daydreaming again.

"Yes, ma'am?" I tried to sound confident.

"Mr. Heraldson will be with you in just a few moments. You can wait in his office. Follow me."

I followed her deeper into the recesses of the cool darkness, down the hall. His door was open; his office well-lit. Walnut panels, forest-green drapes, English hunting prints, a couple of softball trophies, photos of wife and kids. I sat back in the tan wingback usually reserved for the big money men of small town Tennessee. Clark Heraldson was one of those picturesque local boys who had done well for himself. Good athlete, good grades, scholarship to UT, married the local beauty queen (she now ran her own salon, Beauty Transformers). I decided his office reflected his beautiful life too well and I envied his good taste. I wanted to know what he was really like.

Just then he bounded in like a golden retriever, all blond with teeth showing, firm handshake. Sit, Clark, sit. Good boy. He was still larger than life, though, and I admired the ease with which he reviewed my application, asked about school, my parents.

"Let's see, you've worked at your father's car lot for the past two summers. Any reason for wantin' a change this summer?" He folded his arms on his desk. I immediately resented him for asking because it triggered a hidden twinge of guilt for my leaving my father in the lurch. Unknowingly, my dad had still found a way to sabotage my interview.

"Uh, no, sir. I just thought a change would be nice. Good chance to get some business experience." My voice was going to shake if I wasn't careful.

"I see. Well, your GPA is impressive, top 10 percent. Full scholarship to Crescent Community College. Is that where you'll be attendin' this fall?" he patronized.

"Either there or UT, Knoxville. I haven't decided yet."

"Oh, yes, I remember now. You've applied for a student loan with us. Heading for ol' Rocky Top, the University of Tennessee. That's my alma mater, you know." He leaned back and braced his hands behind his head, swiveled his chair.

"Yes, sir, I remember what a great lineman you were for the Volunteers."

"Flattery will get you everywhere, son." He grinned this goofy grin, a row of back teeth showing through the side of his broad mouth. "Well, I hope the loan and everything works out for you to go to UT. Big difference between it and our little community college here. Big difference." He paused and then looked into my eyes with a penetration that made me uncomfortable. I could tell he wasn't going to make this easy. But his next question caught me off guard.

"You datin' anybody? We got some real nice skirts workin' here at the bank. Young fella like you's probably runnin' wild with testosterone." He leaned forward and punched every syllable of his last word, like he'd never pronounced it before. It struck me funny that he seemed so interested in my personal life.

"No, sir, no one regular. I go out with friends, just hang out." I smiled nervously.

He jumped back in his chair, suddenly back on track: "Tell me why you think you'd make a good teller, Bounty. We don't have that many young men apply for this position, you know."

I wasn't sure what to say and before I knew it, I was rambling about dependability, honesty, and courtesy like a boy scout. I think I was on to trustworthy when he interrupted.

"—You've got the job. It'll be good to have you with us, Bounty. Even though you'll be at our Clearfield branch," he said it like they had forty branches instead of four, "I look forward to workin' with you."

It seemed too easy, all my future freedom summed up in his handful of words. I caught a whiff of gasoline and couldn't decide whether to mention it or not, but realized it didn't matter since I had the job. We got up to shake hands and I noticed a ketchup stain on Clark Heraldson's dapper paisley tie. I guess we had something in common.

"Oh, and Bounty, I just remembered, please ask your father to call me ASAP." He paused, smiling all those white teeth. "We have some business to discuss."

"Sure thing, Mr. Heraldson."

My father does a lot of business at the bank, but we weren't exactly rich. Usually he's cosigning a banknote for someone who's bought a car from him. Our financial reputation is probably solid enough, but the fact that my father drinks now and then is just as well known. Now I'd have to tell my father about my new job before Heraldson did. I felt curiously afraid.

"Call me Clark, Bounty." He led me down the hall to the lobby. "You know Mrs. Sherman at our Clearfield branch. She's expectin' you eight o'clock Monday morning. If you have time, stop by today and reacquaint yourself. Judy here will take care of all your paperwork. Glad to have you aboard."

In the coolness of the lobby, I suddenly felt feverish. As he shook my hand for the third and final time, I didn't want to let go. There was something comforting and secure about this celebrity banker's implacable life. He looked into my eyes again with that sparkling blue intensity before carefully pulling his hand away.

"Hope to see you soon, Bounty. Let me know if there's anything I can do for you." He turned and disappeared down the hall.

Adopt me? Love me? Take me golfing at the country club? I wanted something from Clark Heraldson, but I wasn't sure what.

Judy Tate had me fill out some forms—a W-2, an emergency notification card, a fingerprint file (in case I embezzled, an exciting thought), and signature cards for my teller volume reports. I wasn't sure what I expected from this job, but it definitely would shape the rest of the summer.

I debated on stopping at my mother's work and telling her the good news, but decided to wait until she got home. Although

I'd thought she'd be glad for me, now that I actually had the job, I wasn't sure.

I stopped at the Clearfield branch on my way home. Mrs. Sherman was like my grandmother, she'd been there so long, so I wasn't worried about her. She introduced me to the other tellers, Sarah Anne Shelton, I knew her from the drive-thru, BeBe Devereaux, a girl from my high school—she was a year ahead of me—and the new branch manager, Douglas Rosenstein, who didn't look much older than me, recently graduated from Southwestern in Memphis, with the bank six months. I snagged a lemon Safe-T pop from the basket on Mrs. Sherman's desk on my way out.

At the intersection of Maine and Highway 27 I hesitated after the light turned, tempted to head back to the car lot and get it over with. But my mood was too light and too precarious to be snatched away so soon. I'd wait till after supper, when he'd be full and mellow, sleepy and agreeable, and hope he'd be too tired to raise his voice. So I headed home.

Our house is on Hamblen Drive, a dead end off Old Franklin Highway. My parents own twenty-four acres, stretching from Clearfield Creek up to the railroad tracks. A ramshackle estate, like my parents' marriage—a merging of extremes, it's the last house on the left facing the last barn on the right, with the two-car garage parked next to it. At its worst—say when the car lot overflowed and Daddy used our yard as adjunct—you couldn't tell where the house ended and the barn and garage began. The house was the one of old mountain stone and pine shingles, behind the huge beech and ginkgo trees, with the wooden sign (from Gatlinburg) above the front porch eaves reading, "The McGraws" and below it "Jimmy, Eileen, Bounty."

Across the street the barn serves as centerpiece to a part-time eyesore, part-time artful arrangement of used tires, tractor engines, three wagon wheels, a cast iron cauldron (I used it for our high school production of *Macbeth*), barrels, faded picket fence posts, Sun-drop bottles, PBR cans, an oak desk, and half—the front half—of a '64 Ford Fairlane. All this didn't bother our nearest neighbors, the Allisons, nearly as much as it bothered my mother. For all of her fastidiousness inside the house, the outside was Daddy's domain; she made no long-term alterations despite her best efforts. Her attempts always backfired— one of Daddy's ways of teaching her a lesson—and the conglomeration multiplied. The faded red Fairlane half was deposited shortly after Mom, with my help, had moved the wagon wheels and oak desk to the back shed. When it came time to store winter hay, they returned to the front to comfort the severed old Ford.

From the house and barns the land sloped down to the creek, and that June reminded me of pictures I'd seen of the Napa Valley, all green-carpeted lushness, wisteria, vineyards. We didn't have grapes, but since Daddy hadn't had it bush-hogged yet, it looked as free and wild as I wanted to be. I briefly considered setting up my four-man tent down there and living Walden-like off the land. Maybe if Daddy kicked me out for quitting at the car lot I'd end up doing just that.

But as I wandered inside and threw my tie around my bedpost, I still felt a peculiar kind of loyalty to my room. It's the kind of affectionate loyalty you have for brand names or old girlfriends, or tacky souvenirs you can't bear to put in yard sales, a tenderness turning to embarrassment because you've outgrown each other but feel too guilty to part.

My bedroom reflects the exterior of the house more than any other room. Since I turned twelve my mother had not been allowed to clean it. So it became a museum of my adolescence: regional and state science fair trophies, 4-H ribbons in red, blue, yellow-gold, the U2 *War* poster, Grace Kelly and Marilyn Monroe, an Atlanta Braves pennant, an autographed Dale Murphy poster, a UT football schedule from eight years back, an academic achievement trophy, the Rotary Club scholarship plaque, Elvis from *Jailhouse Rock*, and a collage of ticket stubs from every event I'd attended. The furniture, dark, heavy walnut, belonged to my father's grandfather, who supposedly bought it in Ireland.

The incongruity of elements still pleased me, like the arrangement in front of the barn, but I was uncomfortable that my room no longer reflected who I felt like, the new me who was making decisions and taking risks. I was anxious to shed my adolescence and move on to being a man, make my new adult glasses permanent lenses.

"Bounty?" my mother yelled cheerfully from the living room. "You're home early." She stepped out of her Aigner pumps. "Everythin' okay at the lot? Is your father's mood any better?" She headed into the long great-room encompassing kitchen and dining room. I came out of my room and followed her through the kitchen.

"Went fine," I lied. I needed a moment to decide my strategy. The sound of her banging pots and digging through the refrigerator filled the empty space. With my mother the direct approach usually worked best, my honesty cutting through what she perceived as the complexity of her own life.

"I got a job today. Workin' down at the bank, in town." My understatements unnerved her since she was used to my father's exaggerated proclamations.

"You did what?" She turned with a frying pan in her hand and I almost laughed as she held it in the air. "A job? Doin' what? You'll help your father at the car lot like you always do in summer." She placed the skillet on the front eye of the stove.

"I decided I'd rather not work for Daddy, if I don't have to. Y'all just assumed I'd work down at the lot again this summer. Nobody asked me. Besides, I'll make more money at the bank—they pay minimum wage. I'm gonna be a bank teller at our branch in town."

"Well, Bounty, I don't know what to say. You're serious. Who hired you? How'd you find the job?" She doled out a splash of grease into the hot iron.

"Clark Heraldson hired me. I found the application last week when I went in to make the business deposit. I'd been thinkin' about quittin' at the car lot for a while. Since I got this job, I figure it must be the right time. Heraldson knows Daddy anyway. Oh yeah, he wants Daddy to call him ASAP. Be sure to tell him in case I forget," I said, snagging a Coke from the fridge.

"You know what it's about?" she asked.

"Nope, some business he has with Daddy."

"Probably some note comin' due down at the lot. I'm gonna change my clothes. How's pork chops sound?" She disappeared into their bedroom, behind my own.

"Fine. What else we havin'?" I played along, thinking she sounded anxious to change the subject while she sifted through the implications of my new job.

She reentered the room in a cotton house dress with gingham flowers planted on the shoulders.

"We're having peas like you like and potatoes and biscuits. . . . You know your father isn't gonna like this. You should have at least asked him before you went out and got a new job."

"Why? So he could keep me down at the car lot for more slave labor? You know he'd say no. I'm tired of him runnin' my life. I'm out of school now."

"He'll never let you attend college if you sneak around and do things behind his back."

"Who's sneakin'? I'll tell him soon as he gets home. I thought you'd be glad for me."

Even as I spoke, her word *college* produced an automatic reflex: an instant replay of the previous months' discussions of my future options, colleges and trade schools, real estate courses, going into business with my father. My mom said I was too smart not to go to college and my father said I was too smart to need to go. He always told me that I had book sense but no common sense.

I'd earned an academic scholarship to our community college, which my daddy conceded was more than good enough for me; after all, I'd be the first in our family to go to college. But my mom had encouraged me to apply to our state university, over three hours away. She'd brought home the paperwork and helped me fill it out when my father was out of the house. I'd been accepted. The only problem now was the money. My mother checked into student loans and helped me apply for that as well. She said that if the loan went through, then it was meant to be, and we'd worry about telling my father then. If not, then I'd have to start out at Crescent County Community College, home of the Cougars.

But my new restlessness viewed college as an opportunity, a Pandora's box of potential freedoms waiting to be opened. A tense knot formed in my stomach and tied itself tighter and tighter as my mother's voice replayed itself inside my head: "He'll never let you attend college. . . ."

I leaned against the counter next to her. She looked up at me, and I wondered if I had grown in the week since we'd stood side by side for graduation pictures, me all capped and gowned, or if she had shrunk. Her makeup looked weary, unable to hide her forty-seven years. Most people described my mother as "younger than she looks," "attractive," with "gorgeous hair," but hers was a fragile beauty, sustained by an intense regimen of creams and lotions, cosmetics and conditioners.

She really has rather plain features, deep-set blue eyes, dimples. A heavyset woman, thick for her 5'4" frame, distinguished mostly by her hair, shoulder-length auburn, copper, thick—it's why Daddy married her, she claimed. Whenever they argued, she threatened to cut it, but always compromised with just a trim. I've grown up seeing it as a beautiful reminder of my father's possession, like her wedding ring.

She took out another skillet and the late afternoon sun blinked in through the kitchen window above the sink.

My father wasn't home by the time supper was ready so my mother called him. He told her that he had a man coming late to look at a car, for us to eat without him. After two pork chops I retired to the front porch swing with my iced tea glass. My mother turned on the radio—eternally fixed at WKUZ, "your Kountry Kuz"—while she did the dishes. At that particular moment, full of pork chops and gravy, on the chain-creaking, slow-rocking porch swing, with the honeysuckle thick as musk, and the green fans of ginkgoes sweeping me away, I could not imagine ever leaving home. For all the pain I can remember, and all the more I can't, growing up was redeemed by such moments.

I watched the blue gauze dusk settle over our hill and felt my body radiate loneliness. I had theories about only children remaining lonelier all their lives than most people. "Loneliness builds character," my mother had said when I was growing up, whining about lack of playmates. I hated her for it then, like somehow it was good for me, a vitamin for the psyche, but now I realize she said it for herself. If her character had not become a skyscraper, then what did she live for?

Uncannily, she opened the screen door on cue. I stopped the swing and she boarded carefully, as if it were a ferris wheel. The chains creaked again.

"Good supper, Ma."

"Thank you. Stick around and I'll feed you again. Whatcha thinkin' about out here?" She wiped her hands on the dishtowel from her pocket.

"Nothin'. . . . what I'm gonna tell Daddy, I guess." I swirled my iced tea, tracing my glass' sweat ring on the porch rail. Each water ring overlapped another until it looked like a pattern of some exotic flower pressed in wood.

"It won't be as bad as you think. He may even be glad for you. I just hope you haven't left him short for now," she said soothingly.

Chinese linking rings, each one bound to the other, infinitely bound until the magician separates them with graceful ease. I rubbed the water rings with my finger as they all ran together, a cold pool.

"I'm tired of the car lot, Mom. I'm afraid if I don't quit now, I'll be there the rest of my life. I need to decide what I'm gonna do with my life—you know? I don't think I can stay here much longer. . . ." I tipped the last of the melted ice from the tumbler.

She smiled and patted my hand. "I didn't realize you were so miserable," she said. "He hasn't drunk in a long time, you know."

"How long's it been?" I tried to sound casual. As vague as I was, she knew my unspoken question, *How long will it last?* There's a hidden language in families like mine; words themselves become camouflaged vehicles for the unspoken tone, gesture, expression.

"He hasn't drunk in over a year. It could be for good this time. I think he's really changed. This time may really be different."

I frowned and quickly tried to disguise it. She pulled her hand back from mine as if she could feel the heat of my anger.

"I know you must hate him, Bounty, but he is your father. He loves you. God, if he loves anybody it's you," she pleaded defensively.

"I don't hate him, Momma," I said firmly. And if I was honest, at that moment, I surprised myself by hating her.

"This summer will be different," she said, returning to her upbeat incantation. *Say it enough, make it so,* I thought. She rose from the swing and picked up my glass from the rail.

"I'm not through with that."

"You gonna eat the glass?" she laughed. "Want some more?"

I nodded. She mock-curtsied, tea glass in hand, and retreated through the screen door.

It was almost dark by then, the stars shaking themselves out as thick and bright as the lightning bugs. I sighed, and for a moment almost fooled myself into believing that I could return to my aloneness. But the sigh released the tension in my stomach, realized the heartburn in my gut, and forced me to taste how fearful I was. How anxious I always was at home. Magic moments were just that. It always came back to bracing myself for the next blow.

The porch light suddenly illuminated, and it seemed like an omen of agreement, a cartoon character's bright idea. Mom reappeared with a full glass of tea.

"Thought it was gettin' too dark for you to find your mouth."

"No, I always seem to find it. I'm okay in the dark."

"You want me to turn it off?" She bent and kissed my cheek, and I wished she hadn't. She vanished then, simultaneous with the light fading and my vision returning to the stars.

I couldn't release the tension inside, and I knew that ol' Jimbo would be coming over the hill in a matter of moments. It was like an extra sense. Sure enough, I heard the sputter and shift of his Jeep turning off Old Franklin. Two headlights appeared at the top of our hill. I swigged the tea and started to rise. Then for some reason, I sat back down and braced myself for the battle ahead.

-2-

As my father pulled his battered Jeep into its spot across from the house, I felt wooden, immobile, part of the porch swing. In the darkness his silhouette looked frail; I thought of the black cardstock profile done of me at the state fair when I was six.

He hesitated a moment and as he swung the door shut, my stomach tightened more. There was a swagger, an all-too-familiar unbalance, in his steps, and I started when he suddenly appeared before me on the porch.

"Hey, son." He sounded tired, a surprising softness in his voice. I expected him to rail about my not showing up that afternoon. "Feels good out here, don't it? Cooled off a lot." His voice revealed only weariness, and I realized with mixed relief and disappointment that I had exaggerated his tired amble into a drunken swagger. If he had been drinking, I would've stood a decent chance of winning this round.

"Yeah, feels real nice out here. Sell the Mustang?"

"Don't know yet. Sammy Rayburn—you remember Sammy, John D.'s boy, from Pikeville?—came by and wants it real bad, but he just started workin' over at the new Speedy Rentals place. He's expectin' some money in, but I told him, can't hold it forever, so he's gonna try to work somethin' out over the weekend. Let me know somethin' Monday. My knee's givin' me fits today, feels like a lot of fluid collectin' around it. I need another cortisone shot, I bet. Have to call Doc Thomas. If he don't take the Mustang, I may run it through the auction down at Huntsville. Have you seen it since I replaced the chrome? Sweeter than sin. I wish you'd told me you wasn't comin' down today. Mrs. What's-her-name?—you know, over in LaFayette—supposed to pick up that Buick tomorrow."

"I got a job today at the bank. Starts Monday. Clark Heraldson asked about you, said to give him a call about some business he has with you." I poured out my torrent of news fearlessly.

"I know. Done saw him this afternoon. That Mustang, she's smooth, one-owner, man over in Coffee County. I had the engine checked, good compression, needed a tuneup, new points and plugs, put in new floor mats, had Jody vacuum it out good. Sammy's gonna let me know by Monday. That new chrome makes her sparkle like a gem. Where's your mother?"

"Did you hear me say I got a job at the bank? I'm not gonna be able to work at the car lot this summer." I bit my lip and could taste the salt of my blood.

"Yeah, I heard you." His voice became firmer, harder, more of what I expected. "Don't mean nothin'. I told Heraldson you wouldn't be takin' that job after all. Don't try goin' behind my back like that again. I need you down at the lot." He turned to go in and the porch board beneath his feet creaked in relief.

"I'm keepin' the job. I'm tired of workin' at the car lot. I'm not gonna be there all my life." I felt giddy with newfound power, even if it was a suicide mission. I kept going, "You might as well know, I've applied to UT and been accepted. I plan on goin' this fall. You'd have to find somebody to replace me down at the lot then anyway."

"I know all about the University of Tennessee. Your momma done told me. You might as well get that out of your head, too.

Ain't no need to be traipsin' off to Knoxville when you can go to school for free here. I don't understand it, son. I do everythin' I can for you, and you don't no more appreciate it than this porch rail does. What's got into you? I don't plan on puttin' up with no more disrespect. Got any other surprises up your sleeve?"

My father is a big man. Even though we shared the same over-six-foot height, he weighed almost a hundred pounds more. In the shadows and stray arms of light from the windows, he looked immovable, a tactile statue, clothed and detailed down to the beard stubble around his neck and chin. Despite the darkness our eyes locked. At first I thought I sensed a kind of amusement there or joy, not at my powerlessness, but at my attempt to stand up to him. Maybe he'd been waiting for me to rebel before he could respect me. But as soon as I thought about it, that spark of enjoyment in his eyes disappeared, replaced by a dull smolder.

"No, sir, I don't have any more surprises."

He pulled off his cap, smoothed his hair with his hand gracefully, and turned to go. Just as he pulled the screen door in behind him, I said: "But I will work at the bank this summer." Even if I died trying.

I thought about what Momma said, that I hated him, and realized how desperately I wanted to, but couldn't, not even when I tried. He was a mystery, harder to understand even than myself, and I couldn't love him or hate him or respect him or know him. What did most sons feel toward their fathers? The best I could do was tolerate him, polish my ambivalence, while I explored whatever rolled around inside me.

I tried to gain some of my earlier tranquility, release the anger and fear, let my father and mother float out of my head, up through the trees, branches and leaves murmuring, out into the darkness, to become clouds, or better yet, stars, beautiful, at a distance, fulfilling wishes.

Up above me, the Big Dipper hooked its way into my vision with its diamond claw. I played a little game I learned as a boy, to take the Dipper apart, star by star, let it go into the vast collection of other stars until you can't pick out the Dipper at all, just one blanket of pinpricks, light, and dreams. You can play the game with any constellation. As I put the Big Dipper back together again, I wondered about my desire for pattern and design, my longing to see both a field of stars and the great bear of my imagination. I guess it's something we all do. We want it both ways.

By the time I went inside, the ten o'clock news was starting and Daddy was finishing his last biscuit and gravy at the horseshoe-shaped bar counter in the living room. Bought at auction from a Texas barroom, the odd piece dominated the room as much as my father did.

"Momma already gone to bed?" I asked.

She yelled out from the kitchen before my father could answer. "I'm fixin' to go. You need me for somethin'?"

"No, ma'am. Good night."

"I'm on my way, too, son. I need you to work tomorrow. Got a couple of trucks comin' in from Nashville. They'll need cleanin' up before Monday. I'll see you in the morning." His eyes looked drowsy and I regretted not waiting longer to tell my news.

"Good night." I almost added "I love you," completing my childhood litany. My lip was still bleeding.

My father left his dishes on the bar counter and began unhitching his overalls as he staggered off to bed. He must not have told Momma about our talk or surely they would've been arguing over it. What if he told her and she didn't argue, didn't put up a fight? What if she agreed, or worse, was simply too tired to resist his will? I would have to wait until morning to find out.

It wasn't long before Ed welcomed Johnny on TV and I slumped into another auction find—a dentist's chair my father had bought. He had it reupholstered and conned my mother into letting him use it as a recliner in the living room. It was as uncomfortable and out of place as I was.

Johnny's guests droned about their latest CD, their latest movie. I could hear my parents' voices, low and soft, from their bedroom. Maybe they were talking about my future plans after all; only it was too quiet and muffled. Maybe I was dreaming. When I woke up, my back was stiff from the chair and David Letterman was dropping Jell-O off a building. I shut the room down for the night, checked the locks, and tried to recall the dream I was having about my father being a dentist, my mother his assistant. Lapsing into bed, I remembered them strapping me in for a root canal.

Since I didn't sleep well that night, I got up early and decided to watch the sun rise out behind the barn. The sun rolled itself open like a gold flower over the green fields, the sky tinged pink and blue. The morning shimmered in the expanse of sunlight and dewy pasture. I surveyed the hills and fences, walked down to the creek, found the fallen oak, the decay of which I'd documented for the past few years. If only somehow I could fuse myself with the land, become immortal and unpossessable, then there would be no need for escape or even longing for it. I would pass through my father's fingers like creek water when he checked the temperature before fishing.

I sniffed and the wind tasted like fear. Something was about to happen, something unlike the minor crises and arguments I was used to. I looked for confirmation of my feeling in the morning oracles, as if I could predict my future like rain. As if in the breeze, trees turning their heads, I could sense some of the pain that awaited me and turn my own head away from such a sight as well. Looking back it's always easier to find signs and divinations—if only I'd listened to the wind at this point, or counted the stars at that point, somehow things might have

29

been different.

In the hallway of the barn, I was struck by the smell of earth sweating, dung, sweet clover, the moldy litter of winter hay. Sitting on the gray steps leading to the loft, I untied my Nikes and peeled off my socks. Making sure to watch for manure land mines, I waded in the small clover courtyard behind the barn. It felt spongy and springy, cool and damp like hundreds of wet rubber bands. My eyes teared, standing there with my toes scrunched in clover and the barn smelling like my boyhood and the morning sun coming up like a memory. It made me sad to think about ever leaving scenes like this one.

But then I chided myself for being too sentimental; I would never escape that way. For most of my life I've wondered about this, asked what's wrong with me. "It's just a phase you're going through," my mother would say. "Too damn sensitive, can't say anythin' to the boy without him sulking," my father echoed. When I was five I saw a hunting show on TV and cried when the quail fell to the ground in bloody feathers. In third grade I cried when Richie Talbot made fun of my Scooby Doo lunchbox.

By the time I turned twelve, I learned the game, desensitized myself. I still felt things, ached with a longing to understand why, if it meant I was effeminate or defective or something. I forced myself to hunt with my dad, squeezed the trigger again and again, wiped warm blood on my coveralls. I learned who to watch at school in order to fit in. I masked my sensitivity with a calmness, an indifference, a storm window sealed with duct tape during the hurricane.

So maybe I'd let myself feel more this summer to make up for lost sacrifices. Maybe I'd forgive myself for becoming this clay child always conforming to whatever his parents needed, but never himself, flesh and blood. Over my shoulder I heard the hens from the chicken house sounding their alarm of clucks and nervous ticks. My father was coming my way. I wiped my eyes on my T-shirt and went back inside the barn to get my shoes. A single clover, three-tiered, with its thin, chalked, heartlike ridge on each petal, had planted itself between my right toes.

When I looked up from tying my shoes, I remembered.

I'm upstairs in the loft, playing fort, barricaded by a battery of hay bales and salt blocks; it's late spring and I'm about ten. I hear him coming. He mustn't discover my hideout. Brushing through the carpet of hay and baler's twine, I watch him through the cracks. Overalled and shirtless, he just stands there, and I realize he isn't looking for me. I can tell he's been crying, and I become a statue. I have never seen him cry before. He isn't sobbing like I'm prone to when my feelings are hurt, just crying, the tears like sweat dripping down his face.

He goes to the corncrib and plunges his hand in, fishes out a paper sack and slips a pint-mouth out the end. He tilts it to his lips, smacks them. He does it again, only longer this time, like a man pulling water from a well after a drought.

"Whatcha doin' up so early?" My father stood before me and brought me back.

Was it the same man in the barn from my memory? I wanted to touch him, give him a sobriety test of reality. Maybe my memory was only a commercial for a detox program in Nashville or Chattanooga.

"I woke up early, couldn't sleep. Was just rememberin' when I was a kid and how I liked to play fort out here." I forgot his question.

"Yeah, you was a good one. Play by yourself up there for hours. Seems like yesterday, don't it? I wish you was still a boy sometimes, Bounty." He wished I was always compliant and submissive.

"It's gone by fast." Not fast enough.

My father looked caught up in a memory of his own, and I

31

wondered how it compared with mine, where the two met, or if they met at all.

"Guess I better finish feeding. Got to get down to the lot. Got some folks comin' to look at that station wagon. I need you there by nine, get started on those pickups. They both need waxin'."

He turned and headed for the back of the barn. I went back to the house and found Mom, housecoat-clad, reading *The Tennessean*. The aroma of country ham hung in the air and its salty, greasy smell made me hungry.

"Good mornin', early riser."

She sat there with the long kitchen windows behind her, and sunlight pointing fingers at the small lines on her face. She smiled curiously, told me about some article in the paper about a woman who had been adopted and finally found her birth mother right before the mother died of cancer. I thought of a picture of my mother as a girl. She's about six, with her hair in little ringlets and a perky bow placed like a crown. She looks lost in the picture even though she's smiling.

"I talked with your father. About the bank job. I'm sorry, Bounty, maybe this summer isn't the right time to quit. He says he really needs you, that the economy's pickin' up and he'll have a lot of turnover. Maybe in the fall." She turned the page to the entertainment section.

"I thought you were gonna wait to tell him about UT after the loan went through." My voice sounded shrill and flat at the same time, accusatory.

"It slipped out. Last Monday when he took me to work while my brake pads were being replaced. He didn't say much about it, only that we'd wait and see. I told him you'd been meanin' to tell him about it for some time, that you just got your acceptance letter a couple of weeks ago."

Not exactly lies, but the smooth spread of conciliatory half-truths that my mother bridged between me and my father. She was failing me, slipping in her expertise, now when I needed her most. All the school trips and church group sleepovers that she wheedled out of my father paled beside the new stakes of my future.

"I'm not givin' up the job at the bank. I'm callin' Mr. Heraldson today to find out exactly what Daddy told him. Summers are always slow at the car lot."

She stood up and skated across the linoleum to her fixed position in front of the stove. Her eyebrows crossed, and I noticed more crow's-feet.

"Son, don't make this harder on all of us. Just this once try to keep some peace in the family. For me." She added those last words with a kind of pout, an attempt at a kind of Marilyn Monroe-little girl seduction.

I just shook my head and locked the door behind me in the bathroom. My strategy had to be simple and direct, nothing complicated. Maybe if I cornered my father at the car lot this afternoon. Maybe if I could think of some advantage for him if I worked at the bank. Washing my face, I looked up and saw my cheeks flushed with a kind of anger.

     —⊱⊰—

By noon I was finishing up my second wash and wax job on identical Ford Ranger short-bed pickups. My father had been conspicuously absent all morning, drifting in and out of his office a couple times, but for the most part leaving me in charge. Not that it was a lot to oversee.

J & R Motors had a neat, orderly appearance from the high-way—a former service station, remodeled and painted blue, perfect for housing a small office with a garage in the back service bays. In front of this a dozen even rows of American-made cars and trucks, Fords, Chevys, Chryslers interspersed with the hand-ful of oddities that my father accepted in trade. These were my favorites. The sixties-something El Camino with its hybrid blend of sedan and flatbed, a truck in drag. The GMC ton truck with its peeling paint and Texas license plate. The old green John Deere tractor, the yellow VW bug with permanent Grateful Dead stickers on every window (which my father hated).

My favorite, though, was the '67 cherry red Mustang that my father had accepted as loan collateral and eagerly kept when the poor chump defaulted. Daddy had it rebuilt, had Ricky work overtime for two weeks under the hood. I sometimes stayed with him and watched in fascination as he clinked and pinged parts together, piston rings and cam heads, fan belts, radiator hoses, plugs, and cylinders. Despite my exposure, I still knew very little about what went on under the hood of a car. Sure, I knew the basics, but the finer points didn't mean much. It was more fun to watch Ricky, to maintain the mystery.

When my father came in for lunch about one o'clock, I had just finished washing the Mustang for the second time that week. The twin Ford trucks were positioned front row, far right, to allow maximum exposure, and I prided myself on their gleaming shine in the afternoon sun. Daddy had a bag from the diner with burgers and chips, and we ate in silence in his tiny air-conditioned office. I could stand it no longer.

"I called Mr. Heraldson down at the bank today. Told him there'd been a misunderstandin' and I'd be startin' Monday after all." I timed it perfectly to when my father's mouth was full. His eyes rounded themselves, hardened with a glaze. I swigged from my Sun-drop bottle, started to set it down, swigged again.

"You disobeyed me's what you're sayin'. What's so appealin' about that pansy job? If you want the job that bad, then you move out and get a place of your own. We'll see how you like makin' decisions then, big boy." He chomped down angrily on the last half of his hamburger and I thought he might bite his fingers.

"No, Daddy, I'm not tryin' to disobey you. I just need a change. Try to see it from my point of view. I don't want to move out, can't afford to."

"Should've thought of that before you did what you did," he snapped.

"Listen. If you let me work at the bank this summer, then

I'll work here on weekends and evenings. . . ." I sounded desperate and we both knew it.

He pounded his desk with his half-empty Coke bottle, as if he were a judge pronouncing sentence. He surprised me: "I'll let you work at the bank on one condition—you come back to work here in the fall, and if you still got your mind set on goin' to school, you go to Crescent. Put UT out of your mind for good. That's my only offer. Take it or leave it."

In one way this was more than I'd hoped for. But I couldn't decide if my first step of independence was worth the rest of the journey. Things might change. If that loan went through, he couldn't stop me from going to Knoxville, no matter how hard he tried.

"Deal. Thanks, Daddy. You won't be sorry." I hated myself. He ruled my life and I thanked him for it. I crumpled up my foil sandwich wrapper and stuffed it in the barrel beside the first service bay.

"I'll still need you on weekends and evenin's down here."

"I'm through with the trucks. They cleaned up nice. If there isn't any more to do, I'm gonna get a haircut." I said it quickly and again tried to time it to his last bite.

"Go on then. Make sure you get it off your neck and above your ears."

"I'll see you at home." I climbed into the big Merc and forced myself to ease out of the parking lot on to the highway, instead of burning rubber and driving as fast and as far away as I could.

<hr>

As I turned from Highway 27 on to Clearfield's Maine Street—not Main, changed by patriotic city fathers decades ago to remember the *Maine*—my eyes burned and with it my town looked just as sore, just as homespun, as if I were a big city tourist. The spectacle of it was tinged with sadness, like the last night of a traveling carnival. Whoever planned the town, if any-

one had at all, didn't go to much trouble. It was originally
Clearfield Springs, a kind of resort town, with hot springs attract-
ing a variety of ailments. Franklin Roosevelt supposedly came
here for his arthritis and polio. The L & N Railroad made
Clearfield Springs a stopover between Memphis and Chattanooga,
and business grew around the train station. The dissipation of
the hot springs coincided with World War II, and the town's
tourist industry faded, leaving it another back-roads town in
western Middle Tennessee.

I tended to think of Clearfield as a series of parallel lines
stretching for something just out of reach, like me. One traffic
light swings at the intersection of Highway 27, Newberry Road,
and Maine Street, separating the town into "before the stop-
light" and "after you pass the light" in terms of direction giving. Businesses line the fairway—Buddy's Grocery and City
Barbershop, Solid Gold Video, the Qwik-n-Grab, Ray's, the
Diner. Over on Side Street you find city hall, the post office,
the fire department, the bank, Miss Mary's Preschool, Clear
Creek Elementary, Mane Attraction Beauty Shop (which everyone calls Eva's), and the Bait 'n Tackle Hardware Store. You
could find almost anything, except you'd have to drive to Crescent
for a movie theater—the Regal—or all the way to Murfreesboro
for a shopping mall.

Behind Maine Street is Church Street with, you guessed it,
the town's five different churches: First Baptist, Clearfield
Methodist, Church of Christ, Presbyterian, First Holiness. I
grew up in First Baptist, mainly because my grandparents went
there, Grandaddy and Grandma Epperson, and because my
parents wanted me to.

I learned fast that like the small town itself, church amounted
to nothing more than an anthill in which all the other ants
know, or die trying to find out, what you're carrying on your
back. I believe that's why Mom quit attending after both her
parents died. She knows what kinds of crumbs everyone else,
including Brother Bob Stuckey ("Like the pecan log!" he says),
carries and they in turn know about her. Her first marriage at

sixteen, her divorce at eighteen, my daddy's alcoholism, my grandfather's Alzheimer's, everything. I hadn't gone to church since Christmas, and I decided right then that I might try a new one, maybe the First Holiness Church, where I'd heard I could be slain in the Spirit at one of their outdoor revival/healing services. I was open for change that summer.

F or now the changes would be less dramatic, a shorter summer haircut, a new job. The barber's pole was turning that day; it didn't always. I used to imagine it to be a signal to men with hair on their collars. Kind of like musical chairs, you were safe until the pole stopped, then you had to get a haircut.

My father was a short-hair fanatic. If you were respectable you kept your hair clean, neat, above the collar. Until I was twelve, I had a haircut every two weeks. I had planned my exit well—he never resisted my monthly visits now. He only insisted on reminding me how it should be cut.

Being a Saturday, the place was full: a mother with a six-year-old, who wanted a flattop, a father and young teenage son I vaguely recognized, and three old men—in addition to Mr. Melman. The old men were drinking RC Colas. Two wore overalls, one wore jeans and cowboy boots. Co-op caps graced all three heads. They were laughing about someone's coon dog, Whitey Ford, and how he treed a skunk. I sat on the wooden bench that had once been a pew in the old Baptist church and turned through a *National Geographic*. The blue fluorescent light above the mirrors gave Mr. Melman and his six-year-old customer an eerie glow. The place smelled like witch hazel, lemon shave cream, eucalyptus, and mildew from the wrinkled linoleum.

Mr. Melman finished with the boy and gave him two pieces of Double-Bubble. The mother took a five dollar bill from her purse and laid it on the cash register. The teenager was next. I could tell there was some debate over how much needed to come off. His father shot knowing glances, raised his eyebrows.

Mr. Melman would mediate beautifully, enough over the ears, length left in back. The hum of the shears lulled me away so that I wanted to close my eyes. Despite how much I loved this place, something bitter lingered. Whatever boyhood hope I experienced here of being like my father had long been swept away.

I decided to have a Coke while I waited. I took a bag of peanuts from the snack rack and dumped them, fizzing, into my bottle. Daddy used to always do that when we came here. I sipped and crunched and read about Buddhism in the *Geographic*.

I was next after the teenager. The old men were still waiting, but not for haircuts.

"How you been, Bounty? Saw in the paper where you graduated top o' your class," Mr. Melman said.

"Just fine, Mr. Melman. How 'bout you? Busy this morning?"

"Yeah, Saturday's usually my busiest. . . ." He droned on with questions about school, the prospects for next season's UT football team, business at the car lot. His hands were cool and smooth, soft. His was a tender job, and he enjoyed it. And he was good at it. He clipped and sheared—"Tapered in back, right?"—trimmed, snipped. Then came my favorite part. Mr. Melman took the warm foam and smoothed it around my ears and neck, worked the straight razor in neat strokes. It comforted me. This man I'd known all my life, and hadn't known, comforted me more consistently than Daddy ever had.

But it wasn't just the comfort. I had read in *Psychology Today* that getting your hair cut (or letting it grow out) was a sign of control. It was true for me. I liked thinking my cares were less if my head were lighter. Maybe I discovered a new kind of therapy. I thought about getting a radical haircut then, a flattop of my own, my name shaved into the side of my head. But it was too late.

"Well, that'll take you another thousand miles or so," Mr. Melman smiled. He used that line on everyone to indicate he was finished. He handed me the oval mirror and spun me around to see the back of my head. Smooth and tapered, my hair was so short I could see ridges of flesh over my skull. It felt like a Shar-Pei. Mr. Melman removed the seersucker lapcloth as if unveiling a work of art.

"Looks good, Mr. Melman. As always." I took out five dollars from my wallet and placed them on the ancient register. I suddenly realized an impulse to tip this old barber, this man who knew my hair better than any other. My father never tipped Mr. Melman, nor did anyone else to my knowledge. I walked out regretting not giving him something.

Like the sunrise that morning or sifting stars the night before, the barbershop, the very act of getting my hair cut, seemed fleeting, significant, and sensual in its irretrievability. Another eternal memory.

***

Outside, the afternoon gleamed fresh and glorious, so hot you could smell sunlight off the sidewalk. I decided to walk up to the drugstore and maybe to the post office for some stamps. The drugstore was another favorite place; the pharmacist, Pete Williams, collected comic books and always had the latest in stock on the wire frame rack in the rear corner of the store. I stopped reading comics in my freshman year, but quickly resumed when it became cool again my junior year. It disappointed me then to think about stopping something I enjoyed just because of what others thought. My own fickleness frustrated me.

I quickly caught up on my collection, though—Batman, Spiderman, X-men, Titans. But the one comic I followed religiously was called *Arrowhead*. I needed issues 2 and 17 to have a complete set. The story's about John Thundercloud, a Yamzi Indian archaeology student. While on a dig in the Arizona desert, he finds an arrowhead inside the tomb of a Yamzi medicine man. You can almost guess the rest of the story. The magical arrowhead talisman supernaturally endows any worthy Yamzi who possesses it. Thundercloud uses his new powers to become a super-hero of sorts. A superior archer and tracker, he goes to

L.A. and becomes a private eye. When the going gets tough, he becomes Arrowhead. Originally conceived as a Native American Batman-clone, he's been redesigned in the last few years to become a grittier, politically correct urban warrior.

When this second run started about five years ago, it ushered in a "new realism" in comics. Published by Independent Comics, *Arrowhead* runs a small disclaimer in the corner, "Suggested for Mature Audiences." Which means they have the bad guys cuss (and occasionally our hero), and that we get to see the breasts of Arrowhead's girlfriend, Rachel Greene. She's a white reporter for the *L.A. Times* and gives John all kinds of hot tips and news leaks.

Arrowhead 87 was hidden on the top shelf, so the little kids couldn't reach it. The cover showed John looking in a mirror, only his reflection was dark, ominous, more sinister than John himself. Red letters in the corner read, "My Brother's Keeper?" Usually in the summer, comics try to come up with a gimmick, some ongoing storyline to keep students interested during their vacations. I expected as much from *Arrowhead*, which often connected plots and subplots for months before resolving and moving on. Flipping through the new one, I liked what I saw, some conversation between John and Rachel, a chase scene with a mystery man, a confrontation. I felt Mrs. Lowe watching me from the front counter. The ceiling fan whirled and hummed like an old biplane.

I debated on an ice cream cone and reading the comic there, in the corner where two small glass tables were set up. Then I decided I wanted to read in privacy, like on our front porch swing, where I could drift off after pondering Arrowhead's latest dilemma. I picked up some Chap Stick and Juicyfruit and walked to the register.

"Well, if it isn't Bounty McGraw! How in the world are you? I heard you'd be workin' in the bank this summer—that right?" Mrs. Lowe sported short, dark hair; it was rumored to be an Ava Gabor wig. A short, heavyset woman in her late fifties, she knew everything that went on in Clearfield. She'd taught Sunday

40

school when I was in the fifth and sixth grade class. I think I harbored some deep-seated resentments from the time she picked me out to explain what it was like to be a believer in an unbelieving home. I didn't answer her question and later my mother gave her a tongue-lashing. But Mrs. Lowe only smiled and said she was trying to help me express my feelings, that she hadn't meant anything by it.

I felt conspicuous with my comic book since I knew she didn't approve of the Disney ones, let alone those for mature audiences. Mr. Williams had once told me that she continually badgered him to get rid of them, but he'd never budge. If she noticed the disclaimer on *Arrowhead*, she'd be telling everyone by sundown that I'd purchased pornography.

I envisioned myself pulling Daddy's revolver from my pocket and shooting this hair-capped little woman. I was taking too long to respond—what was her question?

"Yes, ma'am, news travels fast." I fidgeted with my wallet, a new one, a graduation present from a great aunt or somebody I hadn't seen in forever.

"Hope this doesn't mean that the car lot is doing poorly."

"Nope, not at all. Better than ever." I smiled wickedly.

She handed my change back, and I declined the bag she offered.

"Good to see you, Bounty. I hope I'll be seein' you in church this summer. Tell your parents hello." She smiled a Cheshire smile, and I nodded and made the bell on the door jingle my goodbye.

Walking back to where I'd parked, I felt dizzy. The three o'clock sun glistened off everything—sidewalks, store windows, chrome on cars and trucks—even other people radiated. The Mercury's steering wheel burned my fingers; I had to use my shirttail to get the key in the ignition switch. It must have been at least ninety degrees and still the first of summer. Something about the heat frightened me, as if the hotter it got, the harder my life would be. Maybe my fingers would melt and meld with the hot plastic steering wheel, the inverse of sticking your tongue to a lamppost in freezing winter. Something about summer had always been hard, because I was home more, no school, no friends. I suffered the heat.

But somehow this summer I knew there would be much more to suffer than the heat. If I didn't escape from our burning house while I still could, pretty soon my parents would drag me down into their own smoky recesses with them.

-3-

"Who are you? What are you doing here?" John Thundercloud charged into his loft apartment to find the latest villain waiting for him.

Slowly the long-haired man he'd been chasing the entire issue turned from the shadows to face him. Because of the cover I already knew what to expect: in the last panel John's twin looked him dead on, only he's dressed in black and snarling his lip, saying, "Hello, Brother!" Behind Arrowhead, his "brother's" henchmen have surrounded him. "Is this man really Arrowhead's brother? Can he claim the secret Yamzi powers as well? Be here next time for a battle you'll never forget in 'Brother Against Brother.'"

It was a good issue. His relationship with Rachel is strained—she wants to get married, he's afraid to endanger her—and now he has to deal with a villain who claims to be his brother, a man who will apparently share claim to his power-endowing arrowhead. It's a satisfying storyline because I was left wanting to know what would happen next, who his brother really is. I felt very sleepy and wondered what it would be like to be John

Thundercloud, dark complected, huge biceps and shoulders, dark shoulder-length hair, and piercing brown eyes. I admired him, a comic book cartoon, and somehow I felt like this wasn't something adults did. Maybe I'd quit reading comics again.

I don't know how long I slept, but I woke up hot and grumpy. My clothes clung to me in sweaty spots—my back, seat, and legs. The pillow was damp from the back of my short-haired head. I had been dreaming about Arrowhead, my hero, and I awoke angry that he was not real. In my dream I was his side-kick. He wasn't a cartoon, but a real man. There was something erotic about my dream. I couldn't pinpoint it—we weren't naked together or anything—but it disturbed me. I desired him.

My mother's Olds came humming over the hill and I bolted up, as if she might read my thoughts, catch me thinking about an imaginary man. I helped her unload groceries.

"You got your hair cut. Looks good," she said. As I lifted a gallon of milk and a bag of charcoal from the trunk, she stroked the nape of my neck.

"You feel like a porcupine," she giggled.

"I think it's more like one of those Shar-Pei dogs." I wondered if she had ever seen one.

"It looks real clean-cut, though. Your father will like it."

"'Cause everthing's gotta please ol' Jimbo McGraw," I said. She'd tapped the leftover agitation from my dream ending.

"Don't be disrespectful, son." Her smile wilted.

"I called Heraldson and I start work at the bank on Monday. I've already cleared it with my almighty father."

"Watch it, mister. You're not so grown up that you can talk about your father that way."

That's nothing compared to what swims below my surface, I thought.

I followed her through the front door and shifted the charcoal over my shoulder.

"Well, don't you wanna know how I got him to agree to it?"

She turned and looked at me funny, placing the groceries on the oak bar.

"You're serious, aren't you? What happened?"

44

"I told Daddy I didn't want to work at the car lot for the rest of my life. He cut me a deal, and I agreed to it—"

"What kind of deal?" she interrupted.

"I go back to work at the car lot in the fall and attend community college here. I got to help out at the lot on weekends and evenings this summer, too."

"You agreed to that? Oh, Bounty." She picked up the bags and turned away from me as if I'd just told her I sold my soul to the devil.

"It's the only way he'd let me work at the bank. I had to agree to it. That don't mean that if my loan goes through I'm not movin' to Knoxville."

She unloaded lettuce and salad dressing, pudding and vanilla wafers, bananas and strawberries, shaking her head.

"So you just lied to him to get what you want," she said.

"No, I mean, yes . . . I mean, I didn't lie to him. But things can change." I tried to help her put things away, but she pointed at the milk I'd abandoned on the table.

"Your father don't like to be lied to. I'm just afraid he'll never let you go away to school now. I want you to have a college education, Bounty, a real one. An education that I never got. You're smart, but I don't know what's got into you these last few weeks. Graduation and all, I know, but it's like you're a different person."

"Maybe I am. I'm gonna get out of here, Ma—one way or another."

"You lied to him. You're no better than he is." She might as well have socked me with the can of pork and beans in her hand.

When I turned my back to walk out of the room, she added, "I've done the best I could. That's all anybody can do, son." She sniffled and I knew there were tears welling up in her eyes. I had seen this performance many times.

From the porch swing I could hear her stacking cans in the cupboard below the sink. They clanged loud with her anger or fear or whatever it was that she really felt. I thumbed through

Arrowhead again and wondered what inspired me to let my own anger spill out. Whatever bargain I'd struck that afternoon was justified, even if I didn't fulfill my end. I had done nothing wrong and no matter what she said, I would never become like my father. If I'd promised myself anything, long ago I'd sworn never to become the kind of man he was. Never.

<hr/>

The next morning, Sunday, I awoke to my mother's laughter. "Doesn't that beat all? How excitin' for you," she said and her laugh faded. I looked out my window to verify that my father was gone.

As I downed some orange juice, I could tell Mom was on the phone with her sister, Rebecca, in Atlanta. She was ten years younger than my mother, conceived after my mother's younger brother died during a tonsillectomy, fatally allergic to the anesthetic. She was a baby-boom baby, Miss Crescent County. After my mother married at sixteen, her parents pinned all hopes on Becca. She became their clay princess, while my mother was the sad divorcee. My mother and Becca were very open about their parents' favoritism, but I didn't think that made Mom resent her any less.

"No . . . you don't say . . . well, I'll be . . . yes . . . uh-huh," my mother smiled at me and rolled her eyes.

"He just woke up . . . yes . . . okay . . . you, too." She handed me the phone.

"Hello, Becca. It's good to hear you too. Fine . . . at the bank, yeah, yup. I'd love to, but I'm not sure if I'll have any days off. I'll be helpin' out at the car lot as well. Uh-huh. Okay, thanks. Bye." I replaced the receiver and sipped the rest of my juice.

"Junior League this and Junior League that. She's still claimin' that Momma told her she could have her rose china because it has more place settings than hers. She's coy, all right, hintin' that I'd trade the china for some 'beautiful casserole dishes,' when I know for a fact Momma bought them at Wal-

Mart a year before she died. I'm keepin' the china. She wouldn't have a life if not for Peachtree Mall and Junior League. Buckhead this, Buckhead that. What do you want for breakfast?" My mother lathered herself into a jealous rage.

"Did you call her?" I asked.

"It was my turn. She called me Sunday before last, so it was my turn. Want pancakes?" She moved to the kitchen and slid a skillet from the oven drawer.

"Great. Why do you call each other if you don't like her?"

"Family is family, Bounty. Whether you like 'em or not. You'll understand someday. Sometimes I wish you had a brother or sister so you'd have someone when me and your father are gone." She took some Bisquick and measured it into a bowl.

I thought about Becca and Lake's mini-mansion in Buckhead and the last time we visited them. My cousin Beth acted like we were old pals. She took me for a beer with her friends at the Big Buck Grill. Beth is Texas-blonde and wears fashions. She would be a sophomore at Duke next year.

My mother's last comment buzzed in my head. That was all I needed, a sibling to share with. I had grown accustomed to my lonely, golden role of only child and couldn't imagine relinquishing it. Thinking about having a brother was more than I could bear. My parents' first child, a son, had died at birth. They didn't name him; the tiny tombstone reads, "Beloved Son of James and Eileen." I used to imagine that he was my twin, and I named him Ken-Wel, after an old baseball glove I found in the barn. After I started school, my teacher and Mom agreed that Ken-Wel had to be abandoned. Good ol' Ken-Wel. I hadn't visited his grave since Christmas when we took plastic poinsettias and planted them below his stone. I decided to visit him at the Clearfield Cemetery that afternoon.

Mom poured batter into neat circles in the skillet, placed Aunt Jemima and margarine on the table before me.

"Aren't you goin' to church this mornin'?" She asked pleasantly enough, but the tone underneath her question was that I needed to go. I had mentioned it the night before when Daddy asked me if I wanted to go with him to a car auction in Chattanooga. It was my only excuse. My mother was determined to hold me to it, especially since my attendance had slacked off so dramatically this year.

After the pancakes, I headed for the bathroom and ran my bath. I wasn't sure why I was looking forward to it, but I actually did want to go to church. It was funny to me that my parents prided themselves on my membership at Clearfield First Baptist. My mother had quit going when I was about ten. She had sick headaches a lot, and then I realized she wasn't going back. She'd go for the Christmas cantata or the Easter sunrise service, to see me baptized when I was eleven. But she quit going.

Daddy never did go, and he carried a large chip on his shoulder about the hypocrisy he witnessed. He considered it shameful that all of his aunts, self-proclaimed fine Christian women, had gone to see *Gone with the Wind* when he was a boy. Even though he raved and ranted too much about the evils of church, he had his points. Since neither of my parents went now, they took it hard at first when I stopped going in January. But then school kept me busy and they let up on me. I wondered if they really believed I could save them.

And I wondered who could save me, because it felt like if there was a Savior he was late in coming, like some dimwitted actor who'd missed his cue. It was something I used to pray about, but then I realized I had to take responsibility myself. I felt that way about most things I used to pray about.

I bathed and shaved, picked out a shirt and tie. I grabbed the Bible my grandmother gave me for my twelfth birthday but planned to leave it in the car.

God could be cruel. I wondered if he ever knew what he was doing. I wondered if I believed there was a God. I still felt like something was about to happen and I wondered if one of us were going to die that summer. I pictured my father having a heart attack down at the car lot in the coming hot August sun. Or Mom having a car wreck on the way to work. Or even me—

shot and killed by a bank robber. I didn't know what was about to happen, but I felt the first loose threads tickling my arm.

The church looked inviting with its red brick and white columns. A car in the parking lot had a bumper sticker reading, "I'll See You in Church on Sunday!" Inside people milled around on their way to classes. So many people—bits and pieces like confetti—from my life. My junior high algebra teacher, my parents' lawyer, my first true love from second grade, Donna Hartford. She was the first girl I ever told I'd marry, and there she was married to a mechanic from Pikeville and with a baby, too. My youth choir leader, Bertha Valley, "The Big Valley" we called her. They were all glad to see me.

I went to the "college and career" class, a promotion since I'd been last, even if the attendees were mostly the same. Seven of us plus the teacher, Clyde Jameson. Most were older than I was, freshman at the community college. A perky blonde in her late twenties—definitely the "career" part of the class—chewed gum and smiled constantly.

"Our lesson today is on joy in the midst of our circumstances. We'll be studying in Philippians. . . ." Mr. Jameson's face was wrinkled and his eyes bloodshot. He had a dopey smile plastered across his face, above a double chin and a prominent Adam's apple. He cocked one eyebrow when he talked, a Southern Hercule Poirot.

"Oh, Mr. J., before we jump in, I want to make an announcement," said the blonde.

"Sorry, Kelly. Go right ahead."

"Well, as social chairperson, I've been workin' out our calendar for the summer. As most of you know, our first event will be next Friday night, here at the church—we're gonna make a ten-foot banana split! Now y'all, this is a great place to bring a friend, even a date," she giggled and smacked her gum, "especially a nonbeliever. Brother Bob will be givin' a brief

49

evangelistic presentation after we build the split. I think almost everyone has paid already. Oh, except you, Bounty—"

"Sorry, it sounds great, but I won't be able to make it," I lied.

"Oh, we'll miss you. But we'll have other socials! Don't forget, y'all, this Friday at seven. Bring some whipped cream and a friend!"

The pancakes churned in my stomach. The old bait and switch. Bring a nonbeliever, like E.T. or a Klingon, for banana splits and then make them pay by having to listen to Brother Bob drone about sin and salvation. I sure as hell wouldn't be there.

I was convinced God tuned in to First Baptist Church, Clearfield, Tennessee, like I tuned in to reruns of *Gilligan's Island*. Brother Bob's sermon, "The A-Team of Christ," confirmed it. A small man, about my mother's age, with a receding hairline and bifocals, Brother Bob Stuckey graduated from Ponce de Leon Seminary in Saint Augustine, Florida, and he never let you forget it. He had a nasal Southern drawl, sounding more Texan than Tennessean.

"Now friends, something good can come from our depraved society. Romans 8:28—All things work together for good to them who love the Lord. I was watching channel 31 out of Huntsville, and I bet many of you know that reruns of *The A-Team* come on at three every afternoon. I just happened to be home sick last week and tuned in. And what I saw stunned me with the power of God. He moves in mysterious ways!" I zoned out, watched other people, studied the angels in the stained glass. The rest of the sermon had something to do with Brother Bob's interpretation of the book of Revelation and how Mr. T represented Jesus Christ. I suppressed a laugh so hard at one point that it hurt. I wish I could remember more of the sermon, but the absurd wears thin for religion. I can take mystery, but not the watered-down magic show he offered.

The only redeeming part was seeing the baptismal. Painted in rich greens and blues, with purple grapes and red apples and a clear stream beside a willow tree, the mural depicted heaven for me. I met the artist once; she was a Clearfield native who moved to New York and made it big.

At the end of the service, I walked through the white double doors, kept a straight face as Brother Bob pumped my hand, and I said, "Enjoyed the sermon! Powerful." He nodded and looked genuinely flattered.

At home Daddy had returned and was watching a race from Darlington. He rooted for Daryl Waltrip in the Tide Clean Machine. Momma made mashed potatoes to go with the fried chicken and gravy. I cut off a pair of old jeans and remembered that I wanted to go to the cemetery after lunch.

In the attic I rummaged through my science fair projects, discarded antiques, and matchbox cars until I found the old Ken-Wel glove. As neat as Mom was, she couldn't bear to throw away something I loved so much and I knew that about her. Even though she'd hidden the glove after my first grade weaning, I'd found it in a matter of days. It stayed at the bottom of a cedar hope chest, beneath layers of old quilts and lace doilies. The leather cracked brittle around the edges, but at the heart felt soft from mink oil applied years ago.

When I left, Daddy was snoring peacefully in the dentist's chair and Mom was washing dishes. I didn't tell her where I was going.

Only two miles away, the Clearfield Cemetery was the most peaceful place I knew other than the barn. Our family plot was toward the back, in the corner, next to the caretaker's cottage. My father's mother was buried there with the stone already cut for my grandfather. My mother's parents were buried about three rows over.

My brother's grave looked like an animal's, it was so small, dwarfed even more by a huge cedar. My old friend Ken-Wel. I took my shoes off and ran my fingers over the moss-crusted stone. He would be nineteen years old. I wondered if I would have even been born if he'd lived, since they had conceived me almost immediately after his death. I wanted more than Ken-

51

Wel, more than imaginary twins. I felt cheated out of a brother.

I looked over at the Confederate soldiers' graves. They were chained off with a stone cannon guarding the entrance. I wondered about reincarnation, Ashley Wilkes, and all that. Maybe I had the same soul as that first son born to my parents. Maybe he wasn't supposed to die and when he did, I was born to replace him.

The sun shifted behind a cloud as I took out the old Ken-Wel glove that I'd brought in my backpack. The genuine horsehide smelled moldy and stale. I could still read, "'Lou' Gehrig Model, The Glove Big Leaguers Use." I placed it reverently on the stone.

"This is for you." The sun shifted again, returned bright and fierce, and I felt foolish.

During the week that followed I learned to be a bank teller. Money became another object, like leaves on a tree or groceries in a store, and I surprised myself with how easily I handled it. The mystique dissolved as I learned interest rates and every function of my Sharp 3500 SE teller machine. Mrs. Sherman was a good teacher and saw that I caught on quickly. By Wednesday I observed her on the teller line, on Thursday she watched me, and by Friday I was set up in my own window.

It's a small town bank, despite what Clark Heraldson wants others to believe, and so operations ran clean and simple. This Friday was not a regular payday, the first or middle of the month, so it was a good day for me to learn. Mrs. Simms, my kindergarten teacher, cashed a check from her sister in Charlotte.

"My goodness, Bounty, you've become the handsomest man. Your haircut is so debonair," she purred.

I tried not to blush. Sarah Anne wanted to know if Mrs. Simms had molested me like that when I was a child. I could tell I would have to adjust to working with all women. Mr. Rosenstein was there, but he wasn't one of us.

Bill Fairday came in to make the deposit for the Qwik-n-Grab and to pick up the change order for the weekend. I felt comfortable waiting on these people I'd known most of my life, felt well-equipped to offer a fake smile, chit-chat about the weather, give them what security can be had in rows of numbers and green paper.

The only hard part about Friday was the hours—open till six—which dragged by from three onward. I took a break at four o'clock, our usual closing time, and downed a diet Coke and M & Ms to get me through. When I got back to my teller cage, I watched my father pull up in front and Clark Heraldson get out of the passenger side. He leaned back in the still-open door, and he and Daddy mouthed indistinguishable words. Heraldson slammed the Jeep door and entered, did a double take when he saw me. Veering from his path toward Rosenstein's office, he made eye contact as I looked up between customers. He winked and gave me the thumbs up. I couldn't help but smile.

My father, on the other hand, pulled away without a wave or any acknowledgment to me. Rosenstein sat calmly behind his desk while his superior stood in front of him. They didn't look like they were discussing their golf game. Nothing unusual, I guess. Heraldson is in charge of all the branches. Maybe he was checking up on me.

The last two hours on Friday are definitely the toughest, even on a slow day. I waited on thirty-seven customers before four o'clock and twenty-eight after. Right away I learned and loved the music of my teller machine. Chuk-chunk, whir-whir-whir, chuk-chuk-chunk, "And there's your receipt. Have a good weekend, Mrs. Bagglioni." At six Rosenstein locked the heavy glass doors and heaved a clichéd sigh. Heraldson had left sometime during my last hour rush.

"You've done a fine job today, Bounty. I had several customers tell me how polite you were. Mrs. Simms wanted to know

53

if she could take you home!" Rosenstein smiled. Sarah Anne, who probably told him to say that, laughed so hard her weight shook the drive-thru teller platform.

"Thanks," I stammered. "I guess the real test will be if I balance or not."

He didn't hear, had already returned to his office. Mrs. Sherman did, though, and maternally reassured me.

"Oh, you'll balance. I've been watchin' you. You haven't made one mistake. You'll do fine, Bounty."

BeBe piped in from the other side of Mrs. Sherman. "You'll do just fine. Unless you gave Mrs. Simms more money than her check was for!" She and Sarah Anne took another belly laugh.

BeBe was a well-formed, stylish young woman, one of the only blacks in our county to work for the bank. She stood out beautifully, like a copper penny in a row of dimes. That week I'd found myself attracted to her easy charm and sharp wisecracks. She wanted to be an actress, wanted to be on *Days of Our Lives*. She attended the cosmetology school at night in nearby Pikeville and had pumped me for gossip about our high school teachers. She couldn't believe that I still wasn't sure where I was going to college, or if I would go at all.

"Honey, smart as you are, you'd be a fool to hang around here. Forget about community college, baby," she drawled.

I explained that my father wasn't too happy about me leaving town. I couldn't decide if I should trust her with the full details of my pact.

Off by a nickel, I wondered if thinking about BeBe had made me miscount. I started again.

"How much you off by?" Mrs. Sherman asked.

"Only a nickel. I'll find it."

She smiled knowingly and, without a word, came around to my cage, pulled out the third drawer, and produced a nickel from a cigar box crammed with rubber bands and money straps. She held it up like a magician and dropped it into my change till.

"Now you balance," she said. I wondered if it had been a hundred dollar bill instead of a nickel if she would've done the same thing. "We don't tell Mr. Rosenstein about this, it would only bother him," she continued. "So when we're over or short, under a dollar, we just use the cigar box." She smiled at me like a child and I wondered what would happen if I told Rosenstein.

"That's a great idea," I said.

"It saves so much paperwork, you know, all those forms we'd have to fill out just for the sake of a nickel. And then, you're likely to be over by exactly that same nickel next week. We're really doin' the bank a favor." Mrs. Sherman had once wanted to be a lawyer, I could tell.

———

The next morning, Saturday, I was at it bright and early at the car lot. My father had gone to an auction at an old garage over in Wartrace and had left me with cars to wash and state title certificates to update. It was this latter task that caused me to stumble upon something I'd just as soon not have found.

Ricky was under the hood of Mrs. What's-her-name's Buick, trying to track down "a sound like my vacuum cleaner makes when it's unplugged," as she put it. Ricky asked her, "Unplugged? How can your vacuum cleaner make a noise if it's unplugged?" He and I laughed, but the blue-haired lady was not amused. "You know what I mean," she ordered.

Jody was washing the oddball row and seemed to be taking his time so he wouldn't have to sweep the parking lot. I sat behind my father's oversized oak desk and was filling out the last form when I came to the blank for the state business ID number. Since my mother usually did this, I didn't have any idea where to look for our number. I called Mom and she told me to look in Daddy's little black book in the second desk drawer on the right. "I really appreciate you doin' those forms for me, son. I'm almost finished here." She was making strawberry jam out of the latest crop of Florida berries so my sacrifice seemed well worth it.

The drawer was locked, but I fished the key out of my father's

NASCAR jacket pocket, its usual location. Crammed with receipts, titles, business cards from body shops and parts stores, the drawer was every accountant's nightmare, and in the very back I found my father's black book, which contained, not names and numbers of other women, but every piece of information my father considered worth saving. Like the desk and drawer itself, the small address book overflowed with more business cards, courthouse tax receipts. There was even a copy of last year's tax return.

I found the ID number after thumbing through pages of my father's blocked scrawl. When I went to return the black book to its spot, though, I noticed an envelope edging out from beneath the assortment of papers. It was smaller than a business envelope, and maybe that's why it caught my eye; it looked like a personal letter. Marking its place with the manila envelope behind it, I tugged it free and found it addressed to my father, Mr. James Bountiful McGraw, General Delivery, Clearfield, TN. No address, not even a zip code, and it still got here. It was postmarked a month ago, recent. Inside was a black and white photo of a man, my father, holding a child, a little boy, maybe two or three years old, hard to tell, and beside them, a woman wiping her hands on a checked apron. No date, no writing, but I could tell it was a copy of an original. No mistake, it was my dad and I knew instantly that the child was his son and the woman his wife, but not me and my mother. It surprised me and it didn't, if you know what I mean. Of course he was married before, of course he has other children. It made sense if you knew my father.

The handwriting on the envelope was slanted as if the writer had been positioned diagonally and stretched to address it. I wondered if there had been a note or letter, if the woman and child were still alive, if I could safely assume that one of them sent it. I wondered if my mother knew about this, either the photo or the family, and intuitively knew that she didn't. I wondered what other secrets my father had. Someone knocked on the door and proceeded to turn the handle.

I jumped and banged my knee on the open drawer. The swiveling, rolling office chair rocked backward and I caught myself just as Clark Heraldson walked through the office door. I carefully placed the photo back in the envelope, threw it in the drawer, and pushed it back in place.

"Mr. Heraldson, good to see you," I offered.

"Bounty, good to see you. Keep your seat. I'm just lookin' for your old man." He winked like he was really hip because he called Daddy "my old man."

"He's gone to an auction. Can I do anything for you?" I stood up, noticing that my knee was scraped. Heraldson stuck his head through the garage doorway and looked down at Ricky still tinkering with the Buick.

Turning around, he groped in the pocket of his expensive chinos, adjusting himself. "No, no. Just tell him to call me at home tonight or tomorrow. Didn't know you were workin' two jobs. How's the bank business goin'? They treatin' you all right down there?"

"Yessir. I'm enjoyin' it, learnin' a lot. I was even in balance this week."

Heraldson was out the door. "Good, good. Tell your father I'll catch up with him."

I stood up and followed him to the doorway. Through the small office window I watched him disappear in his blue Mercedes sedan. Daddy had gotten it in a trade last fall and called Heraldson right away to see if he was interested. I drove it all weekend just to say I'd driven a Mercedes, and Heraldson came and picked it up on Monday. Something was up; he and my father were having too many conversations lately.

And then there was the picture. I returned to the drawer and debated on taking it with me. It felt risky; what if he missed the picture and raised hell? What if I were wrong and it wasn't some secret first family? Maybe this first wife and child had been killed in a traffic accident and this was his only tragic reminder.

Somehow I couldn't believe that. And despite the risk, I

wanted the photograph. I wasn't sure why, but with someone like my father, I figured it never hurt to have an ace in the hole. I took the picture from the envelope once again and placed it in my hip pocket. The envelope I placed back in the loose jumble of papers where it had been.

Maybe for the first time in my life, I felt like I had something on him. At the same time, he didn't seem like my father so much, not the drinking, wheeling-dealing tyrant I knew, but rather just another man, someone in the newspaper or in a book or on TV, someone distant and removed from my life. A man whose past, I realized, I knew virtually nothing about.

-4-

On the Fourth of July my father reasserted his independence by bringing home two six-packs from the Qwik-n-Grab. I should've known it was going to happen by the way the day had started. But life had ironed itself out so smoothly till then that I'd become settled in a kind of pattern where I enjoyed my newfound freedom at the bank, daydreaming about what the fall would bring.

The past month, while weather forecasters predicted the worst drought in thirty-two years, I hibernated in the cool, fluorescent glow of the bank and watched the pavement boil and simmer sunlight a few feet away. I peeled the days off my Crescent Co. Nat'l Bank desk calendar like layers of onionskin. The drought and soaring temperatures provided me and bank tellers all over the South with fodder for customer conversation. We made inane statements like, "How hot is it out there, Mrs. Ferguson?" and she'd say, "Oh, my, it's *so* hot! Your sign

59

says ninety-nine!" I wondered why we all found it necessary to go through the ritual, why it was important to feign human connection.

Whatever the reason, by July 3rd I was ready to break out of my dialogue of transactional chatter. (I still hadn't been out of balance by more than a dollar yet.) July 4th fell on Friday, and since we'd be closed, everyone bombarded us that Thursday. I took only half my lunch break that day, and counted in my sleep that night.

My mother had the holiday as well, but Daddy insisted on keeping the car lot open for all the patriotic shoppers. He woke me up early to help hang red, white, and blue bunting in the windows and over the J & R Motors sign. Mom placed neon price stickers reading "Declaration of Independence!" on all the late model trucks. Although we were through before nine, I resented him spoiling my holiday.

I grumbled even more when he suggested that I mow the lawn that morning instead of waiting until my usual Saturday. It boiled down to, he wanted it done then and it didn't matter when I wanted to do it. So I put on cutoffs and a tank top and dragged the old Snapper mower around the jumbled two acres my parents designated as yard. A hummingbird distracted me as he beat his tiny wings so hard I thought he'd disappear in smoke. He seemed to follow me and found some bloom or blossom to penetrate at every turn.

Lost in the sweet tedium of even rows and hummingbirds, I mowed in concentric squares and fished inside myself for something meaningful. I hovered on my parents and the relative calmness of our lives the past three weeks.

Nothing had happened. I hadn't seen my father meeting with Heraldson, hadn't seen the bank vice-president at all since he came to the car lot that day I found the picture. And the picture—I hadn't forgotten about it, but I didn't know what to do with it either. I almost told my mother one evening on the front porch swing, but couldn't bear to let my father inflict some new wound on her; after all, it might be nothing, ancient history, over and done with. The photo was enveloped and sealed inside my sacred cigar box in my bottom bureau drawer.

Adding more gas to the mower from the half-empty plastic milk jug, I realized the past weeks suddenly seemed conspicuous in their calm indifference of events.

My father had sold over a dozen cars and trucks, my mother processed insurance claims, and I counted other people's money. We'd all come home at night and eat supper together, drink iced tea, watch *Designing Women, Jake and the Fatman,* or Ralph Emery on TNN. I went to Nashville the weekend before last and visited my friend Pace, the one at Vanderbilt with the TVA job this summer. He was one of those close but not close friends, someone I could relax with without having to say much. We drank a beer (only my third time ever—the risky thrill was still there) at his watering hole, Lucky's in Brentwood, played pool, went to Opryland the next day. It was a nice distraction. My mother went on her annual summer diet, taken more seriously because she returned to Weight Watchers and lost six pounds the first week. And my father remained uncharacteristically distracted, quieted by some unknown force. He hadn't required me down at the car lot in almost a week.

As the weed cutter whirled around the roots of apple trees and the foundation of the chicken house, I knew the summer could not pass so artlessly. I sent a whole orchard of dandelions into the breeze. But there was no use speculating.

When my father pulled up for lunch, I was hosing the green sweat off my bare feet in the driveway.

"Finish?" he asked.

"Yessir. I still have some weeding to do out back."

"Your momma got those burgers ready?"

"I think so."

Then I noticed. Like a gun bulging in a bank customer's pocket or spinach in a date's teeth, I noticed the familiar-looking grocery bag from the Qwik-n-Grab. I followed him into the cool of the house wordlessly. Mom mixed potato salad at the kitchen table and was about to add more mustard. She didn't look up as he deposited the two six-packs in the bottom of the refrigerator. He slid one from its plastic sleeve and cracked the pop-top. I stood in the doorway, my hands still tingling from the vibration of the weed cutter. Or maybe they were shaking.

"Wash up, Bounty, we're about ready to eat." My mother mixed harder, and I thought we'd have mashed potato salad if she didn't stop soon.

I headed for the bathroom and lathered green from my face and hands. In my room I tossed the tank top and dug out my favorite concert T-shirt, from *The Joshua Tree* tour. Above the comforting hum of the air conditioner, I heard my mother's voice low and hard.

"What do you think you're doin'?" I couldn't see her, but I knew her teeth were clenched as she spoke through them.

My father must have ignored the question because she repeated it and he laughed. I rubbed the faded Bono on my shirt as if for comfort. I heard only wisps of what he was saying.

"Look . . . hard day . . . defaulted . . . I'll have to pay . . . stuck with that El Camino again . . . my nerves . . . relax . . . need a beer . . . no big deal."

I entered the room and took three plates from the cabinet, scooped up forks and napkins, and set the table. My mother grabbed a platter and went outside to the grill. Daddy chugged the remains of his first Bud and slam-dunked the can into the aluminum can bag. He opened a second and set it by his plate as if it were a Coke.

"Hot out there, ain't it?" I noticed a bead of sweat on his forehead as if he'd produced it for proof.

"You're tellin' me. I got spoiled by that air-conditioned bank." I hid disappointment in my eyes, buried it deep in the green of my iris, through the pupil, locked away somewhere in my cornea with rods and cones. My tenth grade science fair project had been on cataracts.

"You ain't the only one. We're all a little spoiled. Used to be they didn't have air conditioners everywhere ya went. You sweated and made do with fans." He gulped the red and white can until it foamed when he set it down.

Mom returned with a plate of burgers and a wan smile. We sat and ate baked beans and potato salad; Mom's burger had no bun and she ate salad instead of beans. We talked about fireworks at the city park at ten, about six Ford Escorts Dad bought at auction from a bankrupt rental agency in Nashville, about Mom's vacation due in August. It was forcibly pleasant and trivial, roles we all knew and quickly accepted. My stomach rolled and wondered about proportion. No big deal, right? He could handle it. I thought of my own taste for beer, acquired only in the last year in secret, and wondered about their expressions if I popped my own top. Joined Dad for a brewski. I got my wish.

By the time I finished my first burger, Daddy was on his fourth can. Mom picked at the rest of her salad and averted her eyes every time he popped a top. I must've had an amazed look on my face, maybe even one of longing, because my father looked me square in the eye and asked me the impossible.

"You want one of these?" he asked as he crushed another can empty.

My mother dropped her fork on her plate and looked at my father like a crazy man. "Have you lost your mind?" she half-whispered.

I hesitated. It felt like a test, one that I lost either way I went. If I said yes, then maybe I'd please my father, maybe he'd think I was a man now. Wasn't his offer itself proof that he was thinking of me differently? But if I accepted, my mother would panic, would think we'd both end up drunks, probably her worst fear.

"Thanks, Dad. Not right now. Thanks, though," I chickened out. My mother started breathing again.

"Suit yourself." He was disappointed.

That night as I watched Roman candles and Japanese fountains arc and sputter, something inside me burned just as fiercely.

A longing, an ache, something unbearable. When I drove home, with the radio playing low, some slow Bonnie Raitt song or maybe Emmylou, I was relieved in one sense. The calm had broken and the storm was here. No more waiting, no more hoping or pretending. I didn't have to wonder anymore. Once my father started drinking everything was set in motion again; anything could happen, and I'd have to brace myself for all kinds of possibilities.

Maybe this would be the summer that my parents divorced. I tried to imagine—he'd stay in his office at the car lot, drink his liver to hell, go bankrupt. My mother, on the other hand, would move to Nashville or Atlanta, open her own insurance agency, flourish and bloom. She'd lose more weight, color her hair blonde, eat Lean Cuisines, and remarry. I'd go away to school, visit on breaks, and Daddy would ask me questions about her new husband, how much money he made, what kind of car he drove.

My speculations circumvented whatever pain rattled inside me. If I could second-guess the future, get at least a phantom-hold on the possibilities, then I could prepare. I could devise strategies, scripts, defenses. I'd know what to expect. What if this were the summer my father joined AA or admitted himself to the detox hospital in Chattanooga? "My name is Jim, and I'm an alcoholic." He'd stand tall, proud of his new sobriety, the confrontation with his disease. He would do commercials. Car pulls in drive, cut to wife in apron at kitchen sink, cut to teenage son reading in bedroom. Father gets out, shuts car door, inhales the fresh air of his home, wife drops dishcloth, son closes book, both run to greet him. Voice-over for Lighthouse Recovery Hospital. "For you or someone you love. There's one near you. Call today."

Was it really a disease? I had my doubts. At what point do you give up, admit you're powerless? What about the will to choose? John Bradshaw said on a PBS special one Sunday afternoon that all of us are addicted: to coffee, sex, drugs, alcohol, money, relationships. So we're all sick, right? So my father wasn't really responsible for what happened when he drank. I couldn't believe that.

At home I found what I expected, a scene equally as predictable as my Lighthouse commercial. My father sprawled in the dentist's chair, comically, one leg over, one arm thrown back. Geraldo blared on TV that now it could be told. I laughed and bit my tongue. My father's eyes flickered and he smiled.

"Momma in bed?" I asked.

"Yeah, yeah, yeah." He tried to lift himself from the chair. "How's them faircrackers? They shoot 'em all off? Ever tell you 'bout the time your Uncle Pete and me walked to town to buy firewood, I mean works, from Old Man Jack? He'd give us a pack of Black Cats for a penny. We'd shoot 'em off in tin cans, tie 'em to cats' tails. Help me up here, son."

I pulled him from the chair, all dead weight. He smelled stale and sweet, not beer, but bourbon. He dropped his head over my shoulder as if we were dancing and he were my date. I smelled witch hazel and Old Spice in the rough sandpaper of his beard. He slumped, and I staggered him to the sofa. He laughed at some internal joke, some poor cat's tail exploding fifty years ago. I took the green and orange afghan from the back of Mom's rocker and wrapped Jimmy McGraw in its cocoon. I turned off the lights and lowered the volume on the TV, but I couldn't bear to turn it off. I felt as if I were a parent leaving a nightlight on for his five-year-old.

"Love you," he mumbled and rolled over.

It struck me then, his mortality, anew. How much I couldn't not love him if I wanted to. It's how parents must feel about children, the unexpected tenderness when a pop-fly breaks the picture window, and it caught me by surprise. I didn't like loving him when it was so much easier to hate him, the enemy who must be defeated in order for me to gain my freedom. It didn't seem fair that I could feel both of these at once.

On the kitchen counter a bottle of Wild Turkey towered like a monument next to canisters of flour and sugar. I twisted the cap and guessed only a few shots were missing. I considered draining the bottle myself, one gulp. Instead I placed it in the cupboard below next to cans of soup and Green Giant corn.

After I was in bed, I heard my mother sweep through the dark house, imagined her nightgown billowing like a ghost's. She must have checked on her husband. She must have loved him, too.

———

The next morning the house was ominously quiet. Both my parents' vehicles were absent. I poured Apple Jacks and found a note from my mother saying that Pace had called, that he was home for the weekend. I called and agreed to meet him at the Chew-and-Cue for a late lunch. His voice sounded warm and funny, like a favorite comedian's. Good timing—if anyone could make me laugh it was Pace.

I felt as if the day before had been an after-school special on channel 2 and decided that pop culture invalidates our lives when we let it. I watched cartoons and ate more cereal and then emptied the quart of Wild Turkey down the kitchen sink.

My mother was gone most of the morning, her usual beauty shop appointment, running errands, grocery shopping. My father pulled in the drive just as I was dressing, and I couldn't see any way to avoid him.

"Bounty!" he yelled from the kitchen. "Where's your mother?"

His face was flushed—whether from alcohol or anger I couldn't tell.

"Yessir," I answered. "She isn't back yet from shoppin' and the beauty shop." He knew this as well as I did.

I watched him pick up the empty bourbon bottle from the counter, and I thought the glass would shatter in his hand, all the raging force focused into a single act. He muttered something under his breath and grasped the bottleneck, broke the bottle, not with the force of his will, but by a single stroke across the laminated counter, like christening a ship.

"I'll just buy another. She should know better than to pull

this. Did you see her do it?" His hand was bleeding between the thumb and index finger but he hadn't noticed yet.

"You cut yourself. Here," I said, handing him a wet paper towel. "I did it, Daddy," I added quickly and turned to rummage in the bathroom for a Band-Aid.

"What do you mean, you did it?" his eyes flared, red creeping in from their corners.

"I spilled it this morning. Accident, sorry."

"Sorry as hell, you're gonna be. You'll buy me another one then, you will." He continued to bleed and ignored the bandage I handed him. I wasn't about to place it on his wound myself. Let him bleed to death if he wanted to.

"I said I'm sorry," I lied.

"You little pansy, wouldn't even drink a beer with your old man. You're too good for it, I guess. Tied to Momma's apron strings like you always been, a little boy afraid of his own shadow. You won't amount to nothin'," he snarled and blood was dripping, ping, ping, on to the linoleum now. I walked out of the room, out the front door and jumped the fence leading down to the pasture. He was drunk, right, didn't mean anything he said, right? My mind whirled and someplace deep inside I felt cut to the quick and dipped in salt.

⊰⊱

By the time I met Pace it was nearly two o'clock. The Chew-and-Cue, on the outskirts of Crescent near the city dump, beamed like an old friend. Pace and I used to skip out at lunch my junior year and head to the Cue. Opening the door, Clint Black crooned on the jukebox and my eyes adjusted to the smoky dusk inside. Pace was playing Pin-Bot in the corner, juggling a longneck at his side. I ordered a Sun-drop and slid up behind him. I waited till he lost his third ball before popping the back of his neck.

"What the—?" he spun around.

"Good thing it's you, Bounty, 'cause I was fixin' to beat the daylights out'a somebody! How are you?" Pace drummed my shoulder with his hand.

"I'm doing okay, Pace, good to see you. Got a table yet?"

He laughed, since the place was nearly empty. We walked to the bar and ordered two Cue burgers and curly fries. I felt disappointed already, wanted to beg, "Tell me a joke, Pace. Make me laugh, get me out of my life," but I didn't. He began talking as if I'd asked a question. Maybe I had and didn't remember.

"Working at TVA ain't so bad. Good money, floozy secretaries, but I'm still seein' Shannon." He sounded tied down, middle-aged, droning on about his internship, his classes at Vandy, whether or not he should marry Shannon. Our favorite waitress Cheryl brought our burgers, and grease never tasted so good. I realized no matter how settled his life sounded, he was free, freer than I could imagine at the moment.

"How much money you embezzled already?" Pace asked.

"How much you need?" I twirled a curly fry in ketchup.

"You farin' okay with the folks?"

"Yeah, hasn't been too bad, I guess. Pop's down at the lot all the time, Mom stays on me about goin' to college this fall. I'll be glad when summer's over." I didn't know what to say. If I said, "My father's drinkin' again. Who knows what will happen?" it would sound silly and melodramatic. We've all got our problems.

"Can't wait till you're at Tennessee and the Commodores kick your butt next year in football," he said.

"Won't happen," I said without thinking.

"Let's put some money on it."

"No—I mean I may not go to UT. My dad needs me to work for him, and I've got that full scholarship to Crescent and could live at home. I've applied for a student loan, but I still haven't heard anything and it's gettin' late. . . ."

"Bounty, you gotta get out of this one-horse town. Your father's got you under his thumb so tight that you can't see what you're losin' by stayin' around here. Your loan'll go through, I know it will," he reassured me.

My own words had surprised me, made me admit how hopeless I was feeling. I was afraid to hope that I could ever escape, even if I did move away to Knoxville, or even Anchorage for that matter. They would always haunt me, my father red-eyed and snarling, "You'll never amount to nothin'," my mother crying and whispering, "Don't go, son. Don't abandon me to him."

"You okay?" Paced asked.

"Yeah, yeah, I'm okay. Just thinkin'. Let's play some pool."

After we finished our food, Pace ordered another Coors longneck and offered me one. I stuck with my soft drink, chomped the ice. We played pool, eight ball, bet five bucks.

It reminded me of being in fifth or sixth grade. When it was too cold to walk the half mile from the bus stop, I'd meet Dad at Leisure Time Pool Room—where the video store is now—and watch him play. The place smelled like wet tobacco, new paint, and urine from the one-bulb bathroom in the back. He'd let me rack games for a quarter, but I'd have done it for free just to watch the force in some strange, tattooed forearm surge into that cue stick.

Mom didn't like it, me being there, but there wasn't much of a choice, Daddy told her. Either I walked home in the cold (and risked getting sick, according to her), or I hung out with him at the pool room until she came home. That was right before he bought the car lot, when he still drew disability from TVA for having his leg busted by some runaway bulldozer. Those were the days.

I chalked up until my fingers were blue.

"Far corner," I called my shot. The black eight ball rattled into the leather pocket. Pace shook his head and stuffed his five-dollar bill in my shirt pocket.

"You're one lucky son-of-a-gun, Bounty McGraw," he said.

By the time we left it was after four, and I agreed to be at his house about eight to play poker with his neighborhood gang.

———

When I left that night Mom seemed reluctant for me to go, Daddy hadn't been home all day, and I felt more optimistic. My time with Pace had done me good, a brief parole for the prisoner, whetting my appetite for eventual release. I told my mother about my father's outburst with the broken bottle—I couldn't very well hide the broken glass and bloodstains—but omitted his words to me. He didn't matter anymore. It was their problem, not mine. I was no longer required to be the emotional glue.

When I was nine they almost divorced. Mom packed suitcases for her and me to go to Grandma Epperson's. Dad was drinking and crying and bawling over losing me. I came crying into the room that I didn't want to go, that I wanted us all to stay together. It was a scene you might see on a movie of the week. Anyway, they didn't, of course. Mom made Daddy oyster stew with tomatoes in it and oatmeal cookies for me. We were all happy.

———

So I left Mom with Danielle Steele for the night. When I drove past the car lot, the Jeep was still there and the light was on in my father's office. Then I noticed a big Mercedes pulled around to the side. It was Clark Heraldson's.

———

Pace was right, I was lucky that day. I won $2.37 by the time our game broke up around 11:30. Most of my earnings came from an especially exciting hand of seven-card no-peek that I dealt. You deal everyone—there were five of us—seven cards facedown and turn them over one by one, with each player stopping when he's beaten his predecessor. I stayed in with a pair of threes even though Pace's little brother Jason had a full house. I beat him with four threes. It caught me by surprise as much as the rest of them. I'm not even sure what possessed me to stay in when everyone else folded.

Driving home that night I was thinking about luck, fate, and destiny when I smelled skunk. Like manure or gasoline, I liked the smell, long as it wasn't overpowering. This was faint and subtle, like the smell of a clean body sweating, something attractive about it despite the source. I'd won that night and smelled skunk; life wasn't all bad.

About a mile after I passed the cemetery, just before the turn for home, I noticed a dozen cars lined along the road in front of the Crescent Moon Trailer Park. I slowed down, but all I could see was a group of people clumped on the tiny front porch of Mrs. Odell's trailer. The porch light wasn't on, but the kitchen lights inside were glaring. I turned left onto our street still wondering about the attraction. I'd heard she gets hit by a fever of religion and "speaks in tongues."

Once in our driveway, I lingered on the porch, looking at the quarter moon, wondering if a lunar eclipse were due. Clouds passed effortlessly, but no eclipse. The moon shone beautiful up there, white and pure like a sliver of Ivory soap.

"Whatcha lookin' at?" Daddy materialized from the darkness beyond the garage. He held a can, but didn't sound as wasted as the night before. He should have scared me, but for some reason it didn't surprise me; like winning at cards or pool, my father drinking out by the garage seemed natural. He sounded dreamy and far away, an apparition, no longer full of rage and contempt, but soft and mellow, repentant even.

"I was lookin' to see if there was a lunar eclipse or something. I noticed a bunch of people standin' on the porch at Odell's trailer, all lookin' up." I felt foolish trying to explain. He'd think I was drunk.

71

My father laughed his deep, hearty laugh, the kind of belly-roll I expected when he was sober. I felt even more foolish.

"Why, son, I thought you'd heard by now. Two nights ago Mrs. Odell was washin' dishes and happened to look out her window and see Jesus. She called Hubert and went out on the porch, and the face she seen was on the side of Miss Mary Louise's deep-freeze, which sits on the Odell's front porch since Miss Mary don't have a porch. Hubert saw it too, so Jessie gets on the phone and calls her daughter Marie and her husband—you know Barney, he works down at Ray's sometimes, does pot the rest of the time, that's her husband—and they saw it too. So last night I guess the fireworks was a better show, but tonight word's got around. I'm surprised you ain't heard about it. How many people up there?" He was out of breath and swigged his Bud.

The incredibility of the story caught me off guard. To think, I thought it was only a lunar eclipse.

"You're makin' this up—right? That's a good one, Daddy. Had me goin'." Even when he was passing out drunk, he usually made some sense.

"I swear on my mother's grave, Bounty, drunk or not, could I make that up?" He had a point.

"Jessie thinks a picture of Jesus is on the side of Miss Mary's deep-freeze? I don't understand. I lost you." My mind spun with possibilities. They might as well have claimed to see Elvis at the Pizza Hut or the virgin Mary in a radiator grill down at Ray's. Flannery O'Connor rolled somewhere in her grave. Unbelievable. It had to be a hoax, some scheme for Mrs. Odell to raise money for First Holiness Church.

"Have you been up there to see for yourself?" I asked.

My father shifted his feet in the dark. "I ain't goin' up there with that pack of fools. I figure if Jesus decided to come back, he sure as hell wouldn't pick the side of Miss Mary's deep-freeze." My father laughed again, and I heard his jaw pop. "It'll pass, like everythin' else that's full of bull in this two-bit town."

I nodded as if I agreed. We walked in the front door and the glare of the lights, the roar of Sue Ellen confronting J.R.

on a *Dallas* rerun, made me wince.

"Momma know about this?" I asked.

"I don't know. She ain't talkin' to me today. You have to ask her yourself. I suspect she does since she generally makes it a point to know everythin' that happens."

"I guess she's already gone to bed." I noticed her romance novel bookmarked halfway through.

"She's havin' a hard time, I know that," my father said. Then in an undertone, "You know, change-a-life and all that, real hard on a woman her age."

I nodded as if I understood. Somehow it seemed to me, my mother had been going through the change of life for the last ten years. I wondered if it ever ended, or if, like most changes, it went on indefinitely.

My father went into the bathroom. I followed him as far as the kitchen. He was taking his dentures out. I suddenly remembered the Wild Turkey and felt guilty. Then I noticed a new bottle, Jim Beam this time, as if the brand made a difference.

I scooped a bowl of Breyer's vanilla and hunted for the chocolate syrup. I found it next to the pickle relish in the refrigerator door. Two new six-packs, Bud Lite this time. On a diet, I guess.

The chocolate syrup was in one of those new squeeze bottles and I enjoyed the sensation. I started an outline of the state of Tennessee, but it ended up looking like a horizontal California. As I kept squeezing, it became an abstract painting, a Rohrshack of yin and yang.

I returned to the living room and switched channels until I found videos. Some singer I remembered as a "contemporary Christian" artist had gone pop. She had a new look, permed hair, sexy smile, maybe even a new name. I couldn't quit thinking about Jesus on the side of a freezer. I swirled the chocolate into the cream faster and faster until it was like a soft-serve milkshake, the way I liked it best.

My father stood in the doorway in his faded boxer shorts. They had little hearts on them; my mother gave them to him for Valentine's Day several years before. His navel winked at me as he let out a soft belch.

"Good night, son. Sorry about this afternoon. Sorry. Love you." He turned without waiting for a reply. I echoed a curt, "Good night," and began wondering about miracles and revelation, about a father I would never understand. Despite his hangdog apology, I could not forgive him.

Although I dreamed all night about spiritual wonders, I slept through church the next morning. After my initial visit, my mother asked me why I didn't go back. I remained vague. "Kind of a personal thing, I guess." She nodded as if she understood exactly what I meant and didn't ask again. My father didn't seem to notice. They had more important things on their minds.

Things like my father's sobriety. I woke up when I heard them yelling in their bedroom. My mother kept saying, "You'll wake Bounty!" while my father was saying, "Don't tell me to shut up! You care more about him than you do me." I pretended I was dreaming and concentrated on dozing.

Their words stung me as if I were still six years old, overhearing their barbs from behind closed doors. I couldn't enter sleep deep enough to drown them out. Their words and name-calling buzzed around my head like a nest of hornets. "He ain't goin' nowhere fast!" my father barked. I couldn't hear my mother's reply. She moved on to heavier ammunition, something about a matchbook she found in his jacket last week, from some bar in Huntsville. My father retaliated with slurred non sequiturs, "If anybody's cheatin' on anybody, it's you with those painted-on nails and that dyed hair, readin' them Harlequin romances. You're cheatin' on me, don't think I'm a fool." My mother said something I couldn't hear. And then, "... divorce ... leave you." She was crying then.

I couldn't bear it any more. I slipped on a pair of shorts and crept through the house to the porch. Barefoot, I danced with wet eyes over anthills and rotten June apples out to the barn. I hated the fact that they still got to me; surely becoming an adult meant that I could eventually put them away, out of reach, a shadowbox of memory.

I don't know how much time passed, but after a while the Jeep revved over the hill and I sighed in relief. He would be gone for a good while, maybe several days. He disappeared for a week once when I was in junior high. Mom threatened divorce the whole time and we ate out every night. When he came back he was trying to sober up, had a nasty cut on his chin, and told a story about a week-long poker game with friends in New Orleans. They stayed behind closed doors a lot. She made oyster stew and scrambled eggs, brewed coffee, gave him tranxenes prescribed for her. When he emerged sober and clean-shaven three days later, they were like newlyweds. As always, they made up and I felt like a schizophrenic in the spin cycle. That time I remained sullen and silent around him, answering curtly when he asked questions. My mother finally took me aside and told me I better shape up. "You need to change your attitude, son. If I can forgive him, I know you can. You know what they say at church, that means you must forgive him. Cut the pouting." I felt as if I was going crazy, as if my parents had been replaced by clones, the Cleavers on speed.

When I went back inside, Mom was reading her romance novel as if nothing had happened. She looked relaxed, and I wondered what she had taken—tranxene or Xanax. She had the radio turned to a Sunday jazz program, so I knew something was up; she never listened to jazz since my father called it "nigger music."

"I'm sorry, terribly sorry, about all this, son. . . ." She marked her place with a Snoopy bookmark that used to be mine. Tilting her head and half-smiling, she looked sincerely concerned for me, like a high school guidance counselor reporting low SAT scores.

I just nodded in understanding and kept walking when she reached up and held my arm.

"We'll be okay, Bounty—won't we? Here, give me a hug." She stood up and I was amazed at how fragile she felt. My mother had lost almost fifteen pounds but she felt much lighter, like a balloon, an inflatable doll. I didn't feel close to her as I hugged her, but I thought it was the least I could offer.

I read a Stephen King novel that afternoon in the dentist's chair while watching the Braves play the Dodgers on WTBS. Mother cooked lunch, tuna casserole—my father hated it—and read in their room. She didn't say much about what she knew I must have heard. She hugged me again when I thanked her for lunch, then she started crying. "I'm sorry, sorry, Bounty," she trailed off to the bathroom. I ate my casserole and read the Sunday *Tennessean*.

When I heard the Jeep return in the bottom of the eighth, my heart literally skipped a beat. I folded down the page of my paperback, inspired with a kind of terror Stephen King couldn't touch.

-5-

My father sauntered in, casual, as if nothing were going on. "Who's winnin'?" His eyes were covered with red spider webs. My own eyes watered sympathetically.

"Braves, 3 to 2, bottom of the eighth." I couldn't decide what tone of voice to adopt.

"Who's pitchin'?"

"Glavine's still in, but they'll pull him if another man gets on base." Unconcerned, I decided, sound blasé.

"Who's she?" On the screen an attractive redhead sat in the press box with a gray-haired man, calling the game.

"New sportscaster, Jean somethin' or other."

"Stupid dyke. Women don't know baseball. Can you believe that? It's like a woman tryin' to drive a race car, or a nigger tryin' to drive one. Ever noticed there's no blacks or women in NASCAR? Man's sport. Takes guts. Can you believe, a woman sportscaster?"

I tried to nod, like I usually did.

"I said do you think there should be women sportscasters?" He baited me.

If I said no then he'd think I agreed with him and was just as much a bigot. If I said yes . . . I couldn't imagine saying yes. I never had. The silence grew, and he was still looking at me. Glavine lasted and now Dave Justice was batting.

"I don't know. Yeah, I guess if they're qualified, there's nothin' wrong with it."

"What'd you say? Are you crazy? I guess you think women should wear the pants in the family, be on top, be the spouse of the house. That ain't what the Bible says. You've been readin' it at church. Doesn't it say that women should submit to men?"

"No, it doesn't, not like you're talkin' about. Besides, women sportscasters have got nothing to do with the Bible."

"Are you disputin' my word, son?" His eyes bugged, as if they might pop out like big rubies.

"No, sir. You asked me what I thought, you ought to be prepared for whatever answer I give—"

"Don't talk back to me. You got a lot of book sense, but you ain't got a lick of common sense. You can read your books like your mother till you're blue in the face. You're supposed to respect me, dammit!" He grabbed Stephen King from the coffee table and threw it across the room. My father reminded me of a toy balloon full of some deadly gas instead of helium, burst and careening around the room. I sat like stone, cool and smooth, unbreakable.

My mother stood at the doorway and motioned my father into the kitchen.

I could hear my father pouring a drink. And then I grabbed the car keys. By the time I got to Pace's house the Dodgers had won, 6 to 3, Hershiser the winning pitcher.

That night I felt very calm and relaxed, the way you feel after a hard day's work, after a day of physical labor. I knew he'd be gone by the time I came back from Pace's and I knew Mom would be on the sofa finishing Danielle Steele as if nothing had happened—more tranxenes. I was right on the first count—

the Jeep wasn't at the car lot or at home. Mom, on the other hand, was a wreck. Just sitting on the front porch, red-faced and puffy-eyed. There wasn't much I could say.

"You okay?"

She nodded, sniffling. I started to ask if he had hurt her, but I knew he had never hit her so far, so I assumed he wouldn't start. The wounds he gave went deeper, cleaner, invisible to the naked eye.

"Get you anything?"

She shook her head, tried to smile, which seemed odd to me.

"Okay, if you need me, I'll be inside." I walked into the dimly lit house, the ceiling fan whispering. I shivered from the chill of the air conditioner, turned it off, thought I heard him cough in their bedroom.

The house looked worn and tired, preserved like a museum I had returned to visit. I picked up Stephen King from behind the dentist's chair and carried it around like a part of me. I wasn't sure what to do with myself, with my life, where to go, what to see. I thought of the Grand Canyon and Key West, Yellowstone and Disneyland—all the places I could go. I couldn't imagine leaving her, though, and I couldn't imagine taking her with me. My bank account was up to almost a thousand dollars. Air fares were cheap right now, at least until August first.

I lay in bed, still in my clothes, listened to the creak from my mother's heart on the porch swing and wondered where he was, what he was thinking, what he was doing. He was driving somewhere, I felt sure of it, could see him red-faced in the dark womb of the Jeep, the top down. What part of him was in me I didn't know and I wished I could sever it, cut it clean out never to return, or I wished I could give in to it, let it grow like cancer until I was him. But I could do neither, forced somewhere in between, the son, the boy-man of the father.

My mother was up and gone the next morning by the time I hit the snooze button; my father had not come home.

The morning loomed overcast, but the weather forecast promised that we would not have rain and that the drought would continue.

At the bank, the normalcy of the superficial comforted me, the sameness of counting money, the customer chatter, "Gonna rain out there? We sure need it. No more of this drought." I knew I was quieter than usual, but excused it to the others as sleepiness.

"Honey, you depressed about something, ain't ya?" BeBe looked sympathetically through purple mascara. "You just ain't yourself today. I can tell, I'm a good judge of character, I get it from watchin' my stories, and I think you're more than just sleepy. You bummed about somethin'? I know it may not be none of my business, but if you wanna talk to someone, old BeBe has a sympathetic ear."

I didn't know what to say. I impulsively wanted to tell it all, condense my life, even this summer, into a ten-minute paragraph, as if I were a guest with Oprah or Donahue.

"Thanks, BeBe, I appreciate it. I . . . guess I am bummed about something. Things with my parents, you know, we're startin' to get on each other's nerves. But I'll make out all right." I sounded slick and she knew it, but she didn't press me.

"If you want to talk, I'm here." With that she turned away and headed to the counting machine to verify strapped bills. Her bright, flowery skirt, cherries and oranges, billowed and bloomed in sharp contrast to the dark cloudy sky outside.

Just then a customer came in. I was grateful for the interruption. I didn't like staying in my head so much, talking myself in and out of mood swings. That's what I'd done most of my life, siphoned the venom from my family and internalized it to the point where I was immune. Only I wasn't. The older I got the more I realized how far from normal we really were, how screwed up we all were. I was ready for my life to be different.

"Boy, quit your dreamin' and balance that drawer," BeBe laughed at herself as she poked my ribs. "Closin' time, and I want out of here."

I watched BeBe count her money-till, then her drawer, with an unself-conscious grace, an elegance with her purple nails and the jingle of bracelets and rings.

I started counting my own drawer and was short by twenty dollars, which I knew had to be a tray of nickels I'd overlooked. Sure enough, I found it in the very back of my coin vault, hidden behind a tower of quarter trays.

"Aren't you finished yet?" BeBe leaned over and purred in my ear.

"You got a few minutes . . . after we leave here?" I decided to take her up on her offer.

"Sure I do. We'll go get a Coke or somethin'," she smiled sincerely.

We waited until the others had pulled out ahead of us, then BeBe hopped in the big Merc with me. A few fat drops of rain were just starting to plop on the pavement.

"What's up?" BeBe asked, her dark eyes wide and intense. She leaned into the plush velour, toward me, and I noticed the windows were starting to steam up, condensation from the rain or some scientific phenomenon I'd learned in earth science class but couldn't recall.

For a minute I panicked, imagining my father driving by and seeing me in a steamed-up car with a black girl. But then I didn't care, after all he was gone, and even if he hadn't been I'd have risked it anyway. In fact, as I shifted toward her, I felt drowsy and aroused, no embarrassment, only curiosity.

I briefly imagined arranging for my parents to walk in on BeBe and me at home. She'd wear some lacy negligee from Victoria's Secret and coo softly in my bed as my parents charged in. I grinned and then remembered why I'd asked her to join me.

"Where to start . . . like I told you this afternoon, my folks and I aren't gettin' along too well. My father drinks, see, and he started up again this weekend, and now he's gone. He didn't come home last night, and we don't know where he is. My mom's all upset and I don't know what to do." I took a deep breath.

"I'm tired of it, that's all I know."

"Does he hit your momma? My daddy used to beat my momma up, then my brother DeWayne got big enough to hit him back. Momma finally left him."

Her attempt at connection, identification sobered me, attracted me, made me want to ask her what she did with it all, what it meant, if anything.

"So you go off to college, Bounty. Get out while there's an opportunity. Didn't you tell me you'd been accepted at UT? Just wait it out till then." She sounded sure of herself, someone who took action and thought about consequences later—my opposite.

"I don't know if it's that easy, BeBe. I hate to leave my mother with him—you know? Sometimes I even think he'll change, but he never does. I want to leave, but I'm scared to go. I feel crazy sometimes."

She reached across and put her hand on mine, and I was touched.

"We all do . . . we all got things to break away from, things to move on to," she said.

"I'm supposed to go to freshman orientation this weekend, visit the campus, mingle, preregister for classes, and stuff. But I don't know if I should. The timin' isn't so great with my dad gone and all. I haven't reminded my mom yet. . . ."

"You gotta go. Didn't you tell me before that she wants you to go? She cares about you, Bounty, that's why she wants you to go to school and make somethin' of yourself." She paused, trying to think of what to say next.

"I think you gonna be a writer or actor or something. Somebody famous. You ever write about all this stuff you tellin' me? I keep a diary. It helps me a lot. Cheap therapy."

"You sound like Mrs. Hartsel now—did you have her for senior English?—she always told me that I had a way with words. She'd recommend books and poems for me to read. She told me I had a different way of seein' things than most folks. That's what she wrote in my yearbook. I'd forgotten that till now."

I liked the idea of writing, of putting the events of my life into a story, something orderly, controllable. I'd written a few poems before, sappy descriptions of places and sunsets, that sort of thing. In sixth grade I wrote a story that I then bound with a cover in art class. Something about a boy detective searching for his kidnaped father at the Grand Canyon.

"Anythin' else wrong? Anythin' else you wanna tell me?" Her voice was soothing, comfortable. I debated all kinds of things to tell her—my attraction to Heraldson's charisma, my desire to grow up, my fear of turning out like my father—but finally shook my head and smiled.

"I appreciate you listenin'. It means a lot. Thanks. I think I will write about some of this. I think somebody gave me a blank book for graduation. Thanks, BeBe."

She squeezed my hand again, allowing me to avoid the awkward decision of whether to hug her or not. The windows had really steamed up now so I rolled down my side; the rain had eased into a fine mist.

"If you need to talk more, call me. Here's my number. I know there's a lot you're not tellin' me. That's okay. We all got our secrets," she said and winked.

At first I thought the week would pass uneventfully, a pocket of time serving as an indicator of alternate reality, what it would have been like if my parents had divorced and it had only been me and my mother. Or what it would have been like if he had died, leaving the strong widow and junior to carry on. I noticed we were even starting to refer to him in the past tense.

"Damn him—excuse my French," my mother said Tuesday night. "I don't know how on earth I'm supposed to make the payment on that run-down car lot and pay all the other bills. He knows I hate this—I don't even know half of his deals, who he owes and when. And I hate callin' the bank and askin' questions like I'm the man's secretary instead of his wife."

She sat with a stack of envelopes, stamps, checkbooks, and stick-on mailing labels—some with our address, some with J & R Motors'.

"Bounty, is there any way you can check on our accounts when you're at work tomorrow? I mean, just to make sure none of them are overdrawn. Maybe check on outstandin' loans, too—see if he's taken out any I don't know about or don't have coupon booklets for. Could you do that for me?" My mother wore her reading glasses and she looked stern in her request, a teacher commanding a student to do homework.

"Sure, I could do that. I mean, we're not supposed to go accessin' through the computer for random accounts—you know, right to privacy and all that. But it's been a slow week so I don't think that'd be a problem." I debated on telling her that on slow days BeBe and I frequently scanned the accounts of individuals we knew, friends, the mayor, the county commissioner, Pastor Stuckey, even Clark Heraldson (he's loaded, CDs out the nose). But I didn't.

"That'd help a lot, hon, thanks." Her voice softened as she returned to her bill collage.

"Who's runnin' the car lot? What'd you tell Ricky?"

"I told him that Jim had to be out of town unexpectedly this week and if he had any problems to give me a call. He's got enough to do to keep him busy."

"We're okay then, aren't we? I mean, we're not goin' bankrupt or anything?" Even though I had a scholarship, I envisioned foregoing even community college to pay off my family's debt, all because of my father's carelessness.

"Oh, no, Bounty. Don't you be worryin' now. We're covered, at least through August, and your father will be back. . . . We're fine. I shouldn't be talkin' business with you. You don't be worryin' about my problems—okay?"

My mother had a smudge of ink on her chin where she had carelessly idled the pen. I licked my thumb and wiped it away.

"Okay, just checkin' to make sure. I've got some money in savings, you know. . . . I can help out."

"Absolutely not, Bounty. That's your money for school. What if your student loan doesn't go through? No, you hold on to that money. We're fine. Forget I even mentioned it." She had been firmly composed but flared at the last statement, angry, as if I pitied her.

I found myself fidgeting and decided to change the subject.

"This came in the mail today. Have you forgotten about this weekend? Freshman orientation at UT?" I handed the orange postcard over to her. I had decided I wanted to go. BeBe was right. I'd been to football games in Knoxville before with Pace and his father, but I had to go and at least see what the campus was really like. I might not like it, might not want to go there after all.

"I haven't forgotten. I'm taking Friday off so we can get an early start."

"What about Daddy?" I asked.

"What about him? He wouldn't go if he were here anyway."

"But I thought you wanted him to go to help change his mind, help him see how good that college would be for me."

She placed her glasses upside down on a stack of clean envelopes. "Son, I want a lot of things I don't get. We'll go and have a good time this weekend. You wait and see." The old, false optimism crept back into her voice. I knew how to respond.

"Sure, we'll have a good time."

The rest of the evening I spent alone on the porch swing, writing in the crisp pages of my new journal. It had an Indian design on the cover that I liked, a Navajo rug pattern or something. I doodled awhile, sketched the beech tree in the front yard, started putting down sentences about where I was, the questions I had about the future. Then I started writing a story. I wasn't sure what it was about or where it was going, but I thought up this character named Chance who lived on a farm with his parents and wanted to go away to school, only his drunk father wouldn't let him go. It ended with Chance an old man, living on the same small farm, with a son of his own who'd won a scholarship to Harvard. Pretty stupid story, I guess, but I liked the way it made me feel.

That night I dreamed that my mother and I were in a big conference room with hundreds of other parents and freshmen. My father staggered on to the stage, punched the suited speaker, broke a whiskey bottle across the podium, and called out my name. "Bounty! You can't stay," he bellowed. "You'll never amount to nothin'." I woke up in a sweat and kicked the sheet to the foot of my bed.

The next day I enlisted BeBe's help in scanning my father's accounts. This meant, of course, that I had to tell her more details of the story, my father's backhanded deals at the car lot, and more importantly my intuitive sense that my father and Heraldson were cooking up something. I couldn't decide whether to tell her about the photograph I'd found in his desk drawer.

Since the morning was still gray and overcast—it had rained intermittently throughout the night—business was slow. An occasional money order or check to cash, but that was about all. So right before my lunch break BeBe and I strolled over to my computer terminal together. She had a sheaf of papers in her hand, like we were doing important business, entering address changes or purging accounts that had long since been closed. Mrs. Sherman was typing up a report on money-market accounts. The drive-thru kept Sarah Anne busy with a steady flow of folks avoiding the chance of more rain. Rosenstein was at a meeting in Crescent.

We began with J & R Motors' accounts and found five different ones—two checking, one savings, two outstanding loans. Cringing as I rolled the screen, I expected to find some mystery loan that was overdue for thousands of dollars. The carpetbaggers and scalawags would come and repossess Tara while the "massah" was away. My father would return to find Momma and me sitting blank-faced out in the yard with a handful of belongings the bank hadn't auctioned off.

But I found no such loans or anything amiss. My father had, indeed, made the loan payments through September 1, and all the accounts had at least a few hundred dollars. So then I pulled up the accounts in my father's name, and you'd have thought he was Donald Trump or something. "Whoa," BeBe said, "I didn't know y'all were rich." Not exactly, I tried to explain. Many of them were closed accounts but were still on file for record-keeping. In his time in Crescent County, my father had signed on over ten different checking accounts, eight different savings, two CDs, and had cosigned over two dozen loans.

I was just about to quit the search when BeBe pulled my hand back from the keyboard. "What's this?" she asked. The last number on the screen came up as a dormant account.

Usually for the bank to declare an account dormant meant it hadn't seen any transaction activity for five years. Often dormant accounts are those forgotten by old folks or unknown to survivors after someone dies. But I couldn't imagine that my father forgot anything having to do with money, so I pulled up the account history.

Only the computer wouldn't let me, which had never happened to either of us before. "Access denied, enter code 7," it read. I tried every configuration with a seven in it, but the same message beeped back at us. BeBe tried with the same results.

"I'll be right back," I said.

"Where you goin'?" BeBe watched me cross the lobby to Mrs. Sherman's desk.

"Mrs. Sherman?"

"Uh-huh, just a second, Bounty." She typed one last sentence before looking up.

"What's it mean on the computer when you're pullin' up an account and it denies access? It says, 'Access denied, enter code 7.' What's code 7? I don't remember you mentioning it when you trained me."

"That's because I didn't. I'm not sure I've ever seen one myself. Code 7 simply means it's a classified account that needs a password for computer entry. Usually it's a wire-transfer account that some big shot uses to play the stock market, somethin' like that. Whose account is it? Anybody I know?" Her eyes twinkled at the prospect of new gossip, or at least speculation.

"No, ma'am, just an account for some lawyer in Pikeville. We were updating the address and found the code 7. I'll just send the change of address card in to the main branch in Crescent."

"That'll be fine, Bounty. They'll have the access code there."

She turned back to her typing, and I reported back to BeBe.

"That's big stuff," she punctuated with a whistle.

"I doubt it's any big deal. Still, I plan to find out."

"How's that?"

"I'm not sure yet. I'll look for the access code in my father's office, in his little book. If I still don't find it, I'll go to the main branch and get it."

"Your daddy may not like you pokin' around in his business, you know," BeBe cautioned.

"It's too late for carin' what he thinks. I'm entitled to the truth for a change. I'm goin' to lunch—bring you back anything?"

She nodded and pinched my arm.

As I headed to the diner, I let out a whistle and felt a knot in my stomach as big as a ball of baler's twine. My father had too many secrets, and they all seemed to be sliding out of their hiding places. I wasn't sure if I could bear to uncover them all.

My mother made her third casserole of the week that night for supper, summer squash with peas and soup and mystery meat, which I think was chicken or maybe some kind of canned fish. She played the jazz station all the time now and recognized many of the songs being played. "Listen to this," she'd say as if she were playing the sax or trumpet instead of David Sanborne or one of the Marsalis brothers. I smiled and nodded like a doting parent.

"I checked on all the accounts down at the bank. Everythin' looks fine through the first of September."

I dried while she washed.

"Good. That's good news. Did I tell you I'm gettin' a dishwasher, Bounty? I called Sears in Pikeville today, and they'll deliver it and install it next Monday. I'm so excited."

My mother coveted appliances, dreamed about dishwashers and microwaves, refrigerators with ice makers in the door, crockpots with self-timers and multiple settings. She had been shopping for a dishwasher for the past two years, warming my father up to the idea. Like most vehicles of progress, new appliances were something my father held in contempt. He always had a comeback ready anytime the topic came up. "My momma washed all her dishes by hand, so clean you could eat off 'em for a week. Them machines don't get things clean, they leave chunks of dried food. Ain't sanitary."

"That's great, Mom. Can we afford that right now?" I hated to be a wet blanket.

"I've been savin' for it for some time now. Don't worry about the money," she assured me.

"Okay, whatever you say." It was nice to see her happy for a change, distracted by the convenience of modern technology. And I was relieved that she hadn't mentioned the "d" word yet, hadn't confided in me about what she didn't get from her husband. This happened the last time he left, the time he went to New Orleans. I tried to get my mother to confide in Sally Kelly, a woman she worked with at the insurance agency, but Mom said Sally meant well and could be trusted, but her husband couldn't, and Sally told Harold everything. So that left me as confidant.

I folded my dishcloth across the little towel bar adjacent to the sink and headed to watch some TV. My mother continued puttering around the kitchen, measuring the counter with a

J & R Motors' yardstick, sketching a floor plan, in anticipation of the dishwasher. She couldn't decide where to put it.

During a commercial—I was watching a John Wayne movie, made in the fifties, I think—I went to make some popcorn and saw my mother sitting on the end of my bed, tears running down her face, my journal in her lap.

"What are you doing?" I grabbed the multicolored cover out of her hands as if I were rescuing her from a burning coal she was unable to release herself.

She sniffed. "I read your little story in there. I can't believe you hate us so much." And then her clenched teeth softened to a pout, all pitiful and childlike, the little girl not invited to the birthday party.

"I can't believe you read this. I had that in my dresser drawer, closed. Not that it would have made any difference if I'd left it face up on the kitchen table. You don't have any right to snoop in my journal; it's private. Damn, I can't believe this."

She had started crying again as I ranted, then her mood shifted as if she remembered she was the parent.

"Watch your tongue, mister. Don't you cuss at me. I won't tolerate it. Who do you think you are?"

"Who do you think you are, is what I want to know? You just randomly go around lookin' for things in my drawers? Were you lookin' for pot or a pint bottle or old *Playboy*s or somethin'? I'll be glad to accommodate if you tell me what you're lookin' for." My heart drummed in my head and I could feel a vein protruding from my neck.

"I was puttin' away your clean laundry, for heaven sake. I just saw it there and opened it to see what it was. I wasn't snoopin' around. Don't talk to me like I'm some kinda dog. I'm still your mother. I got a right to read what's in my own house. You're the one who's breakin' my heart. If you hate us this much, why don't you just leave?" She stood up and went to my window, pulled the cotton curtain back as if she were expecting someone.

"I don't believe this. You're makin' me feel like I'm the one who's done somethin' wrong, when I haven't. You're the one who violated my privacy." I relished the word *violated*.

She was crying again, almost rhythmically, but my heart had hardened toward her.

"Son, promise me you won't ever write about me . . . about the family. Not till after I'm dead at least. Write about anythin' you want, just not my life. Promise?"

I was stunned. "That's not fair to me. I don't know if I can do that."

"I guess it doesn't matter what's fair to me? Let me tell you something," the fierceness in her voice surprised me, "you're not the only one who wants to leave this place. Some days I wake up and I think about packing a suitcase, walkin' out that door and never lookin' back. I've done the best I can for you, Bounty. If that's not good enough, then I'm sorry."

"It's a story, Momma. Somethin' I made up, don't mean anything, don't take it so literally."

"I won't be goin' with you to Knoxville this weekend. If you hate me as much as you hate your father in this story, you don't want me there anyway." She wiped her nose across the sleeve of her gingham house dress.

She played her trump card against me, a strategy for shifting the burden of guilt back on my shoulders.

"You know I need you to go with me this weekend—I need at least one parent there."

She walked to the door and added one last blow: "You're turnin' out just like your father."

Outside on the porch swing I heard a gunshot. It was Mr. Allison next door shooting a possum down from the persimmon tree in his back yard. I fantasized momentarily, not about taking my own life with his shotgun, but about my mother thinking I had. Maybe she was inside at that very moment wondering if I were slumped in the yard, bleeding out all the guilt she stirred in me.

Somewhere in one of the shoeboxes under my bed I had some fake blood left over from a Halloween party. Or what if I went for the real thing? Daddy's extra pistol was loaded and waiting in the second drawer of the china cabinet. It made me nervous sometimes to see it lying there when I'd be rummaging in the drawer for a deck of cards or a rubber band. It looked so powerful, so permanent. I had once imagined myself picking it up, walking into the living room where my parents sat watching TNN, and smiling through tears as I placed it to my temple and pulled the trigger. They'd never get over it.

But then neither would I. Effective revenge is so permanent, not to mention melodramatic. Is that what I wanted?

Revenge? A payback for what? For making sure I've always been clothed and fed, for giving me the Mercury when I turned sixteen (I'd wanted a motorcycle), for loving me too much? Or was it more for escape—I didn't want to die so much as I wanted out of a situation I couldn't handle.

Walking up our street, past the hedgerow of honeysuckle and kudzu that separated us from the Allisons, I realized how young I really was, how everything in life really was before me, only out of reach. The streetlight at the top of the hill cast my shadow diagonally away from me, stretched itself into the dark field on the other side. It depressed me to think this way.

On my twelfth birthday I had told my mother that I was tired of being a child and that I wanted more than anything to be an adult. Her eyes teared and she said, "Enjoy your childhood while you can. Once you're grown, everythin' changes and you'll look back to your childhood as the best days of your life." She robbed me of some hope that day, but she didn't drain it all. I couldn't believe those were the best days of my life. Hell, if it wasn't going to get any better, I wanted out. Despite her words I hung on to my belief—being an adult had to give you more freedom, more hope for happiness, for some semblance of a normal life.

But how to get there? If only it were a matter of geography, I could cross the state line into Adulthood, safely out of my parents' jurisdiction. And wasn't that what I was banking on, going away to college, leaving the car lot, leaving them behind? Somehow I couldn't imagine my life separated from theirs, though. Like trying to pull one thread from a bolt of cloth, only to watch the whole fabric come undone.

I reached the end of our street and cars were lined up in the ditches on either side of Old Franklin Highway. Families walked by flashlight over to the cluster of trailers dotted along the roadside next to our pasture. The only other light was from a single porch bulb. I was remembering what Daddy had told me about the Odells' divine apparition. I couldn't believe that many people were out on a weeknight looking at an upright deep-freeze, but my own curiosity edged me closer.

Elbowing my way to the small cement porch wasn't as easy as I'd thought. Folks lingered as if it was a church service, chatted quietly, murmured among themselves. Some left little gifts, bouquets of flowers, apples, scented candles, photographs, a rosary. Jessie Odell worked the crowd, guided her best friends and neighbors up to the rail for the best view. Hubert, her husband, stood in the shadows on the dark side of the freezer like a bodyguard. I edged closer and turned to find myself face-to-face with Miss Jessie.

"Oh, Bounty, I'm so glad you've come to share our miracle. Did your momma and daddy come too?"

"No, ma'am, just me tonight. They send their regards."

She took my arm and gently guided me up front, the small crowd parting in her wake. "That's too bad. Tell them I'd love for them to come over. Look here, son." She pointed a bony finger. I had to angle my head back and forth, holding it just right, to find the image.

Sure enough, there was a profile there on the side of the deep-freeze. Various dents and scratches caught the light, panned shadow and reflection into the profile of a long-haired, bearded man. It could have been Jesus, but it could just as well have been Willie Nelson or a ZZ Top band member. It reminded me of those paintings of Jesus where he looks all moon-eyed and frail, hands folded in prayer, pale and fragile as a ghost. I laughed out loud.

Miss Jessie looked up at me with raised eyebrows as I turned my laugh into a cough.

"That's something, all right," I said politely.

"Don't you see Jesus, Bounty?" she asked.

"Well, it sure looks like him, doesn't it?"

"You are a believer, aren't you?" I realized my mouth was open. She continued: "—be right back, I've got a little pamphlet from my church that will explain all about how much you need the Lord. Wait right here." She hurried up the steps and disappeared into the trailer.

A man behind me whispered to his wife, "Pray for Jimmy

McGraw. Down at the diner I heard he's drinkin' again."

I slipped into step with a family of four as they were leaving and mingled my way out into the darkness.

The car ride to Knoxville was laboriously long, green hills refreshed by the recent rain and gray interstate pouring by slow as molasses. I drove my mother's Cutlass, and she sat in silence for the first half of the trip, all the way to Chattanooga.

"Traffic's heavy for middle of the afternoon," she finally said.

"Hungry? Cleveland's the next exit."

"That's fine. Whatever you want." She turned her head back to the window, folded her hands across her lap.

"I appreciate you comin' with me, takin' today off and everything," I said. We'd already made a kind of peace the night before, the night following our big blowout. She'd apologized and said we had to stick together, that I was all she had. "Of course I'm goin' with you this weekend," she'd offered. I accepted and tried to forget about our fight, but she wasn't making it easy. Or maybe she was depressed about Daddy; I never could tell since her moods often stayed the same even though the catalysts behind them would swing.

I pulled into a Wendy's in Cleveland. After we'd ordered and sat down with our food, I asked, "Why didn't you ever go to college? You're smart." Some attempt to change the subject.

She nibbled her cheeseburger and looked me in the eye, half-smiling.

"You know I was married before . . ." she began.

"Who says divorced people can't go to college?"

"It was different then, Bounty. Divorce wasn't as commonplace as it is now. I had to move back in with Mom and Daddy, take a job at the hat factory in LaFayette. Money was tight." She paused to sip her iced tea and looked at me as if I was too naive to understand what she was trying to explain.

"So how'd you meet Daddy?" It came out before I could

help it, before I remembered I was trying to distract her from her present circumstances.

"Did you know I almost married a different man?" She sounded coy, her voice suddenly infused with energy, a fisherman telling about the one that got away.

"*No*, you never told me. Who was he?"

"His name was George Grisham. From Murfreesboro, sold insurance there. We met through mutual friends at a VFW dance at the armory. He was tall, had a moustache like Clark Gable. We dated four months and he asked me to marry him."

"Why didn't you?"

"He had been married before, had a little girl by his first wife. I wasn't sure I was ready to be a mother. I was afraid he drank too much, wouldn't settle down."

"So you broke it off?"

"Worse. He got drafted and went to Vietnam. I wrote him a letter, mailed the ring he'd given me back to his parents. I never heard from him again . . ." her voiced lowered, trailed to a whisper.

I tried to imagine my mother breaking some soldier's heart.

"A little over a year later, he came back, moved to Nashville, but I had met your father by then."

"How'd you meet Daddy?" I repeated the question deliberately this time.

"Same way—at a dance. I didn't like him at first. He was sellin' used cars in Fayetteville, wore the loudest ties I'd ever seen. Kept callin' me at work, pesterin' me to go out with him, sent me flowers, yellow roses with baby's breath. I finally gave in. A month later we got married. . . ."

I thought she was about to smile.

"Did you love him?" I thought about the picture in my cigar box then, my father with his other family, thought about telling her about it. But I caught myself, wondered what that would really accomplish. I thought about George Grisham and his little girl, wondered if he ever remarried, wondered if he hated my mother, if he ever thought of her.

"What a question! Course I did." She paused. "Love makes you do strange things, Bounty."

"Ever think about what would've happened if you'd married George?"

"Sure I do. I read where he's a lawyer up in Louisville now. Imagine me a lawyer's wife, we'd have a big, fine house with white columns, some horses. You'd be goin' to Vanderbilt or Sewanee this fall. We'd travel in the summers, Europe. . . ."

"If you'd married him, you wouldn't have me." I sounded afraid, as if her imagining an alternative life could somehow erase me. A woman at the table beside us looked over at me curiously.

"Of course I would. I mean, you'd have a different father, but—"

"And a different name. I'd be a totally different person. Without Daddy as my father I wouldn't be who I am. Know what I mean?" I lowered my voice.

She considered it a moment. "Yes, I guess you're right. Maybe you're the one good thing that's come from our marriage. One." She patted my hand.

The rest of the drive was interspersed with lighter chatter, we didn't mention my father or other alternative lives she might have lived. We checked in—we were staying in dorm rooms for that authentic college experience. I carried her red overnight bag to her side of the dorm before finding my room on the opposite wing.

At the get-acquainted mixer that night we stood in line at the buffet and talked with a couple from Memphis and their daughter Marybeth. I knew how her name was spelled because we all had to wear name tags, which I knew my mother hated. She much preferred being a wallflower, a silent observer, the shy one who never danced.

The mixer was held outside and a breeze sighed through

the courtyard. It was actually cool and refreshing, unlike the tepid wind that occasionally whispered at home. There was still light even though the sun had set. Folding chairs had been set in clusters across the patio, facing a makeshift stage. While we munched sandwiches and chips, some genuine college students—student orientation assistants, they were called—rambled over the loudspeaker about tomorrow's agenda, the history of the university, and the wonderful journey we were all about to embark upon. I sat next to Marybeth and noticed how pretty she was, short blonde hair and brown eyes, and wondered if she was as nervous as I was. Her parents asked questions about Clearfield, my job at the bank, what my parents did.

"Did Mr. McGraw come?" Marybeth asked politely.

My mother went stiff in her chair, a paper plate balanced precariously in her lap. "No, he had to be away on business," she responded, smiling weakly. My mother wasn't a good liar, I realized.

On the way back to her tiny dorm room, my mother said, "Do I embarrass you, son?" It was a loaded question, of course, but she sounded so pathetic that I had no choice but to reassure her.

"No, of course not. Why would you ask somethin' like that?" The elevator was empty except for us, and I smelled stale beer as we were lifted to the twelfth floor.

"Oh, I don't know. . . . I just see all these young people with nice lookin' parents, respectable mothers and fathers in nice clothes who lead nice lives. It makes me sad for you." She lowered her head as we came to a gentle stop on her floor.

As we walked down the long corridor of the east wing, all was quiet. Most of the other parents were still in the courtyard or else out on the town. I didn't know what to say in response to my mother.

I unlocked her door for her and said, "Can I have the keys to the car? Thought I might go explorin' a little bit. You can come with me if you want." It was a genuine offer.

"No, I'm gettin' a headache, think I'll turn in early. Here's the keys, but please be careful, and don't stay out late—okay? We got an early start tomorrow, breakfast at eight, campus tour at nine." She sounded more like herself, and I jangled the keys around my finger.

"I'll remember. And I'll be careful," I said.

"Would you check in with me when you come back, just so I'll know you're okay?" Her voice pleaded again and I couldn't turn her down.

On my way back down to the lobby the elevator stopped on the seventh floor and Marybeth got on.

"Get your parents tucked in okay?" I asked.

"Are you kiddin'? They're out at some bar with one of my dad's old buddies. He's an alum so they know people in town." She brushed her yellow-white bangs out of her eyes. "Where you headed?"

"I don't know, out to discover the big city. Wanna come?" I really added the invitation to be polite and was surprised when she accepted.

We drove down Cumberland Avenue—the Strip, as it was called—with its fast-food places, bars, and bookstores. Marybeth did indeed know the city, as she took me out west to view the big homes on the Tennessee River, then downtown to the World's Fair site with its big gold eye, the Sunsphere, looking over the city.

"Let's have a drink, Bounty," she said as we watched huge goldfish in a murky pond. "I know a place that'll serve a ten-year-old," she laughed.

I felt nervous and uncertain. I'd drunk with Pace a few times when I'd visited him in Nashville, but never with a parent so close in proximity. I didn't think my mother could bear it if she caught me with a drink in my hand. After my father had offered me the beer at our Fourth of July picnic, she told me that she had dreamed the scene over that night, except that I'd accepted

99

and split a six-pack with him. Then we were shooting bourbon, and pretty soon both of us had passed out in the living room. My mother said I was on the couch and she kept trying to rouse me and couldn't.

But her dreams were not my own.

"You drink, don't you? How about a beer?" Marybeth took a penny out of her jeans shorts and tossed it in the pond among the fish.

We ended up at a place called The Aquarium that she had discovered with an older cousin the previous football season. It had fishnet everywhere, not just on the walls, but over door-ways and tables, with seashells and plastic fish. The floor was covered with pale red gravel that crunched when I tilted back in my chair.

Marybeth kept me entertained with stories of her job at a woman's clothing store in Germantown. "So snobby," she said and rattled on about selling a rather large, affluent woman a leather mini-dress. I felt pretty good, actually forgot where I was and that my mother was only a few blocks away. By the time Marybeth poured the last amber drops from our pitcher it was after midnight.

She held my arm and then my hand as we walked from the parking lot back to the dorm. I felt so warm and unself-conscious from the beer that I kissed her when we were in the elevator alone. I couldn't believe it; the old Bounty would never have been so bold, regardless of the buzz. She pressed back and promised to see me at breakfast in the morning.

I floated all the way back to my room, then I remembered I was supposed to call Mom and let her know I was okay. I found her waiting for me outside my door and I literally almost wet my pants, my bladder full and relaxed.

"Where have you been? I thought you were just goin' for a short drive?" Her eyes were red, and I dreaded the conversation because I knew I couldn't win.

"Yes, ma'am, I was, but then I ran into Marybeth—you remember, from supper?—and she knows Knoxville pretty well so she showed me a few sights. You know, the World's Fair site, Neyland Stadium, downtown. The time just slipped away from us. . . ."

We were inside my room now, the tiny window overlooking big elm trees in the corner of the courtyard. There was no air conditioning so the room felt claustrophobic and stuffy. My mother turned her face so close into mine that I thought she was going to kiss me.

"You've been drinkin', haven't you? I smell beer on you." She kept shaking her head and I wanted to grab it in my hands and hold it still.

"We had a beer, no big deal."

"I don't believe you, son. You're a mystery to me. Give me the car keys." She held out her hand and held back more tears.

I handed over the keys, saying, "Don't make this a big deal. She's a nice girl."

"That's all you need is a girlfriend."

"What's that supposed to mean? I'm not a kid, not your little boy."

The tears were flowing in small rivulets down her cheeks, and I handed her a tissue.

"You'll always be my little boy. Damn you," she said and blew her nose. I didn't understand and didn't want to.

"I'm tired, Momma, we both are. I'll walk you back to your room."

"No, I'm fine. We're not through talkin' about this. Good night."

I lay on my bunk bed pressed against the wall and listened to her footsteps pad down the hall to the elevator. My body felt tired and worn, a piece of wire bent back and forth until it was fatigued to the breaking point. I had to get out of my parents' house, out of Clearfield for good, and that night only confirmed it.

———

The rest of the weekend also confirmed my feelings. Despite my mother's icy words at breakfast—she said we would discuss the previous night on the way home—I thoroughly enjoyed Saturday and spent most of it with Marybeth.

Along with four hundred other prospective freshmen (out of the several thousand who would attend that fall), we toured classrooms and laboratories, had our picture taken in front of the Torchbearer, and lunched in Smokey's in the student center. In the afternoon we met individually with student advisors who were no help at all—I signed up for psychology, calculus, biology, English, and philosophy—and told us that we'd have to change our schedules anyway when we arrived in the fall.

My mother hit it off with a widow her age whose son would also be a freshman. They chatted nervously about the weather, about raising children, about small town life. Orientation was over before I knew it.

Marybeth and I exchanged phone numbers and addresses, and I told her then that I might not see her in the fall.

"What do you mean?" she said.

"If my student loan doesn't go through, I'm stuck at home," I answered.

"You'll be here. Find a way." She smiled seductively and kissed me on the cheek in front of my mother. Her father shook my hand and said he'd see me on football weekends in the fall.

***

As we headed down I-75 out of Knoxville, I felt triumphant, elated. I would find some way to slip out of my parents' grasp. I was a son, not a slave, not a psychologist or marriage therapist. It was time for them to let me go. I decided then and there that no matter how much they resisted I would do whatever it took to break free and attend the University of Tennessee.

While I was savoring my freedom vow, my mother sat staring out the window, more subdued than I expected. Finally she closed her eyes and propped herself against the headrest. When she finally spoke we had already put an hour's drive behind us.

"Slow down, please; you're speeding," she said calmly and evenly.

"Yes, ma'am. . . .Tired?"

"Yes, I am." She was suddenly animated. "And you know what tired me the most? Worryin' myself to death last night about you. What if you'd had a wreck? Or been stopped for DUI? Bounty, I can't handle you actin' up on top of everythin' else that's goin' on. Surely you can understand that. Please. For me." She paused and swallowed hard. "You've always been so good. Why now? What's got into you?" She asked this as if I were deliberately plotting to drive her mad.

"I told you before. I'm not a kid anymore. I'm an adult, and it's time I started makin' my own decisions. If you and Daddy can't accept that, it's not my problem." I was suddenly doing seventy miles an hour.

"You're eighteen years old. I'm still your mother. I'm tired of talkin' about this. But I promise you this: If I catch you drinkin', let alone drivin' too, I'll ground you. Take your car away so fast it'll make your head spin. Don't forget who pays your insurance."

She snapped on the radio and I thought the knob would come off in her hand. The "seek" button cruised up and down the dial until my mother stopped it on a station blaring a dixieland blend, heavy horns, drums, piano, and bass. My earlier bravado seemed silly and inflated, a pipe dream as implausible as my marrying Marybeth. I drove seventy-five the rest of the way home.

We spoke no more than the necessary monosyllables on Sunday, but by Monday morning we were both trying to act as if nothing had happened. My father had now been gone for a week, and I didn't like waiting for my mother to fall apart even further. Even anticipating her new dishwasher, to be delivered that afternoon, hadn't cheered her as I'd hoped it would. I didn't think I could bear it when that night she asked me what I thought she should do.

"I can't live like this," she said as we sat watching Vanna White striptease the alphabet on *Wheel of Fortune*. Mom had brought home a deluxe pizza from Terry's Steak and Shake—a conciliatory gesture, I'd thought—and the gutted crust lay in the box at our feet.

"You think I should divorce him, don't you?"

"I don't honestly know, Mom. I know it's hard on you. Course, he'd be hard on any woman. I honestly don't know." I picked a mushroom off the last slice on my plate. Pat assisted the lucky contestant in the bonus round and the answer was "Double Indemnity."

"I wish I could tell you," I added.

She collected the plates and forks she'd insisted on us using and hurried to try her new dishwasher while I retreated outside.

From the porch swing, I watched the clouds collect for a thunderstorm. The breeze blew cool and smelled so much like rain, it was like watermelon, sweet and wet. The leaves unfurled and turned their backs to me, further proof. Lightning cracked against the back of the hillsides, and I felt the first big drops splatter my arm.

As it thundered, I noticed my mother standing in the doorway, stoic and lost in the distance. I motioned for her to join me.

"How's the dishwasher?" I asked.

"Fine. I love it," she responded halfheartedly.

"Reach any life-changing decisions?"

"No, Bounty, I'm tired. . . . I don't know what to do."

"It'll be okay, Momma—one way or another." I suddenly felt tender toward her, wanted to protect her, felt the weight of our latest skirmishes rise out of me.

We sat and rocked as the storm picked up, blowing rain away from us.

"We better go in, lightning." She started to rise. "You know what happened to Gloria Cameron's brother-in-law, fried him black as coal."

"He was on a golf course, Mom, holding a metal rod in his hand, not on his own front porch. . . . Come on, it's just a little storm."

"I'm scared, Bounty."

"You're scared of everything," I said without thinking.

"Maybe I am." She sat back down beside me, rubbed her arms.

The rain came down harder and cold, as only a summer thunderstorm can rain. We sat there letting the wind move the swing. I held the chain and wished it were a lightning rod. I'd go up in smoke, spontaneously combust before her very eyes.

"Do you ever think about dyin'?"

"Bounty, my God, as if I'm not scared to death out here already." She hit my arm lightly, like a pal.

"No, seriously, I mean—if you don't want to talk about it, that's okay—but what do you think death is like?"

She paused dramatically: "It's like dark velvet, maybe blue and crushed, or black. . . . It's peaceful and beautiful, forgetful. . . . It's not as bad as we all think it is." She smiled.

"So you're afraid of lightning, but not afraid of dyin'?"

"I didn't say I'm not afraid of it. . . . I'm just not as afraid as I used to be. . . . There are worse things than death. . . . I look in the mirror in the morning, and know what I see? I see Momma, your grandmother, looking back. The older I get, the more I see her, she's in me, her eyes and mouth, coming out a day at a time. . . ."

"I agree that death isn't so bad and there are worse things than death, but I'm not so sure that we agree on what those things are. . . . I know you hate the idea of being alone, but I don't think it's so bad. . . ."

"You're young, Bounty, and it's not so bad. But you can't see what I see. You don't see your daddy lookin' back at you in the mirror yet. . . . Someday." She looked solemn, touched her hair. "Being alone . . . is . . ." she didn't finish.

"I'm sorry I brought it up," I said.

"I'm not. I'm okay, Bounty—I'm gonna be okay, I'm stronger

than you think. I'll have what I want. I'll pay the price, and I'll be happy. . . ."

I looked at her, puzzled.

"What is it that you want?"

"I want to not be alone. I love your father, and I'm not sure I could divorce him. I'm just not sure if I can wait on him or put up with this crap—excuse my French—much longer. He and I aren't kids anymore. You wish we'd divorce, don't you? Do you hate him?"

"I don't hate him, and I don't wish you'd divorce him. That's ya'll's business, not mine. If you stayed together in the past for my sake, I'm sorry. I just want to see you both happy. I don't know what I can do for you, Mom."

"You do a lot for me, son. I just don't want you to hate me either way—if I stay with him or if we separate. I still have some thinking to do. . . ."

We rocked awhile longer, till almost dark, and then she got up.

"I love you," she said.

I wondered how I could ever leave a woman who needed me as much as she did. I guess I loved her, too. I wondered if I'd ever be forced to choose.

No word from my father, dead or alive. The rain continued most of the week, and customers at the bank mocked the weather forecasters for predicting drought. "I told you it weren't gonna be no drought this summer, could tell by the way the clouds been lookin' since May," said Old Man Hurley, with tobacco juice dripping down his chin.

"You're always right, Mr. Hurley," said Clark Heraldson from behind him, just coming in. His fancy raincoat was finally put to good use and even though his hair was wet, making it look brown instead of blond, he still looked handsome.

I turned back to rolling pennies, expecting him to head for Rosenstein's office. But instead he bounded right over to my window, purposefully. A woodsy-sweet cologne smell preceded him, Aramis or Obsession or something. He leaned into my window as if he were an old person without a cane and was so close that I could smell his breath, the corned beef smell of a man's breath, not horrible or anything, just stale. Was that gin I smelled, an early martini perhaps? Probably just the corned beef smell mingling with aftershave or cologne. Either way I liked his attention, having him so close.

He awed me with his presence, not like a movie star, but like an accomplished athlete or musician, someone with talent you envy. And what talent did I envy in Heraldson?

"How's it goin'? They treating you all right?" He flashed that golden retriever smile.

"Yes, sir. It's goin' really well. Kinda slow right now with all the rain. Folks prefer the drive-thru," I nodded in Sarah Anne's direction.

"How's your father? Haven't seen him in a while." His smile had faded.

"He's been out of town for a few days. Big buyin' trip." He nodded as if he knew I was lying.

"Well, I didn't come to check up on him. Bounty, I have an offer for you. My wife and I wondered if you'd like to go to church with us Sunday and then come home for dinner. I realize you probably attend your own church, but this Sunday is special for college and career young people at our church—we go to Crescent First Prez—I thought you might enjoy it. Give me a chance to get to know you better. Never know when I might need a good banker in the future." He smiled again, knowing I couldn't resist his charm, but there was something behind the smile, the light in his eyes perhaps, that seemed forceful and cruel, a Mafia don making an unrefusable offer.

Wasn't this what I wanted? Before I responded an entire vision flashed before my eyes. We'd be best friends, like brothers, golfing together, discussing new bank procedures, fishing, playing softball for the bank team. After a while I'd start to look like him, blonder, handsomer, tanned. Customers would ask if we were related. I'd hang out at his house, baby-sit his daughters, swim in his pool. He'd personally loan me the money to go to his alma mater. He'd come up in the fall and show me the ropes, take me to football games and tailgate parties.

"I appreciate that . . . thanks very much. . . . I . . . I'd love to go. I think they can do without me for one Sunday at First Baptist," I stammered. Looking him in the eye, I wondered if he felt the same rush that I did, if this was how girls felt when asked out for a date.

As Heraldson bounded out the door, I felt ashamed, even pathetic. He was merely doing his good deed, probably would get extra deacon points for bringing a real visitor to "college and career Sunday." And there I was acting like a middle-aged hairdresser at Graceland. I hated myself for this weakness, for wanting whatever it was I wanted from him so desperately. It was the same longing that had kept me in the cast-iron role of peacemaker for my parents. Maybe hate's not exactly the word—more a convergence of fear and anger, internalized.

"So, you're in with the management now," BeBe purred. She slunk back to her teller cage next to mine and made me feel even more ashamed, as if she could read my thoughts.

"Not exactly. I figure it's a chance to be out of the house away from my parents, a free meal. No big deal." I tried to sound nonchalant.

"Well, I didn't see him leapin' over here to ask me to his big white church. Why don't ya take me as your date, Bounty? I am a college coed, you know." She smiled, showing perfect, Cheshire white teeth. "I'm a good time, too."

"We're talking about church here, BeBe, not a dance at the Armory. Thanks for the offer, though." I didn't know what to say, even though she was kidding.

"Uh-huh. Well, this girl's expectin' a full report on what Mr. Clark J. Heraldson's house looks like on the inside. All the details."

<hr />

Heraldson's visit reminded me of the account BeBe and I had found the previous week under my father's name, the one requiring a code 7 to access. I'd put it out of my mind over the weekend at orientation, but now my curiosity peaked stronger than before and I was determined to know what the account was for. I figured I could rifle through Daddy's desk drawers down at the car lot, hoping to find it in his little black book. Or I could take a more direct route. Our phones had a direct extension to the main branch in Crescent. I made the call, and Judy Tate sounded startled on the other end of the receiver.

"Ms. Tate, this is Bounty McGraw workin' over at the Clearfield branch. I need a personal favor, please. . . . Yes, ma'am. I need a code 7 for one of my father's accounts—he's out of town and can't remember where he left the code written down. . . . Well, no, I don't sign on the account, but. . . . I'd really appreciate it. My father would too. . . . Yes, ma'am, bye." I scribbled down the five-digit number and hung up.

BeBe's ears perked up, and she came over to my computer terminal.

"What're you up to now? Judy Tate give you that code number just like that? . . . She had a facelift, you know."

"Yup. Now let's see what's in that dormant account." I pulled it up and punched in the code. The screen flashed and pulled up the columns with credits, debits, and balance summaries.

"What's this mean?" I pointed at code classifications on the screen.

BeBe scanned. "It's a special wire-transfer account, for fixed withdrawals at regular intervals. Some people have these set up for insurance or car payments so they don't have to worry with coupon booklets and mailin' checks."

But my father's account was different. It had been opened almost ten years ago. The last installment had been made just over five years ago. The authorized party, the recipient, was Cypress Springs Mental Health Corp., Cypress, Florida. The fixed monthly amount was $367.89 and the payments ended in June of that year. The account now showed a balance of $122.12.

"You got relatives in the loony bin in Florida?" BeBe asked.

"None I know of."

"Uh-hum. Well, your daddy's payin' for somebody to be crazy. At least it looks that way to me."

I scanned through the five years since, the same balance maintained for all that time. I was about to switch off the screen

110

when BeBe's bangled hand stopped me.

"Wait. Look at this," she whispered. Her eyes opened wide and I could see her pupils dilating.

In the last six months over $300,000 had passed through the account. It had been deposited, usually in amounts of ten to twenty thousand, and then wire-transferred out in larger lump sums, not to Cypress Mental Hospital, but to an unidentified account in a California bank.

"Your daddy's in the Mafia, son—in the laundry business. We better stop while we're still alive." She quickly hit the button to exit the account.

"He's not in the Mafia. This must be a mistake. We don't have that kind of money, BeBe," I said reassuringly while my thoughts raced. *Could he be in the Mafia?* My father had been a wheeler-dealer all my life, but I didn't think he had ever done anything really illegal. Sure, he occasionally rolled back the odometers on some of the cars down at the lot, and he'd embellish the qualities of his vehicles to anybody who'd listen. But Mafia money?

My mind spun like a kaleidoscope with my father's image, dressed not in overalls, but in dark suits with colored shirts and a white tie, Don Corleone of the South. This only got more and more unreal.

Then I remembered the mental hospital. I wasn't shocked or even puzzled about it—somehow it fit in. The photograph that had come with its Florida postmark burned in my mind even from the safety of its hiding place in the cigar box. I felt like a Hardy Boy solving the "Mystery of the Phantom Father," only it didn't feel like my father, just some man I knew little about, a suspect I'd been hired to follow. I decided to keep going and give Cypress Hospital a call. Since the computer record didn't give an address, I'd have to call directory assistance for a number.

Lucky for me, there's a phone in the lunchroom connected to an outgoing WATS line for banking business. I told BeBe my plan, and she switched lunch times with me so I could be alone in the tiny kitchen and make the call. The operator gave me the number, and as I dialed I had a curious feeling of gravity, soberness, as if I were calling to find out the results of a biopsy.

"Cypress Springs Mental Health, how may I direct your call?"

"May I speak to someone in accounts and billing, please?" Covering the phone receiver with my tie, I tried to demand confidently, not ask.

"One moment, please." I heard Kenny G. on the call-waiting music. It made me think of my mother and her new passion for jazz.

"This is Ramona Raymond," said a soft female voice.

"Ms. Raymond, Clark Heraldson, Crescent County National Bank, Crescent, Tennessee. We've got a customer who's closing a wire-transfer account with Cypress Springs as the recipient, and we just need to notify you of the closure."

"Okay, fine. What's the name on the account and the number?" I rattled off the numbers and my father's name.

"Just a moment, Mr. Heraldson. . . . Yes, I have it here. Mr. McGraw's account with us has been paid and inactive for over five years . . . real shame," she sighed. I realized this might be easier than I'd thought.

"Yes, sure is. Do you know Mr. McGraw or just his family?" I tried not to sound obvious, even though it probably didn't matter. In the South everyone's so obviously nosy that not to be curious would be conspicuous.

"Oh, I never met Mr. McGraw. But Miz Carnes was a dear woman, real tragedy what happened. Well, thanks for calling, Mr. Heraldson." And she hung up. I debated calling back and pretending to be a reporter, but decided against it. I wasn't sure how much more I wanted to know, wasn't sure I could stand to see where someone else's tragedy intersected with my father's life, with my own.

On the way home from work I stopped at the car lot, hoping to find some clues as to where, why, and how my father was coming up with such large sums of money to pass through that account. At the lot, business was slow so Ricky was sitting out front reading the *Crescent Courier*.

"When's Jimbo comin' back?" he asked.

"Should be pretty soon now. Everythin' goin' okay? Sold anything?"

"Nope. But I'm keepin' busy."

Yeah, reading the paper, I thought.

"I been stackin' the mail on your daddy's desk."

"Thanks, Rick."

Inside the cramped office, the place was a bigger mess than usual, as if my father had quit caring about order or had left in a hurry. I saw Ricky look through the window, and I shuffled nervously through the mail—mostly bills and advertisements, circulars for parts stores and car auctions—as if I were deeply engrossed in its importance. Discreetly, I opened the junk drawer and found the little black book, but found nothing helpful about the mystery account. I sorted through receipts, old registration transfers, and all the other junk my father stored there, but could detect nothing amiss.

I closed the drawer and was about to leave when a familiar corner caught my eye, the edge of an envelope I'd seen before. Peeking out of the assorted junk mail was a plain white, personal size envelope with a slanted script and a Florida postmark, addressed to my father, just like the one that had brought the photograph. Inside this one was an equally plain note-size page in the same handwriting, which read, "Will be coming to visit you around August 1. Hope you don't mind. We need to talk." The signature was hard to read, but looked like Jack or maybe John.

I didn't like it. What if my father still hadn't returned by then? What if he had? Who was this Jack person? My father's past snowballed before my eyes, each secret leading to another—a scavenger hunt of discovering who he really was. Was someone blackmailing him? At that moment it seemed within the realm of possibility; anything did.

Waving to Ricky, I backed the big Merc out of the parking lot. The note rested in the inside pocket of my navy blazer. At home I placed it with the photograph in a newly sealed envelope in the cigar box, my case file.

I still couldn't decide whether to tell my mother about all this or not. She was busy using every pot, pan, dish, and utensil in the kitchen making a new recipe of lasagna from *Southern Living*. I ate and ate the rich, warm cheesy squares with salad and garlic bread, and we still had over half to freeze. The whole point, of course, was to give the new dishwasher a run for its money. I decided not to interfere with her enjoyment of her diversion for as long as possible, at least until I figured out what was going on.

"Did I tell you that Clark Heraldson asked me to go to church with him and his family?" I said with my mouth full. "They go to First Presbyterian in Crescent, and he thought I might like the speaker they're having for college day or something. They want to have me over for lunch afterward." I felt indifferent as I explained, but knew she'd be excited.

"Bounty, that's wonderful. Clark Heraldson's a good man. I'm thrilled that he's takin' an interest in you. That's just wonderful. I'm sure you'll have a good time."

"Yeah, no big deal really." A strand of mozzarella cheese stuck to my chin.

"If he likes you, Bounty, he'll make sure your student loan goes through. You've made it clear how important that is to you now." She was already loading her new pet appliance and her voice rose on the allusion to our previous weekend, a time that in my mind already seemed long ago, out of reach.

"Maybe he's checkin' you out to see if you're serious about college. Didn't you say this is college day at his church?" she continued.

"Yes, ma'am. Could be." I didn't like this idea, that I would be scrutinized and held to an unknown standard to determine if I was worthy or not. Everyone deserved the chance to an education, to a clean break from their past and their families.

"I hate to change the subject, son, but there's somethin' I want to tell you," she said. The dishwasher hummed neatly and flashed a small, green lighted dial. It looked out of place, surreal, modern, an alien space probe landed in our old-fashioned kitchen. I braced myself for whatever my mother had to impart. She dried her hands on a dishcloth and sat at the table across from me.

"Bounty, I haven't said anything about this till now, 'cause I haven't had any proof. But I think I know where your father is. I think he's shacked up with that tramp who keeps books at the car lot. . . ." She used the dishcloth to wipe her eyes, but I didn't see any tears. It appeared as if she were merely rehearsing a scene from a play.

"Janet? You think Dad's with Janet? What proof are you talkin' about?" I swirled a thin film of lemon sauce on my dessert plate. My father was gone, maybe forever, and at that moment I thought I'd lost my mother as well.

"You know, Janet hasn't been down at the lot in over two weeks. I've tried callin' her at home every day—no answer. I called her sister this afternoon, made up some story about needin' to get in touch with her. Her sister practically laughed in my face, said, 'Didn't you know? Janet's on vacation. Didn't your husband tell you?' I felt like the biggest fool. I swear he'll never humiliate me like this again."

My mother's cheeks turned red, redder than her copper hair, and she looked alive, passionate for perhaps the first time that summer. Maybe this was the catalyst she needed to divorce him finally.

As she wiped away more imaginary tears, I realized I could fuel her fire by showing her the photograph, the note, telling her about the wire-transfer account, the mental hospital in Florida.

"That don't mean anything necessarily, Momma. I'm not defendin' him, but Janet, well . . . she doesn't seem his type." I thought about my father being attracted to sure and steady Janet, her low-cut blouses and sagging cleavage, ample perfume and tailored slacks. She was older than my mother, twice divorced, quiet and country bred, shrewd-eyed behind glasses that she wore on a chain. Thinking about her seducing my father, or even vice versa, made me chuckle. But my mother could, she could imagine it all. In her mind it extended itself beyond plausibility to fact, certainty, the logical progression of their lives—destiny.

"I intend to find out one way or another. When the time is right." She sounded determined.

I wondered if such a time would present itself and if it did, I prayed that I wouldn't have to be there, wouldn't have to watch like a voyeur, intrigued and repulsed by the final wreck of my parents' marriage.

On Sunday I met the Heraldsons in the vestibule of their massive church, the largest in Crescent County. In fact, they didn't refer to it as "church" or "the church grounds," but as "the church campus," as if you needed a map to walk across the sidewalk to the other building.

I'd heard people around town saying they were planning phase three of the building program—a gym with indoor pool, basketball courts, nautilus equipment, and racquetball facilities. They called it the "Family Life Center," but it sounded more like some kind of holy health club. Within the first five minutes Carole Heraldson gushed about all this as if we were at Club Med. She looked older than I remembered—heavy eye makeup, neutrals and grays—but was still a handsome woman with defined cheekbones and deep green eyes. Being a beautician, Carole was up on her hairstyles, but her dirty blonde swirls looked overdone, something Julia Roberts might get away with but conspicuous in small town Tennessee.

As we sauntered into the lobby, I took in the plush burgundy carpet and linen drapes, the classical art reproductions, Madonnas and crucifixions, potted palms and peace lilies. It looked like a kind of Catholic hotel lobby—it even had a front desk of sorts, a visitor's information station. I guessed there must have been about five hundred people milling into the sanctuary. As we went through the double doors, Heraldson clasped my arm and turned me to face a man about my father's age with tortoise-shell glasses and a chin cleft.

"Dr. Milhouse, I want you to meet Bounty McGraw—"

"He's one of Clark's employees at the bank," Carole inter-jected as if I were a leper they wouldn't ordinarily be seen with. Her husband shot at her with his eyes.

"Bounty's a friend of mine, and he is indeed working at the bank this summer.

"Bounty, this is our senior pastor, the Reverend Dr. Mitchell Milhouse," Clark dazzled his most brilliant smile to cover his wife's putdown.

"A pleasure, Bounty," Dr. Milhouse beamed.

"A pleasure to meet you, sir," I returned. His hand was smooth and limp and jiggled mine. Combined with his short stature, I could guess right then that behind his back his con-gregants called him "Dr. Mouse."

"So glad you could be here for our college day speaker. He's an old friend of mine from seminary, a truly gifted, inspira-tional orator. I hope you'll want to come back, Bounty. A pleas-ure to meet you. Enjoy the service. Clark, Carole Ann," with that Dr. Milhouse turned and scurried up front to the pulpit.

I felt like I had met the owner of a nightclub, and I won-dered if he had said, "Enjoy the service," or "Enjoy the show." I couldn't remember. By this time the Heraldsons had guided me to a green padded pew, off the left and to the middle of the center section—obviously their usual spot.

As the organ began moaning and I was reminded of a Bela Lugosi film, I inquired about the Heraldson children—Heather Ann, six, and Margaret Grace, four—and was informed that they were in "children's church." I imagined a miniature sanc-tuary just like this one, stained glass, organ, and all, with chil-dren dressed like little adults. Maybe you had to be trained to participate in a church like this one.

With regards to our speaker, I might just as well have been in First Baptist, Clearfield, listening to Pastor Stuckey. His message was "Youth—Hope of the Future" and sounded more like a graduation commencement speech than a sermon. I wondered if Dr. Milhouse's good friend from seminary—Harvard Theological Seminary, they'd printed it in the bulletin—had not, in fact, spoken these same words to some private Presbyterian college graduates just a couple months ago. For Heraldson's sake ("Call me Clark, Bounty," he reminded me in the lobby) I tried to look interested and nodded at appropriate places, even jotted down a quote or two.

Following the Heraldsons' Mercedes after the service, I tried to imagine their house and could only conjure up variations of the church sanctuary. Even though they lived in the new subdivision—they called it a community development—"Weeping Willows" on the outskirts of Crescent, their home was relatively modest by my expectations. A wide two-story home with porch and brick chimneys, it looked conspicuously middle class for the bank vice-president.

The inside, however, made up for the difference. Oak hardwood floors and Persian rugs, wildlife prints, family photos, Carole's wedding portrait, china cabinets and rare books, antique tables, and barrister's bookcases. The place had class and I liked it; refined and yet homey, tasteful but not overdone. Carole received my compliments like a schoolgirl. Her enthusiasm almost made up for her crack to Dr. Milhouse about me being a mere "employee."

She served roast beef with vegetables, fruit salad, homemade rolls. Heather and Margie changed out of their lacy Laura Ashleys into shorts and T-shirts. Clark slung his navy jacket over the sofa and loosened his tie. Chatting with the girls, I had them giggling as they told me about their pet bunny, Mr. Cotton-bottom. We three adults made comments on the sermon, ensuring that we had indeed been paying attention.

The funniest part of the whole conversation for me was when Carole asked about Mrs. Odell's freezer.

"What's this I hear about Jesus appearin' on the side of Mrs. Odell's freezer? Doesn't she live close to you, Bounty?" she asked innocently. From outside we could hear the girls talking and laughing as they fed Mr. Cotton-bottom leftover carrots. His cage was perched on a stand to the right of the pool and patio. Distracted by the gloss of the blue water, I wasn't sure what approach to take in explaining—the skeptic, the believer, the uncertain. I chose the latter.

"Yes, she does. They live about a mile from us, really just across our front pasture, in one of those trailers facin' the highway. She claims that when her neighbor's porch light's on, there's a picture of Christ, kind of a profile on the side of Miss Mary Louise's deep-freeze, which they keep on their porch, since she doesn't have one." I wasn't sure what else to say.

Clark chuckled, "Doesn't that beat all? Can you imagine what some people won't do for attention? I even think I saw somethin' in the paper about this. I don't suppose you've been down to check it out?"

"*No*, not yet, anyhow," I lied. "I've thought about it, but I'm afraid I'd get tickled and offend Mrs. Odell or some of the other pilgrims." At least that part of it was true.

Heraldson thought that was the funniest thing since he foreclosed a mortgage on the A-1 Massage Parlor in Pikeville. He was almost in tears, and I enjoyed joining his guffaws— "Pilgrims!"—as if we shared some private joke. Carole smiled politely.

"You two best be careful. I don't believe it's Jesus any more than y'all do, but you got to respect other people's beliefs. Now me, for instance," she put down her fork, "I was raised Church of Christ, but now I'm Presbyterian. My beliefs have changed, but I still respect my parents' faith. . . . Folks are entitled to believe whatever gets 'em by," she pronounced, startling us with her seriousness as much as she did herself.

"Maybe you're right, Care," Clark offered. He composed himself, swilled his iced tea, wiped tears from the corners of his blue-sky eyes. "Tell you what. Carole Ann, you go change, and Bounty and I will do the dishes—how 'bout that?"

I nodded as his wife protested. She finally agreed and ascended the staircase. Clark began rinsing plates and loading the dishwasher as I cleared the table. In the spacious, sunny kitchen, with his little girls chasing a rabbit through their mother's petunias, Clark Heraldson had it made, I figured.

As we stood side by side, I felt secure and sure of myself. I'd be okay. Someday I'd have a life like Clark Heraldson's. As he sponged the silverware, I noticed his hands. Long fingered and strong, tanned and supple with ridges of veins like roads on a map, strong hands. The backs of them were dusted with a film of gold and I wished his hands were mine. I even like my own hands, but his looked so much like, well . . . like a man's hands. His wedding band cast gold sparks of reflected sunlight across the pastel wallpaper. Maybe one day I could look down at my own hands and admire them as much.

"Still not datin' anybody, Bounty?" he asked sheepishly.

"Well, no, not really. Workin' too hard, I guess." I felt embarrassed.

"That little black BeBe at your branch sure is a looker. Great body. Maybe I need to transfer her over to our main branch. Make her my own private assistant—if you know what I mean," Clark chortled.

A dry, raspy sound escaped from the back of my throat. He loaded a bright, lemony-smelling liquid into the dishwasher and flicked it on. I still didn't know what to say.

"Don't look so shocked, Bounty. It's okay with me. I'm cool." He smiled the same full-toothed smile that won accounts and charmed preachers. "We men are sexual animals. Hell, I remember what it was like to be your age. Those were the days. . . . Hey, I've got a stash of magazines out in the garage if you want to borrow a few—" He paused as we heard Carole's footsteps winding down the stairs before she burst into the kitchen.

"How're you boys making out down here? All finished? I thought we could all go for a swim." She tidied up the counter.

"We're doin' fine, just havin' some man talk—right, Bounty?" He winked at me.

I grinned back, "Yeah, right, you know how we men are. . . ." I still didn't know what to say.

In the swimming pool I thought twice about my wish to be just like Clark Heraldson. Since I hadn't brought my swim trunks, he loaned me a pair of his, a little big, but not much. Changing clothes in their bedroom, I felt dizzy and at the same time some faint tingling within. His trunks were red with blue fishes on them, Ralph Lauren, of course. As I pulled up the trunks, complete with mesh lining, over my pale midsection, all I could think about was what he'd said in the kitchen. Something stirred inside me and I shuddered. Out the bedroom window I could see him pushing Heather and Margie on their Ninja Turtles float. Carole looked all Hollywood lying on her chaise in her sleek, black suit and sunglasses, her head tilted with a half-smile.

The tepid water felt refreshing on such a hot July afternoon. I splashed the girls and tried to suck in my gut so I wouldn't look so flabby. My body's not bad, but it was a far cry from Heraldson's. In his tropical trunks and wet-dog hair, he looked like a surfer, or one of those beach volleyball players, all muscles, tan, and teeth. I liked wearing this man's swimsuit and wished I could keep it, a souvenir.

He didn't mention the magazines again, and I wondered if he'd really said what I thought I heard. I tried to imagine him seducing BeBe in his preppie office and I almost laughed. It was ludicrous, like the porn film Pace and I had seen at a stag party for Shep Dawson—a football player who married his pregnant girlfriend my sophomore year. BeBe would come into his

121

office for a loan or something, then Clark would make all kinds of suggestive remarks, banking double entendres, that kind of thing. I couldn't believe I was imagining this.

After thank-yous had been properly exchanged—I didn't keep the swim trunks—I drove home wondering about sex. Thought about how I learned in third grade from a boy on the playground that people do more than go to the bathroom with certain parts of their bodies. I was incredulous; he had to be making that up. But he said, "Could anybody make that up? I swear, I'm tellin' you the truth. I'll bring pictures tomorrow to prove it. My brother's got pictures in books under his bed."

Sure enough, the next day he brought a Swedish manual, *Sexual Intercourse and Desire*, with pictures of men and women doing things I never imagined. I couldn't bring myself to ask my parents about it. I vaguely remember asking where babies came from when I was a preschooler and Momma replying that God gave man the seed and man married woman and gave her the seed and it grew in her belly awhile and then a baby came out. I had imagined that something like a watermelon seed or peach pit fell from the sky and a man handed it to his wife and she placed it—I don't know—in her navel or somewhere, and then a baby grew.

The most education my father offered on the matter was once when I was thirteen. We were in the barn delivering a calf, and after it was over he said, "If you ever have any questions, you know, about any of this, let me know." I averted my eyes, watched the new calf totter back and forth, and thought to myself that by that age, I could probably answer more of his questions. Nothing more was said.

Unlike my father, my mother consistently warned me about my sexual potency during my early adolescence. I can still hear the tone of her voice when I was in sixth grade, telling me about Marsha Baines, a ninth-grade girl in my youth group at church who "got herself in trouble." I felt ashamed and dirty, like my mom had tuned into my dreams, rampant with female body parts and speculation at that age, and knew that I was capable of the same kind of trouble. She told me that I was too smart, had too bright a future, to ever get a girl pregnant. "You don't want to throw away your future like I did. Don't marry young, and don't ever put yourself in the position to have to marry young. Do you know what I'm sayin'?" She tried to sound helpful. "Yes, ma'am," I'd answered.

I imagined myself a living time bomb waiting to explode into some innocent girl merely by thinking about what might be beneath her clothes. I was dangerous and I had to somehow beat the clock, get through school and college before my sperm bomb exploded and I had to get married. And the way my mother talked, from there life would be downhill, saddled with burdens and responsibilities.

That night I dreamed about Clark Heraldson in an Olympic-sized pool with hundreds of women lounging in the blue water. He saw me watching from a distance and smiled that smile, beckoned me with his arm. Then he started coming toward me and talking to me, telling me what a great spot this was, and then I couldn't understand his words anymore—gibberish.

I finally started walking with him back toward the pool, but when we got there, the women had disappeared. Clark wasn't disappointed, though. He dove into the water, and I realized I was wearing trunks just like his. He got back out and pushed me in, then I started enjoying myself. We splashed and wrestled, raced from one end to the other. I had just jumped off the high dive and was free-falling when I woke up. It all seemed so vivid and real as I roused from sleep and shucked off my sweaty T-shirt.

I lay awake for a long time then. Thinking about the craziness of it all, church that morning, his words in the kitchen, my

123

feelings that afternoon.

What was wrong with me? Surely other guys my age didn't think that way. They were all off doing what Heraldson did, chasing every woman who came their way. I could count the women I was attracted to on one hand—Miss Richards in eighth grade with those long, full legs, or Sonia Fletcher last year at my prom, maybe Marybeth from orientation, or even BeBe would qualify with more time.

I felt ashamed and abnormal. Most men could evidently be sexual with any woman. That's what I'd gathered from locker-room talk, but I'd always dismissed it as just that, bragging for bragging's sake.

Before I fell off to sleep, I admitted to myself that I was attracted to something about Clark Heraldson. But that's as far as I went; I couldn't bear to think about the implications.

-8-

Monday night my mother had something like a nervous breakdown. She came home from work shaking, and I thought it must be diet pills or something. I'd been down at the car lot making sure Ricky was still there. I'd even pumped him for information about Janet, and about the possibility that she and my father were involved. He just looked at me funny when I asked if he thought they were more than friends.

"That's a good one, Bount," he said, adjusting his crotch and leaving a grease mark beside his fly. "Your momma's way too nice lookin' for your daddy to go messin' around with old stuff like Janet." He laughed again and stuck his head back under the hood of a Ford Explorer.

So I'd felt better about that possibility, looked forward to reporting it to my mother, but it was too late for her.

Like I said, she came into the house shaking and when I asked her what was wrong she put her purse on the table and said, "Janet's back from her 'vacation.' I called her place and she answered the phone. I know your father's there, could tell by the sound of her voice."

She was beyond reason, and I didn't know how to calm her. I told her about my chat with Ricky and how absurd he thought it was. She looked at me wide-eyed like I'd revealed our darkest secret.

"Ricky don't know his head from a hole in the ground. What he says don't mean nothin'." She dismissed all I had to offer.

"After supper, after it's dark, I want you to drive me out to her house," my mother said calmly.

I finally realized what a toll my father's absence was taking on Mom. I could detach myself from her casseroles and crying, but this was her life. She wasn't my mother any longer, only a woman afraid of being alone, afraid of cutting herself on loneliness. I couldn't stand it.

We drove to the Western Sizzlin in Pikeville, and it depressed me deeper than I thought I could go. I found myself saying things like, "He'll be back," "It'll be okay," or as I swung to the other alternative, "Divorce him," "You'll be okay." My steak was tender and done well, but the emptiness of the place poured through me. A few singles eating alone, a couple of families with little kids, an older man in overalls and boots, his wife who wore too much makeup. Ranch salad dressing and wheat crackers, a baked potato, a dessert bar with two flavors of ice cream.

I wanted more. I felt as if I was looking at my life through the sneeze guard on the salad bar. I saw myself moving before myself, listening to my mother, chewing, cutting, chewing, going through motions, loading my plate with more lettuce—but removed, separated by glass.

"This is what we'll do . . ." she started to tell me her plans. I noticed she actually had an appetite, was eating voraciously. "We'll drive over to her house—I know where she lives—and we'll cut the lights before we turn down her street. We can park a block away and walk to her door. I intend to find out the truth." I couldn't believe she actually had a plan, had envisioned this ridiculous reconnaissance mission, as if we were recovering a POW or something.

"I don't think this is such a good idea, Mom. What are you gonna do if Daddy is there? Or even if he's not?" I was genuinely scared.

"I want to drive by Janet's house and see if they're there." She said it like we were going to drive by and see some old friends, ignoring my question.

"What good will that do? I don't understand."

"Peace of mind, son. Maybe you're too young to understand. But you will someday."

I imagined the possible scenes we might find at Janet's house: the scorned wife confronting the other woman, the cheating husband caught in the act, gun shots and screams, ambulances, headlines. This could be interesting . . . if only it weren't my parents.

What we found was much quieter and more disappointing and, if such a thing is possible, broke my heart more than if we had found my father naked with Janet in the front yard. On the drive to Janet's house—she lived in the boonies off Highway 99 between Crescent and Pikeville—my mother sat upright and nervous, a bloodhound tracking a scent.

By the time we turned off the highway to Janet's modest brick two-bedroom, the sun had trailed off into just-dark, cicadas chanted incessantly, omnisciently. They knew what I did not.

"Cut your lights," my mother whispered. I obeyed and braked the car a few feet from the house.

Janet's Chrysler was parked in the gravel driveway. "Keep going. Block her in," the general instructed.

For a brief second as we pulled in behind the potential getaway car, a light flickered across the corner window.

"Did you see that? They're here, all right. That's her bedroom window. She flipped the light out. They're lyin' in there, and she flipped the light out." She sounded like a child, so excited by the discovery of something previously contained by imagination.

"Are you sure? It looked more like a car headlight reflected back, maybe a streetlight. I don't think it was inside, Mom."

"Of course it was. She's lyin' in bed with her big, drunken, married-man lover. I—" she sobbed. Before I could say anything, she opened the car door and leapt up the front porch.

"I know you're in there, you're not foolin' me. You whore . . . I always knew you were sorry . . . Jimmy, you sorry piece of trash . . . your son's out here. . . . Why don't you come to the door and show him what a man you are? . . . I hate you both . . . ." She wept hysterically into her hands, and I had no idea what to do. I only remember thinking a son should never see his mother like this.

If I had remained her son at that moment I couldn't have helped her, so I quit. I took her shoulders, quieted her, guided her off the porch into the car. She began sobbing, "Sorry . . . sorry . . . shouldn't see me like this. . . ."

No one came to the door.

Back on Highway 99 I turned the radio on and let Garth Brooks break up our silence. Mom composed herself with Kleenex and a cough drop and gazed ahead, trance-like.

Dark nestled itself against us, summer dark with few lights off the highway, only an occasional house lit by a TV set, a streetlight, the moon. Garth wailed, "Papa loved Mama," and I changed the cruel station, hoping my mother wasn't paying attention.

I could only think, *It shouldn't be this way.*

At home she took a tranxene and went to bed. I had nothing to do with myself, turned on MTV, and sat in the dentist's chair. I became restless and sat cross-legged on the earth-orange carpet, pulled all the photo albums out from the end table crypt. They were out of order, so I arranged them chronologically, the cracked tan cover first, the two blues, the flowered one, the new brown ones.

The oldest album had little tab corners where you inserted the photos to fit. All the pictures were labeled and dated. The only picture of my parents together before they were married— fresh and giddy at a county fair, my father in a sleeveless T-shirt, my mother in jeans and white blouse, holding a stuffed polar bear. My eyes teared, and I wanted to yell out a warning like you yell at a pedestrian before he's hit. "Don't do it. You don't see what will happen, how you'll hurt us all. Stop while you can."

Outside the moon was high even though it couldn't have been later than ten. I locked the door and walked around the house. The creek glinted light through the pines, winked white flashes like Morse code. I could not decipher it so I walked out back beyond the barn, through the gate, to the pasture, and over the hill. I kept walking till I could see the road down below me, the few trailers, a passing car.

At the Odell's trailer, the pilgrims had dispersed, even though, with the porch light on, I assumed Jesus was still shining. I edged up to the fence to see for myself. Sure enough, the profile was still there, smoky and luminescent at the same time.

My father's a drunk who'd left his wife, my mother's about to have a nervous breakdown, if she hadn't already, and I was standing there looking at Jesus on a freezer in a trailer park. It all made about as much sense as anything I'd known.

I crawled over the fence and inched closer, noticed that the offerings people had left were multiplying, more flowers and trinkets piled below the side of the deep-freeze than I could imagine. I dug in my pocket, said a prayer, and pitched a penny on to the porch. A light went on in the Odell home and I ducked behind another trailer, climbed back over the fence.

I stood in the dark out behind our barn for a long time, wondering why I had pitched that penny. But then, what else could I do? Maybe it's all I had to offer, the only amount of faith to be mustered under such circumstances. It's funny, because part of me wished that it really was Jesus on that deep-freeze—that it was that easy, the way some people made it. If you read your Bible, give money to the church, feed your kids, sleep with your wife, God'll treat you right.

But I didn't believe that. I knew people who did those things, grew up with them, and bad happened to them like everyone else. Their tires went flat, they lost jobs, they got divorces, their children got leukemia, their daddies drank like everyone else's.

If I'd learned one thing in life so far, it was that nothing went like it was supposed to, not parents or jobs, car engines or computers. Even our bodies could betray us with cancer, a brain tumor, whatever.

I used to think money could make things run right, but standing out under the summer stars with the breeze smelling of clover and honeysuckle, I knew better. Somehow money didn't guarantee things either; that stuff I counted five days a week couldn't tame the human heart. There's wasn't much you could count on.

And for that I felt bitter. What a hard, crusty, crystalline time in my life. The summer was only half over and already it felt like a corroded battery, all dry-caked with acrid powder, entrenched in a hidden compartment, leaking its oily, metallic residue. Everywhere I turned I found more and more pain or disappointment, a nightmarish house of mirrors.

I thought about how melodramatic this all seemed when I tried to remove myself, detach. But I realized so much of its power was the old snowball effect. It wasn't just this painful summer I hated, I despised them all, the little shreds of memory that haunted me—my father faltering into my fourth grade class party with a bottle of Canadian Club, my mother refusing to let me have friends over in a cheerful voice, "You never know what might happen." Christmases and vacations, the summer we went to Florida and spent the whole time in bars and at the horse track.

Somehow this summer I thought all that would begin to fade away with my decision to create a new future for myself, shed my old snakeskin and begin a new life. But it wasn't working that way. Everything in my past intruded into the present and tried to eclipse the future as well. I envisioned myself taking care of my mother in an institution the way my parents tended to my grandfather in the nursing home. All the result of my father. Damning him to the lowest level of hell wouldn't have been enough.

I felt so desperate that night I even thought, momentarily, of confiding in Pastor Stuckey or Dr. Milhouse or even Clark Heraldson or BeBe. None of them could help. I was in it by myself. Is this what it felt like to be an adult, to be a man? If it was, I'd been an adult since I was about six years old, and I didn't like it.

I was so tired of giving with nothing in return. I felt like Kevin Costner at the end of *Field of Dreams* when he explodes and wants to know, "What's in it for me?" You can go only so far, then you want to know. If there were guarantees or if life balanced out, then I could stand nights like tonight, summers like this summer. But there aren't. If life balanced out the good for the bad, the rest of my life would be a cruise on the Carnival line. "In the mornin', in the evenin', ain't we got fun," Kathie Lee bubbled in my ear. But it seemed to me that the vacations didn't ever outweigh what the world dished out the rest of the time.

I considered martyrdom for its own sake. What's noble about that? I wasn't a saint and didn't aspire to be one. So why did I stick around? Why didn't I tell my father off, leave my mother for someone else to take care of? I didn't know why, I only knew that I couldn't.

My heart felt buried deep in a hole somewhere, at the bottom of a dormant volcano, or maybe in our root cellar. Spooning handfuls of dirt and rock, I kept clawing and clawing, but when I reached the door, it was barred shut from the outside, our house pressed against itself.

I woke up and found myself slumped in the back of a rickety hay wagon next to the barn. Dew was collecting on my camp shorts, and my bare legs felt clammy and cool. The stars winked through the beech trees beyond the barn, and it felt very late, an endless night.

"**A**re you payin' attention?" BeBe whispered. She jarred me out of my reverie with a pinch on the arm. We sat in a semi-circle in front of Rosenstein's desk for our weekly staff meeting, which amounted to nothing more than a guarantee that everyone showed up on time Tuesday mornings.

This morning Rosenstein made an unusually fervent pitch for "customer products," as if we were in a department store or fast-food place. "When your customer cashes a check inquire about a savings account. Recommend an IRA or CD, especially if they have a high checking balance—say over a couple thousand dollars." Poor Rosenstein droning on and on when all it amounted to was "Would you like fries with that?"

I decided Rosenstein would never fit into the South, even if he did go to school in Memphis. He just looked Northern, not even Midwestern, with his dark suits and laundered, bachelor button-downs. The tortoise-frame glasses didn't help. He looked more like an accountant or engineer than a banker. Not that bankers can't be just as anal retentive. Maybe he was working undercover to crack the "Crescent counterfeit case." I chortled into my coffee thinking about Mrs. Sherman and Sarah Anne in the supply room cranking out twenty dollar bills.

We wrapped up and headed to our windows to work the drop bags, deposits that businesses clunked into the heavy steel drawer, like an oversized mailbox, after regular hours. It wasn't hard work, just took some time. It's what we did before the bank opened.

"Aren't you finished yet?" BeBe again. She looked like an African safari guide today, khaki dress with epaulets and pockets everywhere, short sleeves. She completed the part with a leopard-skin headband and beaded earrings. I liked the way BeBe looked, the sweet spur of her perfume in the air.

"Where're the elephants?" I opened another deposit bag—
Ray's Shell Station, all greasy gas-soaked bills. The women
always made me do this one.

"The elephants? What you smokin' this morning, Bounty?"

"You're on safari, aren't you? So where're the elephants?"

"You're a funny boy, Bounty McGraw." She shook her bam-
boo bracelet further up her dark arm and reached across the
counter to take one of the deposit bags still unopened.

"How you been makin' it with your folks? Heard from your
daddy?" Her tone shifted, full of concern, while I noticed her
full lips were pouting and sensual.

"All right, I guess. No sign of my dad yet." I opened a grape
Safe-T pop from the box usually reserved for five-year-olds and
teenagers. It tasted too much like a cough drop that early in
the morning, so I tossed it.

"Y'all thought about callin' the police and filin' a missin'
persons report? If he's just hidin' out somewhere, that'd teach
him a lesson." BeBe opened a lemon sucker and savored it.

"If it was anybody besides my daddy, it'd make sense to follow the normal procedures. But Momma hates for people to
know what's goin' on. She'd die first before she'd call the cops
and have everybody in town know. She thinks he's havin' an
affair with this woman who keeps books at the car lot."

"Is he?"

"How should I know? We drove out there last night—to the
woman's house—and my mom swore Daddy was in there with
her. But I don't think so. I think she just needs somethin' to
blame . . . someone to blame."

"Who do you blame?" BeBe asked.

"Hell, I blame him for all this. I blame God, too, I think."

"Don't be blamin' God, Bounty. He don't like your daddy's
antics no more than you do. God'll take care of you. . . . Don't you
pray?" She bit the head off the lollipop and threw the stick away.

I thought about my trip to the Odells the night before, about
my doubts and anger, about my longing for some kind of meaning behind all this.

133

"Yeah, I pray. Just not hard enough, I guess. Things I pray for don't happen the way I want 'em to."

"That's part of the problem right there, Bounty. The world don't revolve 'round what you want. It revolves 'round what *he* wants."

"He wants some strange things then," I huffed and recounted a stack of twenty dollar bills until its total matched the deposit amount. "What'd you do last weekend? We were so busy yesterday, you never told me."

She looked knowingly at me, silently agreed to my change of subject, and became animated again. Her tale of her weekend kept us preoccupied until we opened. She had gone with her cousin to a favorite bar, "Pearl's," over near Manchester— a real juke joint it sounded like, a tonk she called it. She'd flirted her head off with some man at the bar, asked him to dance. "He turned out to be gay!" she shrieked. "A gay black man, here in Crescent County. I wanted to call the newspaper!"

When I asked her how she knew he was gay, she gave me one of her "you're so naive" looks. "I can tell, you know. I mean, I couldn't tell at first, but then after we talked, no doubt about it. He didn't look at this gorgeous body of mine like most fools do. . . . And sure enough, before we left I saw him leave with the good white fairy, some blond college boy from Nashville or somewhere."

And that's the way BeBe was. She entertained you, no matter how disturbing you might find her material. She went on to describe her Sunday church service, reviewed what everyone wore, who said what to whom, and ended with a list of who went down the aisle at the invitation hymn and what she knew they needed to be repenting for. BeBe needed her own talk show, and I told her as much.

"You got that right, just call me BeBe Winfrey, Oprah's baby sister." She liked it so much that she had poor old Mrs. Robertson, who came in to get a money order, believing that she really was Oprah's sister.

"I just love her programs, BeBe. You tell her that next time you see her, okay?" Mrs. Robertson smiled blankly. BeBe just nodded and smiled back.

Mavis Jones came running in the bank then looking like she was about to give birth. She worked at the Crescent Moon Motor Lodge halfway between Clearfield and Pikeville. She usually knew who's sleeping with whom and had been known to take money to keep her mouth shut.

So anyway, she ran in all excited straight to Mrs. Sherman, but loud enough for us all to hear: "You won't believe who checked in this morning. Two photographers and a reporter from New York City, *People* magazine. They're here to see Jesus at Jessie Odell's trailer. I tried callin' her, but the phone must be off the hook. Can you imagine? *People* magazine? This has got to be one of the most excitin' things to ever happen in my life. Mr. Myerson—he's the reporter—even took a quote from me about what I think it looks like. I said, 'Why, it might be Jesus, our Lord works in mysterious ways.' That's what I said."

The whole bank buzzed the rest of the day. That night would be the biggest crowd yet; it would be hard to tell who came to see Jesus and who came to be in *People*. I was probably the only person in the whole county who didn't plan on being there.

After lunch, good ol' Clark Heraldson strolled in, and I figured he didn't want his picture in *People* magazine beside the sacred appliance any more than I did. As he approached, he didn't look so great, as if he had the flu or something, puffy eyed and red nosed. He needed a haircut, which surprised me since he always looked like he'd just stepped down from the barber's chair, which was usually true since his wife was a hairstylist.

He headed straight for Rosenstein's office. I could tell something was wrong by the faces Heraldson made. He wasn't a happy banker, and I couldn't help but wonder what our small-time branch manager could've done to incur such wrath. Rosenstein just sat there, though, calm and collected, the implacable professional. I figured Rosenstein saw a therapist, someone in Nashville or Chattanooga.

I cringed a little then when Heraldson came out, recollected his poise and ambled over to my window. He gradually shifted his face into a happy one, just like the theater symbol, masks flip-siding from tragedy into comedy.

"Thanks again for Sunday, Mr. Heraldson," I began.

"It's Clark, remember? Carole and I enjoyed it too. We'll have to have you over again real soon. . . . In fact, why don't you come over for a swim this week? How 'bout tomorrow after work?"

His offer excited me, but then I felt wary, uncomfortably afraid of more out-of-control emotions. "Sure, sounds good."

"It's a deal then, good. . . . I wanted to ask you, Bounty," his tone shifted, his voice quieted, "if your father was back yet. He and I've been workin' on a deal, and I need his signature before the end of the month."

This was all I needed. "Uh, he's been detained on his buyin' trip, Clark, but should be back soon, this week, he hopes."

"Where'd you tell me he was? Atlanta?" He leaned forward into my window, rested on his elbows and forearms.

"Well, I don't think I mentioned it, but as a matter of fact, it is Atlanta."

"Do you have a number where I can reach him?" he pressed.

"He's stayin' with a friend who doesn't have a phone."

"Mighty sorry business practices. I was tellin' him last time I saw him that he needs a cellular phone. . . ." He leaned back again, ran his hand through his hair. The red in his eyes stood out to me.

"Yessir, I've told him the same thing," I laughed nervously.

"Well, please tell him to call me next time you talk to him," he said. "And I'll see you tomorrow evenin'," he smiled again, the sun out from behind its cloud.

The next evening I left my mother reading a Judith Krantz novel on the front porch. She seemed to have bounced back, hadn't mentioned Daddy or Janet since her scene Monday night. She apologized Tuesday morning and actually sounded chipper about some things—gardening, sewing, going to the movies—she intended to do on her vacation the following week, the first week of August.

She encouraged me to go to the Heraldsons', saying, "He must really like you to invite you back so soon."

I wasn't so sure—rather I felt like he wanted something from me. I told Momma about his inquiries into Daddy's whereabouts and she said that Heraldson had called her as well that week, asking about her husband. At least our lies coincided since she'd also told him Daddy was out of town on business.

So I left the house with some trepidation, nervous about leaving her by herself, anxious about the swim at Heraldsons'. In fact, the only reason I went was the thought of my loan application on his desk, his signature short of its being approved. Surely, I'd hear something this week; school started in September after Labor Day weekend. Pulling the big Merc into his smooth-paved drive, I decided to look for a chance to ask ol' Clark about the loan.

"Bounty, 'round here," Clark bellowed from around the side of the house. "I'm already in the water," he echoed.

I opened the small wooden gate and sidestepped Carole's petunias and marigolds on my way to the patio. The water looked inviting, reflecting the last shards of sunlight edging through the trees. I looked around for Heraldson and found him toweling off and coming toward me. A bottle of Scotch sat on the patio table beside a glass of ice.

"Hey, Mr. Heraldson," I offered my hand.

"Clark, now," he shook back.

"Where's Carole and the girls?" I asked politely.

"Oh, Carole's mother took sick yesterday, so she and the girls headed up to Louisville for a few days."

"Sorry to hear that. Nothin' serious, I hope." The pool and porch lights suddenly came on, an eruption of white, even though it was not quite dusk. I suddenly felt awkward standing there next to this man I admired.

"Timer," Clark explained and continued, "I'll be sure to tell Carole you asked about her. Well, shall we take a dip?"

I could smell whiskey on his breath. "Sure." I shucked off my T-shirt. "Brought my own trunks this time," I said and he laughed before diving off the side.

While Clark Heraldson swam laps I floated on one of the kid's green floats and enjoyed the coolness, even peacefulness, of the water, the time of day. Dark finally billowed itself across the sky, and I liked lying on my back and facing starlight. Just then I remembered my dream about being in the Olympic pool with Heraldson, and it startled me.

"Race you," Clark said, suddenly beside me. "Winner gets a beer."

"Deal," I agreed. We lined up in the shallow end and counted in unison before plunging in. He was fast and I knew if I beat him it would be at the turn in the deep end beneath the diving board. I used a somersault turn that Pace had taught me in eighth grade and came up about two seconds ahead of my boss.

"You're a fish, Bounty," he panted. "Let's have that beer."

Inside, the house was cavernous and dark, silent in its lifelessness. We were dripping on the kitchen linoleum when Clark said, "Guess we better change first. Come on up."

I brought a pair of cutoffs with my towel and followed him up the stairs. The wet hair on the back of his legs made a strange pattern, like blond seaweed glued in long strips. I felt the funny tingling feeling in my gut that I'd felt before in this man's house.

"Help yourself." He motioned to the bathroom while he headed into his bedroom. I dried myself off and looked at my body in the full-sized mirror that covered one wall of the bathroom. Goosebumps chased themselves up and down my flesh. I threw on my clothes, combed my wet hair, and opened the door, then I saw him. Through his open bedroom door, by the light of a small bedside lamp, Clark Heraldson stood naked, rummaging through a dresser drawer.

"Come on in, I'm almost dressed," he said.

I averted my eyes but couldn't help stealing another glance at his body, the pale, furry midsection highlighted against the tan trunk. Standing in the doorway, I watched him pull on a pair of white briefs.

"I'm hot, how 'bout you?" He walked toward me and I wanted to run down the stairs, out of the house, and sprint all the way home.

"Yeah, me too." But it seemed obvious I was lying as goose-bumps continued to race across my bare chest.

"You okay?" He stood before me, still in just his underwear, grinning.

"Yeah, I'm fine." I think I was shaking.

He placed his hand on my shoulder, then down to my bicep. "That's a fine muscle you got there. You're a good lookin' young man, you know that?"

He gently tried to pull me into the room, out of the doorway, and I resisted, planted firmly in place, wooden.

"I won't hurt you," he said. "You'll like it, I promise." He smiled the twenty-four-karat smile.

I felt like a fool. It was all a trap—he knew his wife and kids would be gone, probably sent them away himself. I wondered if my feelings had shown on my face or if he was just taking a chance that I wouldn't punch him and get the hell out of there.

His hand had lowered to my waist, and he was still trying to pull me in with his other.

"You know, Bounty, I was reviewin' loan applications today. Yours was at the top of the stack." He kept smiling.

I suddenly realized what was happening, like waking up under water, and my fear and desire turned to loathing.

"Be a shame if your student loan wasn't approved. No goin' away to college. Stuck here at the community college, workin' at the car lot. Sad future for a boy as bright as you." His grin turned into a snarl, the golden retriever transformed into a Doberman.

"I think I better be goin' now." I had trouble finding my voice; it came out flat. "I gotta get home," I added with more energy and backed away. His hands fell to his sides.

"If you want your student loan, think about it. Hell, if you want to keep your job the rest of the summer, I get what I want. And if you're as smart as I think you are, you'll keep your mouth shut about this. Nobody'd believe white trash like you anyway, you little faggot. Get out of here. Now." His voice crescendoed into a shout as I turned and ran out of the house like I wished I'd done five minutes earlier.

My eyes burned with chlorine and fear all the way home. Once there, in the darkness behind the garage, I vomited.

-9-

I lay awake all that night, stunned and restless. My mother had been watching TV when I came inside, a movie of the week about a woman who hired a hit man to kill her ex-husband.

"You're home early," she said. "Have a good time?"

"Yeah, fine. Water felt good." I headed straight for my room. The sounds of the television, my mother turning pages of a magazine, the hum of the ceiling fan, even the rhythm of her breathing were comforting. I wanted to cry, to have my mother hold me and stroke my hair as if I were five years old and had scraped my knee.

My life was falling apart, collapsing upon itself. With every effort I exerted finally to take control of my life, something happened to kick me back into place. Images of my future flashed before me—thirty years old, still working at the car lot; forty years old, still not married; fifty years old, taking care of my parents in this very house. My room felt smaller and tighter, the walls pressing slowly in on me. I ran to the door and Clark Heraldson blocked my path, to the window and he's sneering in at me, "You can't get out, you little faggot."

After I woke up from that, I wouldn't release myself to sleep again. The house was dark, and my digital clock read 1:24 a.m. My mother must've come in and covered me with a sheet.

I wrestled with myself over what had happened that night, what would happen as a result of it. I couldn't shake the feeling of desire I'd had, like somehow I'd missed an opportunity to get what I wanted. And then I'd fluctuate to contempt, repulsion, and break out in a sweat. I didn't know what I wanted, but the thought of Heraldson touching me, taunting me with my student loan, threatening to revoke my ticket to freedom, made my insides roil.

After I lay there for another hour or so, I decided to get up and take a bath, wash away as much of the night-memory as water would allow. I was afraid it would wake Mom, but with all the doors shut between her room and the bathroom, I didn't think she would hear the water running. The warm water covered my pale body as I sank deeper into the worn porcelain cocoon.

My weariness dissolved. I made patterns on my belly with my wet chest hairs and realized that this was perhaps my favorite spot in the whole house next to the porch swing.

All my life I had loved to take baths. It's what I remembered most about winters growing up, getting ready to go to school, the space heater droning its soothing voice throughout the tiny bathroom. The yellowed tiles and warped floor, the forever embarrassing box of feminine hygiene products on the back of the commode, the smell of Momma's hairspray and Daddy's Old Spice.

On really cold days, I'd put the space heater as close to the side of the tub as possible and enjoy the warmth almost as much as a human touch. I'd flick water into the red glowing units to watch them sizzle like a summertime grill.

It was a favorite place because I could lock the door and be myself. As I got older I'd read comics or a Mike Hammer mystery, careful not to dampen the pages. I loved the bathtub.

But then I felt guilty again, drowsily uncertain about how much of what had happened tonight was my fault. Then it hit me and I sat up in the water—it would repeat itself unless I was sure never to be alone with Heraldson again. The water suddenly felt cold to me and my wrinkled skin shivered. I got out and went back to bed.

I didn't tell anyone, not that there was really anyone for me to tell, my mother or BeBe, I suppose. BeBe knew something was wrong with me at work the next day, but assumed it was just more worry about my parents. My mother was too preoccupied with her own worries to notice. I tried to put it out of my mind.

After work the next day I headed down to the car lot and found Jody talking to a man with a ponytail.

"Here's his son now," Jody said, looking up and seeing me.

"Can I help you?" I asked.

"Yeah, I'm lookin' for Jim McGraw. That fella there said he ain't been around in a couple of weeks. Know when he might be back?"

I looked him over. He was taller than me, deeply tanned, wearing jeans and a chambray shirt, cowboy boots that were worn and scuffed despite a recent polishing. He obviously wasn't from around these parts, I concluded. Then I remembered the note that I had, addressed to my father, announcing someone's arrival. Saturday would be the first of August.

"No, sir, sure don't. He's away on vacation right now. Can I help you?" I tried to sound tough, made my accent thicker.

"You his son?" He looked me in the eye.

"That's right. Can I take a message for him?"

"Nope. I'll try back." He turned and walked away. I looked around for his car but didn't see anything I didn't recognize.

"Hey," I yelled into the heat, "what's your name? Who can I tell him came by?" But he was out beside the highway then,

143

walking toward Crescent, too far away for him to hear me. I momentarily toyed with the idea of driving after him.

"Who was that guy?" Jody asked, coming around from the garage.

"Don't know. Somebody lookin' for Daddy. Did he tell you his name? Or what he wanted?" I tried to sound matter-of-fact.

"No. Just said he had some business with Jim McGraw, said he'd come a long way, and asked when Jimbo would be back. Then you walked up."

"Let me know if he comes back, Jody. I don't like the looks of him."

Maybe he wouldn't come back, I hoped on the way home. But then if he was the mystery man from Florida he probably wouldn't leave until he saw my dad. But who knew when that would be. I decided it was time to tell Momma about all this, but when I got home she was in such a good mood that I couldn't bear to spoil it. She had finally made up her mind to divorce my father. So she claimed.

I barely got in the door when she sat me down at the dining room table and said, "This is it, Bounty. I hope you won't mind. Maybe when you were small I was afraid of leaving your father, afraid of what the future would bring, afraid for you not havin' a daddy, but you're grown now and I can't spend the rest of my life like this. I just can't," she preached and I felt almost proud of her.

"I understand, Mom, and I don't blame you a bit. It is time for you to get on with your life—how long has he pulled these stunts now? All my life. You'll make it fine without him. . . . All men aren't like him, Momma." I decided to encourage her as strongly as I could, no holding back.

"You're right, sweetie, it is time for me to move on. . . ."

Then she got all wistful looking and turned her head to stare out the window beyond the clear creek and green trees.

"I don't want to be alone. If I thought he'd ever straighten

144

up and quit drinking, I'd stay. But if I'm gonna be this alone while I'm married, I might as well be single. At least then I won't have to worry about him, about the future." She ended in a low whisper, a shadow of her initial resolve.

"You'll be okay, Mom, trust me. You're better off without him. We both are."

"He's still your father. Even if I divorce him, he's still your father."

"I know that. I know."

Was she trying to decrease her pain by increasing mine?

"Well, my vacation starts Monday; I'll call Stan Howard and get the paperwork in motion." She sounded strained and sad, and it reminded me of the time she had to take Kalija, our Irish setter, to the vet to be put to sleep. He had cancer and moaned in pain a long time before we realized what was causing it. It had to be done, though.

As she opened the refrigerator and popped a diet Coke, I felt tremendous relief. It would finally be over. Sure, there'd still be some hard parts, moving out of the house, settling the property, but it was decided. Finally, some closure on a lifetime wound. Whatever it took to get there was more than worth it to me.

I was so distracted by her decision and the fact that she actually sustained it for more than a day that I didn't tell her about the odd clues I'd discovered. Maybe they didn't mean anything at all.

I checked with Jody at the car lot on Friday, and he hadn't seen the ponytail man.

Saturday morning Mom acted as if nothing was wrong. She was almost chipper. She cleaned house and baked a peach cobbler, made a shopping list—she had to pick out a birthday present for my grandfather—and prepared to go Eva's for her weekly hair appointment. When she returned, her long red hair had become her short red hair, tapered at the neck, a few curls on top with bangs. I had to admit the style was becoming to her, made her look younger, more glamorous. Giddy with change, she giggled at my compliment.

"I had to do it, Bounty. Had to. I think I'd go crazy if I hadn't got my hair cut. I've always wanted to, you know, but your father.... Well, nothin' to stop me now. Eva loved it, said it took years off my looks, the best thing I could've done for myself."

She put groceries away and turned the radio on, changed my country station for jazz, the Tower of Power blowing their horns and brains out. I marveled.

"Look what I got for Grandpa Mac," she said, rummaging through another bag. "It's a flannel bed jacket. Do you think he'll like it?" She held up a tartan-plaid flannel shirt, something between a pajama top and a smoking jacket.

"I thought bed jackets were for women," I said.

"Well, whatever you want to call it. It'll keep him warm in that drafty nursin' home. I want you to go with me on his birthday this week—I think it's Friday. I got a card for you to give him." She handed me a smiling sun card with the usual poem inside, "another year and birthday cheer" sort of verse.

"He's eighty-three and has Alzheimer's, Mom. He'll like anything. He won't know we're there, or even remember it's his birthday." I suddenly felt very sorry for him even though I hadn't been to visit all summer. On Father's Day I was supposed to go, but I got only as far as the parking lot. It depressed me too much. I could not bear to see him that way; I would have had to bring him home with me.

The grandfather who took me fishing, carved penny-whistles, and told me about shooting Japs in WWII was not the man in room 212 of Pine Haven Nursing Home who sported Depends undergarments while drooling over *The Price Is Right*.

So I had lied and told my parents that I stopped in briefly. I paid a kid in the parking lot a buck to take my card and gift in for me.

"Bounty, he's still a human being, for heaven sake," she said, exasperated.

"He'll love it, Mom. The bright flannel will cheer him up. Yeah, I'll go with you." I couldn't see any way to get out of it.

Just then somebody knocked on the door. My mother went to answer it, and I could hear a familiar male voice. I sauntered into the living room and saw my mother talking to the pony-tailed man I'd met two days before at the car lot.

"You don't know when he'll be back?" he was asking. "I've come an awful long way to see him, from Florida. I wrote and told him I was coming."

"I'm sorry. He's been out of town for some time. Is there somethin' I can help you with?"

"Can I come in, Mrs. McGraw?" His eyes met mine through the doorway. "You might need to sit down for what I've got to tell you."

"I'm sorry, but I don't know you. You'll have to tell me whatever it is right here." My mother turned to make sure I was hearing all this. I had my eye on Daddy's shotgun a few feet behind the bar.

"I'm your husband's son, ma'am. Jim McGraw was married to my mother. My name's Jake Carnes."

My mother's mouth opened and closed several times, like a baby bird's, but nothing came out. I came up behind her in case she started to faint or something.

"I see. Why don't you come in?" she said, and I couldn't hide my surprise.

"Thank you." He was wearing the same shirt, jeans, and cowboy boots he'd been wearing the day I met him. There was no car in the driveway, and I wondered if he'd walked all the way from Crescent or wherever he came from. Maybe he'd walked from Florida.

"Why don't you sit down and tell me what this is all about." My mother's voice had an excited edge to it, like the night we went to raid Janet's. I didn't like the fact that she was letting this guy in, but I was as curious as she was. Maybe I'd finally be able to put the pieces together.

Mom perched on the edge of the sofa and I leaned against

the bar, still within arm's reach of the loaded gun. Our visitor sat sideways in the dentist's chair, facing my mother. I studied his face, a handsomely familiar face; it looked like mine, except with finer cheek bones, darker complexion, darker hair. He reminded me of a picture I'd seen of my father when he was about twenty-one and in the service. I maintained a poker face and glanced at my mother. But her eyes were locked with his as he spoke.

"Where to begin . . ." his voice came out in a rich drawl. "Like I said, my name's Jake Carnes. Jim McGraw married my mother, Patty Carnes, in Huntsville, Alabama, in 1959. They moved around a lot since he was drivin' the Southern regional stock-car circuit—Alabama, Georgia, the Gulf Coast, Florida, that's where I was born a year later. He left us when I was about four. I haven't seen him since, haven't heard from him. Have I got the right Jim McGraw?"

"What makes you think my husband's your father?" my mother asked slowly. "Besides the name."

"Well, I got this address from the hospital where my mother spent her last few years. Seems your husband paid some of her bills."

"I see." My mother leaned forward. "Do you have any proof of all this?"

"Yes, ma'am, I believe I do. Here's copies of my parents' marriage license and my birth certificate. See for yourself." He would make a good lawyer, I thought, in his calm, fact by fact manner. He wanted something, I decided then, probably money. He took out several quarter-folded sheets of paper from his hip pocket and handed them to my mother. She unfolded them carefully as if they were about to detonate in her hands.

"I see," she repeated. I leaned over her shoulder and looked down. Daddy's name was on both documents.

"And there's this." Jake handed her a photograph. It was the original.

"I've seen it before," I blurted out.

"What do you mean, you've seen it before?" Mother looked more shocked than she had when Jake said he was Daddy's son.

Her short hair suddenly surprised me, like she was wearing a wig.

"I found one like it in Daddy's desk drawer down at the car lot about a month or so ago. I didn't know what to make of it, so I didn't mention it. I guess I forgot about it with all that's been goin' on." She looked betrayed—it was my worst offense of the summer—as if I were the one who had a secret life and a secret family, not my father.

"Yeah, I mailed a copy of the photo and a note introducin' myself to Mr. McGraw a couple months back. He didn't respond to that or to the note I sent tellin' him I'd be comin' now."

My mother handed the papers and picture back to Jake and started shaking her head.

"So what do you want, Mr. Carnes? I told you my husband's not here."

"Yes, ma'am, I know. But I need to know when he'll be back. Like I said, I've waited a long time to meet him. I hope you understand."

"I'm not sure I do. Why now? Why haven't you tried to contact him before this?" She leaned back now, crossed her arms.

"Well, honestly, ma'am, it's like this. I've been in the Florida State Penitentiary the last twelve years. I just got out two weeks ago." He watched our expressions carefully, but my mother didn't blink, literally. She just looked him in the eye the way she looked at me sometimes and tried to tell if I was lying or not.

I had a lot I wanted to say, but didn't know where to start. I didn't believe him, didn't trust him. I thought about mentioning the big money and the wire-transfer account but decided to hold on to it for the time being, not give everything away at once.

"So, what do you want—money? We're not wealthy, Mr. Carnes." My mother stood and headed toward the door.

"No, ma'am. Although, I admit I'm not exactly wealthy either at the moment. I just have some business to settle with my father. Your husband. Can you at least tell me where he is?"

"No, I can't. We don't know where he is."

Jake looked at me. "Didn't you tell me he was on vacation?"

Mom looked at me again for an explanation. "He came by the car lot on Thursday when I was there. He didn't tell me who he was."

"My husband's out of town on business, and he didn't tell us when he'd be back. Your guess is as good as mine."

"Well, would you call me when he comes home? Right now I'm stayin' at the Crescent Moon Motor Lodge, number three." Jake stood up to leave.

"I'll tell my husband when he gets back. One last question, Mr. Carnes. When did your parents divorce?"

Jake was in the driveway and he turned and looked at my mother funny. "They never did divorce, Mrs. McGraw. They were married until my mother died five years ago."

My mother didn't respond, just closed the screen door and watched him walk away. His boots echoed up the hill and into the distance.

"Do you believe him?" she asked.

"Are you okay, Mom?" I tried to guide her back to the sofa, but she stood fixed in the doorway.

"Tell me whether or not you believe him, Bounty." She sounded angry.

"I don't know. Everything looks real enough. But I don't know. Do you believe him?" She let me help her now, and we both sat down.

"Yes, I do."

She was silently hysterical the rest of the weekend, going through picture albums and drawers, all my father's possessions for some verification of his bigamy. I tried to talk to her, even to assist in the search, but she just ignored me, fumbled hurriedly from drawer to drawer, closet to closet. When she headed out to search the barn and garage on Sunday morning, I let her be. I didn't like the way this was turning out.

And I didn't like leaving her alone on Monday, but at least

she was speaking to me. "I'm fine, I promise. It's my vacation—remember?" she said and sat a plate of scrambled eggs in front of me.

"What're you doin' today?" I asked.

"I need to clean house, put things back in order from my, uh, search, weed the vegetable garden. All kinds of things. Maybe we'll go to a movie tonight." She sounded like her old self in some ways. But she made no mention of calling Stan Howard and implementing the divorce. I could only assume that this stranger showing up, claiming to be her stepson, confirmed her decision. I didn't bring it up.

When I came home from work, though, my mother was gone.

She had left me a note and a freezer full of casseroles. I can't recall exactly what it said, only that she had to find my father and find out the truth. There was enough food in the refrigerator and freezer for at least a week, and she'd signed blank checks in case I needed them. She said she'd call as soon as she found Daddy.

I looked in their bedroom and noticed the red suitcase was gone, her makeup and hairspray absent from the dresser. She planned to be gone awhile, no doubt as long as it took to find what she was looking for. And if my father's quest was any indication, then I might be alone for the rest of the summer. From the freezer I chose a Mexican casserole with ground beef, green beans, Mexican corn, and tomato sauce, a recipe that served eight.

I stayed up all night that night and lived. I paced from room to room, searched my mother's desk drawers, my father's oak file cabinet, looking, hunting for whatever had convinced my mother to take off after him. In the top drawer of their dresser I found a stale pack of Marlboro Lights, lit one, trailed ash across the kitchen floor.

The TV blared its shrill laughter, like some perverse Greek

chorus, till I could stand it no longer. I turned it off and stood there chewing my lower lip till it bled.

My circuits were blown, nothing left to feel, not glad or disappointed. Maybe if I felt anything it resembled relief, perhaps even deeper relief than I'd felt when I thought she'd divorce him. About midnight I was rummaging in the refrigerator and found over half a Bud twelve-pack. That's when I realized I was relieved, like the feeling you get away from home for the first time—summer camp or something. I popped a beer and ate the last serving of casserole, then retired to the porch.

The streetlight from the top of the hill gave me strange comfort. The night air felt thick, yet cool, sympathetic to my plight, dew starting to cover the ground in tiny pearls. I sipped my beer and thought about calling the Crescent Moon Motor Lodge. I called BeBe instead. She said she'd be right over. After about fifteen minutes, her headlights shone over the hilltop, and I could hear her downshifting her old Rabbit.

"That you, Bounty?" She squinted at me on the porch.

"The one and only, James Bountiful, Jr."

I rocked the swing so she could at least follow the creaks while her eyes adjusted to the dark. She felt her way along the porch and sat next to me.

"Poor baby." She clasped my hand and I let her, her palm warm and dry.

"Want one?" I held up the remains of the twelve-pack.

"Sure. Pop it for me so I won't break a nail." The can made a small fizzing sound and foamed at the mouth.

"What'd you mean on the phone—your mother left you?" She took a healthy drink from her beer.

"Just what I said. She's gone after my father. Left me a note and everything. Said she'd call when she finds him. If she ever does." I downed the rest of mine and opened another.

"But that's only the half of it," I continued. "There's some things I didn't tell you before."

She sat close to me like we were on a date while we held hands. I could smell a musky sweet scent like a ripe melon.

"I found a picture in my father's office back at the beginnin' of the summer—him with a woman and little boy. I didn't say anythin' about it, just held on to it. Then Saturday mornin' this guy shows up, thirty-somethin' with a ponytail and cowboy boots, says he's the boy in the picture, my father's son."

I let her take it all in, like someone arriving late at the theater.

"You're foolin' me, now, aren't you? This is like somethin' on TV." She sipped more brew. "So what'd your momma do? That why she left?" BeBe sounded angry, as if she were the woman wronged.

"It may be part of the reason. But I wouldn't be surprised if she had been plannin' this for some time. Her vacation started today. She asked the guy a lot of questions and he answered 'em all, even had a marriage license and birth certificate with my father's signature. Had the same picture I'd found in my father's drawer. Momma told him Daddy wasn't here and she didn't know when he'd be back." I slowed down. "And get this. The guy just got out of prison, in Florida."

"Bad news. That's where those wire-transfers were goin'— right? He wants money, I bet. Wants somethin'."

"Says he just wants to talk to Daddy. Stayin' over in Crescent till Daddy calls him. I don't know what to make of him. I don't trust him."

"And you shouldn't. Ex-con ain't nothin' but trouble, I say. He's here for a reason—M-O-N-E-Y—might as well get the checkbook out now. Remember what I say, Bounty. Stranger showin' up out of the blue claimin' to be your brother means nothin' but trouble. Wait and see." BeBe slurped the last of her beer as if to emphasize her prophecy. I opened another one for her.

"Well, you're havin' one hell of a summer," she announced.

"Thanks for makin' it official." Her empathy caught me off guard and I wanted to hold her. "There's more. . . ."

"Mercy, what d'ya mean, there's more? Let's see . . . you've got a brain tumor?" We both laughed so hard our eyes watered. Then I sobered up.

153

"Not a brain tumor. But there's probably no way I'll be goin' to UT this fall. My loan's been turned down. I'm stuck here."

"Turned down? As chummy as Heraldson is with you, I just knew he'd take care of it," BeBe said.

"Oh, he took care of it, all right." I figured she might as well know the truth. Maybe she could tell me what the truth was.

"What d'ya mean? Did you ask him about it?"

I tried to remember how many beers I'd had by then and couldn't.

"You remember Heraldson invited me over for a swim Wednesday night? Remember?" I put my arm around her, needing her comfort.

"I remember. So? What happened?" She became impatient.

"His wife and kids had gone to visit his in-laws. It was just me and him." I connected with her eyes. "He wanted me to do somethin' I couldn't do. He said if I didn't that my loan wasn't goin' through."

"Heraldson tried to mess with you?" she asked incredulously. I nodded. Her mouth was open and her eyebrows raised. "I can't believe it. I mean, I believe you, but he's such a macho jerk, always rubbin' up against me at teller meetings. Did you hit him?" I felt relieved that she couldn't imagine me responding to his advances, trading my future for a few minutes of the unknown.

"I wanted to. But I ran like hell out of there. I got sick." There was a lot more I wanted to say, but I couldn't find words for it all, couldn't think clearly enough to know how to focus my mouth into the words I did want to say.

"I'm sorry, Bounty." It was simple, heartfelt, what I needed to hear.

I kissed her then and she didn't resist, full and welcoming in return.

"Would you spend the night?" I asked.

-10-

She kissed me again, full on the mouth, before pulling back.

"I'm flattered, Bounty. I like you, too. But I don't think spendin' the night's a good idea."

"Why not? I need you. You may be the only person who cares 'bout me right now." I removed my arm from her, and she squeezed my other hand tight.

"You need some comfort. And maybe I am the only person you got right now—I don't know. But don't confuse wantin' comfort for desire, for passion. After we've spent more time together, if somethin' happens, well, then it was meant to be. But you got too much goin' on right now to be givin' your heart away."

I looked at her in the dark, traced all the curves of her face and neck with my eyes, settled on her mouth with teeth whiter than the moon. I wondered if I was even capable of loving someone. That circuit felt inoperative, shorted out long ago. She was right.

"Nobody's ever turned me down so nice before," I laughed, trying to make light of it.

155

"I'm not turnin' you down. I'll stay with you tonight as long as you need me to. But I won't love you yet."

The stars were out, all prickly pear diamond light, placid and quiet, unmoved by my plight, or anyone's, below. There was no breeze, but it didn't feel hot, only tepid, a comfortable bath of warm air generated as I settled back beside her, our shoulders touching. The chains creaked as we swung.

And then the most remarkable thing. I found the moon above the beech tree leaves and realized that it was disappearing. A lunar eclipse, of all things. Slow and undulating, subtle and yet brilliant white, the moon slowly hid itself in curves of black ink. It reminded me of a lady slowly dipping her beautiful fingernail into a bottle of dark polish. I pointed it out to BeBe, whispered, "Look," and she leaned her head across my chest to see through the dark foliage. Ten minutes went by and a few more degrees of moon were swallowed up.

I started to cry then and wept hard. The salt water taste was sharp, and I was afraid that someone might hear me. But I remembered that there was no one to hear but BeBe, and it didn't matter if there had been.

She rocked me to herself, my head on her bosom now, and I prayed. I prayed for my father and about his need for drink, for my mother, her need for him. I prayed for myself, that things would change, that if God really was up there, that'd he'd do something. I prayed that my parents would come home and that I could go on vacation. I prayed for the moon being nibbled up by the dark shadow of the earth.

I sat up, wiped my face on the sleeve of my T-shirt. "Listen," I said.

"What is it?" BeBe sounded scared.

A bobwhite called out his lonesome cry.

"I remember readin' in *Field & Stream* that a bobwhite who's still callin' in summer, especially this late, never found a mate," I explained.

"*Bobwhite*" he called again. My father had once taught me how to mimic the female reply, an equally forlorn warble, and

I returned his call. We traded calls back and forth.

BeBe hit my shoulder: "You're cruel to be teasin' that poor bird with false hope."

"Maybe it'll keep him alive," I said. Maybe he needed me as much as I needed him. With the moon eclipsed and unanswered prayers, maybe that's as good as it gets. "Maybe false hope's better than none."

"I don't think so, Bounty," she challenged. "False hope's a contradiction. There's gotta be somethin' real underneath it all, or else you might as well believe in . . . I don't know, the moon or somethin'."

We were sitting back, shoulder to shoulder. I felt dreamy and warm, my face still wet.

"What do you believe in, BeBe?" I asked as sincerely as I could. "I really want to know."

She took a long time to answer.

"When I was a little girl, my momma's brother came to town preachin' a revival. At the end of the service one night, my Uncle Theo called me up front—in front of all these people, mind you—and picked me up to reach the microphone. 'Tell these kind people what you told me this mornin',' he said. I looked at him funny and everybody laughed when I said, 'You mean, when I asked to go potty?' He was sweatin' bullets. He tried again, 'Tell these people what you told me you believe in.' I dropped my little purse then—a little white one with all my doll clothes in it—and said, 'Jesus is my bigger betterness.'"

I looked over at her as if she were speaking French.

She continued, "I believe in somethin' bigger than all this, somethin' we can't usually see or understand. Someone hopeful and in control of all this mess we get ourselves into. Somebody who has a bigger plan than just us all bein' rich and famous. I still believe."

In my dreams that night as I rocked gently back and forth on the swing, long after BeBe had gone, the bobwhite perched on my shoulder like a parakeet and whispered in my ear. I was afraid he'd be angry at my deception, but he wasn't. He thanked me. And then he said, "You're welcome, welcome."

Something about the dream comforted me and I turned on my side, careful not to fall out. I could hear the creek then, faint, droning on like water does when it's running.

For some reason this night seemed important, a kind of turning point. Something new was going to begin, and I could only hope it was better than what had happened so far. As strange as it sounds, I felt lucky. Lucky to be lying with my back hurting from the swing's stiff planks. Lucky to see the moon eclipsed on a summer's night and to dream of lonely birds. Lucky to know a woman who believed in something I was looking for.

For the next few days I grew accustomed to living alone, accepted the quiet like a bachelor, ate defrosted food, and drank beer.

My mother didn't call, but I didn't expect her to until she found my father. In the meantime, it seemed as if the days were longer, the nights longer yet. BeBe and I talked every day and even tossed a frisbee at the park on Tuesday afternoon. Her presence comforted me, but also made me uncomfortable. I didn't want to rely on her.

Wednesday after work I drove into Pikeville, ate at McDonald's, and then stopped at the new Kroger SuperStore. Standing in front of the magazine rack, I thumbed through *People* and *US*, *Esquire* and *GQ*, read about famous people's problems: bulimia and bankruptcy, adultery with sexy co-stars, spoiled child stars doing drugs. It was little comfort. In fact, it only fueled my indifference. I found myself wondering about those people I read about. I wondered if they were as lonely as everyone else.

I looked up from *Rolling Stone* and saw an overweight home-maker with a little girl in her shopping cart, reading *Soap Opera Weekly*. Somehow I knew that this was a thrill, a highlight for her week, catching up on the episodes she'd missed, shocked at the latest kidnaping or lovers' triangle. A man on my right in sweats and dirty Reeboks browsed through *Golf Digest*.

Prolonging my visit, I followed aisle after aisle of the maze, looking at shelves of cat food and detergent, frozen dinners and canned juices. The bright neon glare of the overhead warehouse lights, the sheen of the polished off-white floor brought me down.

In the express check-out I found myself worried about the world, no, about all the other single people in the store that night. I worried about single cans of soup, fruit that would spoil before it could all be eaten.

Something peculiarly poignant struck me about my own chips and salsa, large box of Cap'n Crunch, another twelve pack, and the new issue of *Arrowhead*. The middle-aged mother-cashier made me even sadder, with her gold rings on every finger and her name tag reading "Margie." I hoped she'd card me on the beer, but she only smiled when she rang it up, as if she knew I needed it, knew we all needed it, would share it with me if I asked her.

The feeling I had that night reminded me of the way I usually felt at shopping malls during Christmas. This past year in particular I got so depressed. Waiting on my mother in the Murfreesboro Outlet Mall, I sat with other sons and husbands in one of the little lounge areas with fake palms and ashtrays. I watched people passing by with shopping bags and presents, children overdressed for a ten dollar photo pose with Santa, old people who never came to the mall except at Christmas.

I can't explain it. When my mother came out of the store I didn't recognize her at first, just another mechanical shopper. She worried about me all the way home, but I tucked it away. Pace once told me I have a messiah complex—I want to be everyone's savior. He may be right.

On my way home that night, traffic slowed to a crawl on Old Franklin Highway as people searched for parking places or just idled as they drove by. The *People* photo shoot had increased notoriety. The miraculous profile of Jesus had appeared in the *Crescent Courier*, the *Nashville Banner*, and the *Tennessean*.

WKUZ made up a song to the tune of "Amazing Grace" that went something like "Amazing face, how neat and round, to appear on my wretched GE, I once was lost, but now am found, if you don't believe, come see." Not to be outdone, a Nashville station had started playing a country song called "Deep-Freeze Jesus."

So everybody in town had seen it at least once, and traffic' was getting out of hand. Here it was a weeknight with well over a hundred cars lined up and down the roadside, and the previous weekend, Deputy Parker had to direct traffic for two or three hours a night.

If Daddy had been there, he would've raised hell about them parking in our vacant pasture. But it didn't bother me.

By Friday, I was thoroughly enjoying my "vacation." My parents seemed like distant relatives in another state, second-cousins you see only at family reunions. Between Deep-Freeze Jesus in *People* (what was next, the *Enquirer*, *The Star*, the *New York Post*?) and drinking a six-pack while watching MTV, I was a happy student, home for the summer.

Then that morning, as I crunched my Cap'n Crunch, I remembered my grandfather's birthday when Willard Scott congratulated Mrs. Margaret Cornell of Phoenix, Arizona, on her 100th. I'd have to take him his present that evening, a chore I dreaded.

For a Friday it was slow. Since the previous Friday had been the end of the month, most folks had already been paid. The morning crept along, propelled by an occasional savings withdrawal or cashed check.

News of the previous night's photo shoot kept everyone chattering, replacing the weather as topic du jour. Mrs. Simms

160

came in and acted like she hadn't seen me the entire summer, giving Sarah Anne and BeBe wisecrack fuel for the rest of the day. Clark Heraldson stopped in around ten and marched straight to my window.

"Hey, Bounty, how's the bankin' business? Make me a loan?" He rested his Brooks Brothers seersucker arm on the bullet-proof glass partition. His voice betrayed nothing about what must have been going on inside his head. But his eyes lanced holes through me.

"I'm doin' good, Mr. Heraldson, real well," I faltered.

"Clark, remember? How 'bout comin' over for a swim this weekend? We're havin' over some college kids from church for a pool party on Saturday night so Carole thought it'd be a great chance for you to meet new people. You know how fast our little county's growing! And besides," he lowered his voice to a whisper, "there'll be lots of swimsuits—not many bikinis, church function and all that—but still plenty of centerfold material, if you know what I mean." And he winked. I couldn't believe his nerve.

"Uh, thanks, Clark, and tell your wife thanks, too." I wasn't about to fall for this one. "My grandfather's birthday is this weekend and we're havin' a little family party. You know, cake and all that. Not every day someone turns eighty-four. Thanks anyway." I could tell this made him mad.

He lowered his voice again and leaned into my window: "Two things, McGraw. Where the hell's your father? And have you thought about my offer? You wouldn't want to lose your student loan—would you?" His eyes danced.

"He's still not back. He hasn't called since you asked last time."

"I'd hate for him to get arrested."

"What's that supposed to mean?"

"Just tell him. About the loan?"

I wasn't sure what to say, couldn't bring myself to cut off my options totally. A customer came up behind Heraldson; BeBe already had a line. Clark straightened up and resumed smiling.

"Well, I understand. I know all about those family special occasions, it's what keeps a family together. . . . Well, wish your grandfather a happy birthday from me and the bank. And if the party breaks up early, come on over. Take it easy, Bounty." Before he trotted into Rosenstein's office, he clasped my shoulder, the way politicians do when they work a crowd and want to break up the handshake monotony.

I waited on the next customer and wondered if Heraldson was blackmailing my father. Maybe he knew about the bigamy stuff and was making my dad pay him to keep quiet. Maybe that was where all that big money went to. But where'd it come from? Maybe my dad and Clark Heraldson were mixed up with the Mafia or the FBI or something. Maybe my father was never coming back but had been forced to go into the witness protection program and assume a new life. Somewhere in Boise or Boston he was working as an engineer with a new nose and hair color and a split-level in the suburbs. My mom had joined him, and now I'd never see them again. Maybe they were dead.

I couldn't think that way anymore, so I started thinking about my grandfather's birthday and decided to order a cake. What the heck, go all out, right? I mean, surely no one needed something to celebrate more than an eighty-four-year-old man with Alzheimer's and I did. The Crescent Roll Bakery had the best chocolate cakes anywhere. I chose an airplane motif with toy biplanes perched among blue cotton-candy clouds. Maybe going to the nursing home wouldn't be so bad after all.

BeBe agreed to go with me, and on the way to my house after work she asked, "What did Heraldson want? After what happened, I figured he wouldn't dare show his ugly face around."

"I wish. . . . He's lookin' for Daddy. Seems almost desperate. Today he threatened that Daddy could go to jail if he doesn't show up soon. I think he was bluffin' though. He asked me to come to a church swimmin' party Saturday night, then reminded me about the loan."

"So, did you tell him to take a flyin' leap?" There were sparks in her voice. I wanted to kiss her.

"Not yet. I still need that loan, BeBe. I don't wanna be stuck here the rest of my life." I pulled in my driveway.

"Don't whine, Bounty. It don't look good on a man." That stung me, but I didn't let it show.

Inside the house I rummaged around my mother's closet looking for the flannel bed jacket while BeBe called the bakery to make sure the cake was ready. As I clipped the price tags off the red plaid, I discovered shoulder pads and realized I wasn't about to give this to my grandfather, Alzheimer's or not.

"Look at this." I held it up for BeBe to see.

"How pretty," she replied and meant it.

"I can't give this to my grandfather. He'll look like Liberace or something. . . . Here, help me look for another present." I handed it over, and she caressed the flannel. Inside one of the many shoeboxes under my bed I found a penny whistle my grandfather had carved out of cedar. He had given it to me for my seventh or eighth birthday—I'd played it until my parents heard "Mary Had a Little Lamb" in their sleep. It would do fine.

On the way to the nursing home we picked up the cake, and I had to admit, it looked more like the console for a new video game than something edible. Together with the penny whistle (which I'd wrapped in the Sunday funnies), we might have been going to play pin-the-tail with a bunch of five-year-olds. But it felt right, what I really wanted to give to the old man, not a pretense of caring more than I did.

But somehow that bothered me as I pondered this concept, what it would be like if we all stripped pretense and gave whatever we really wanted to give. I thought of the way my father always insisted on me picking out and purchasing his wife's birthday and Christmas presents. He'd give me money, usually a lot, and relieve himself of the burden of fulfilling his wife's wish list. But something was lost. Something strange had always rattled around in me as I handed the cashier a hundred dollar bill for the perfume or terry bathrobe or gold earrings or whatever it was that year. No son can pick out what a husband should give.

"What're you thinkin' about?" BeBe asked.

"My parents. How they should be the ones doin' this and not me. Surely my mother's found my father by now. I picture them on a beach somewhere, Daytona or Pawley's Island, in a motel with a sign saying 'Blue Dolphin Motel, Free HBO, Kitchenettes.' My mother's fixin' tomato soup on a hot plate, and if my father feels well enough, or sober enough, they'll take a walk on the beach, maybe go out for shrimp on the pier."

"You hate them so much?" Her question surprised me.

"Why shouldn't I? Don't you hate yours?"

"Sometimes. But you sound different. Eventually I forgive 'em so I can get on with my life."

I thought on this a minute, but couldn't get past the fact that I belonged on the beach, sunning, learning to surf, deep-sea fishing. Instead I was pulling into the gray parking lot of Pine Acres on a Friday night with a mound of plastic airplanes trapped in a web of cotton candy. It wasn't right.

Inside the steel, institutional double-doors the poignant smell of old people assaulted me. This was why I couldn't come to this place. I know everybody hates the way hospitals and doctors' offices smell, but nursing homes are different. Not only do you have your antiseptic, ammonia, medicine smell, but you smell death. Or what I always imagined death to smell like. And not death like decay or decomposition, but living death. The lost memories, the sagging flesh, wheelchair grease, and aluminum walkers.

My eyes teared from the newly mopped ammonia floors as I turned the corner and found the nurses' station. They seemed chipper and at ease, the kind of folks you want nursing your elders. One young man with a beard seemed especially pleased that I was here to see Mr. Mac, as he called my grandfather. (I'd

called him Gran Mac or Papa Mac since I could remember.)
The male nurse told me that Mr. Mac had even "seemed himself" for a while, that he smiled when everyone sang "Happy
Birthday" in the cafeteria at supper. I felt funny when he said
that.

"BeBe, I can't do this," I said. "You take the cake and the
present in. He'll never know. Please."

"What's got into you?"

"What if he's dead? I feel like somethin's wrong."

"Uh-huh, and we all know what a psychic you are. Come
on." She nudged me through the door before I could resist. I
knew we'd find him dead. It was the same feeling I'd had at the
beginning of summer and later dismissed until it came true.
It's like on a day you have a flat tire, you just know you're going
to bounce a check or need a root canal or something. Misfortune
usually attracts itself and is rarely satiated until there's an
epidemic.

But he wasn't dead. He was snoring lightly while the TV
hummed with a *Star Trek* rerun.

"How y'all doin'? Come on in."

I froze. There sat the ponytailed man, Jake Carnes, my half-
brother, in the big recliner next to the bed.

"What're you doin' here?" I barked once the door was shut.

"I figured somebody'd come to see Mr. McGraw on his birthday. I was hopin' it would be our old man," he drawled.

"He's not back yet. You shouldn't be here."

"I got just as much right as you do. I probably been here
more times this week than you been all year. He's my grandpa,
too, you know." His voice took an edge, fierce and keen, as if
we were fighting for custody of the man sleeping before us.

BeBe broke the tension by cutting the birthday cake, dol-
ing out pieces on the napkins we'd brought. It was mindlessly
quiet for a few minutes while the three of us sat around the
cramped room eating cake and licking crumbs from our fingers. BeBe kept stealing glances at Jake as if she were my guard
dog or something.

Dudley J. Delffs

Jake seemed unaffected by it all, seemed to be enjoying himself, as if he'd been waiting for this all day, his birthday instead our grandfather's. Just then the old man mumbled something and turned on his side toward the wall.

"I need to talk to you and your mom. I need a place to stay until my father gets back."

"And what're we supposed to do about it? I thought you were stayin' at the Crescent Moon?" I shoveled the last bite of icing into my mouth, the edge of a spun-sugar cloud.

"Ran out of money. Thought maybe I could stay at your place awhile. That way I'd be there when he shows up." Jake stood and stretched, leaned against the window sill, a bleak square looking out over a parking lot.

I snorted, and BeBe shifted her eyes back and forth like she was watching a tennis match.

"Let's go, BeBe. I got nothin' more to talk about here." She picked up her straw purse, and we headed out the door.

Pulling away from the brick institution, BeBe searched my eyes.

"Maybe I shouldn't say this . . . but I like him." She leaned over and I smelled fruit, sharp and sweet.

"Are you crazy? You're the one who told me never to trust an ex-con. Didn't you offer to have your brother DeWayne beat him up and scare him out of town?" I felt like my father, all mad and bug-eyed.

"Keep your shorts on, white boy. I said all that before I met him. But I know people. I'm never wrong about first impressions, and I think he's tellin' the truth. I think you could trust him."

"Even if he's tellin' the truth, that doesn't mean I can trust him."

"I'm just tellin' you my first impression."

"You really are nuts, BeBe. . . . So what am I supposed to do? Invite him over for a slumber party so he can murder me in my sleep and steal all the silver?"

I pulled up in front of her house in Benton, "dark town" my father called it, on the outskirts of Crescent. She had to

166

baby-sit her younger sister since their mother had the grave-yard shift at the hospital.

"No, I didn't say that. I just said that I think he's tellin' the truth." She started to get out. "You wanna come in? I'll make some popcorn, we can watch a movie."

"No, thanks," I said.

"Suit yourself." She leaned over and kissed my cheek and disappeared through the yard full of black-eyed Susans and wild roses, up the dark porch front, and into the house.

I drove through country back roads full of ditches lined with burger wrappers and beer cans, Queen Anne's lace visible even in the shadows. The darkness, uninterrupted by streetlights, had an ominous feel: Anything could happen.

Back in town, I drove down the boulevard where all the high school kids cruised. Fat-tired, jacked up Camaros and TransAms, sporting metallic paint jobs, honked and chased after one another.

I saw a guy I went to high school with in his four-wheel drive—I recognized the glittering "Rude Dog" license plate on the front bumper. Little twinkling lights outlined the rectangular plate, as well as his license plate in back, like a neon marquee.

The strip was crowded, a Friday night in August—what else was there to do but get drunk at the drive-in and cruise the boulevard? The Dairy Queen packed in the post-softball set with men and boys in grass-stained polyester baseball pants milling around the picnic benches outside. The Boulevard Liquor Store and Toodle's Drive-Thru Package Window had a steady stream of customers.

Two girls in an Impala convertible slowed to take a look at me. As the light turned, they honked their horn and then gunned the old Chevy's accelerator. I thought about following them, but my heart wasn't in it. I felt like a spy, an undercover agent blending into the local turf, on the surface invisible from any other eighteen-year-old, cruising the strip from town square down to the new Taco Bell. The rest of the time I could be lifting

weights and drinking beer, playing softball and working at the
co-op to pay off a new truck. But inside I would never be one
of them. It's how I'd felt all my life—the rural foundling waiting to be reclaimed.

By the time I got home I was worn out. The traffic alongside the holy trailer park annoyed me. I couldn't imagine how
much longer the novelty would last. The moon was high, no
eclipse tonight, and as I pulled into our dead-end drive, through
the whitewash of my headlights, I saw someone sitting on the
front porch.

It was Jake Carnes.

-11-

"What are *you* doin' here?" I said and slammed the car door shut.

"Told you. I need a place to stay. At least for tonight." He leaned back against the porch column and took a drag off a cigarette, then snubbed the butt and threw it into our yard.

"This ain't a boardin' house. You knew I didn't want you here." I eased onto the porch, cautious in case he had a gun or knife. The boards creaked under my feet.

He laughed and it grew until he couldn't stop himself.

"Are you crazy or just drunk? I'm callin' the cops."

He stood up. "I'm laughin' at you, boy. Creepin' up here like I got dynamite strapped to my chest or somethin'. I'm not gonna hurt you." He lit another smoke.

"Yeah? You say a lot of things. I'm still callin' the cops. You're trespassin' on private property."

"Go ahead. I'll be glad to show 'em my birth certificate, tell 'em my whole story. Maybe I should've done that in the first place."

He had me. The only thing juicy enough to knock deep-freeze Jesus out of the headlines was a local scandal like this one was shaping up to be.

"Came to talk to your Momma, anyway. She disappeared too, or you expect her back tonight?"

I just looked at him a long time in the shadows. A Roman nose like mine and my father's, a lankier frame than mine, long hair, the orange tip of his cigarette glowing like an ember.

"She went to get my father." I moved over to the porch swing and sat down.

"So does that mean we know where he is? When they'll be back?" he asked.

"No, it doesn't."

"Well, then, I guess you got a houseguest till they get back. Got anything to drink? Maybe a beer?"

"You got some nerve—you know that?" I noticed his boots propped beside him, white socks dangling out their tops. Below them, on the lowest porch step, was an army duffel bag. And of all things, a guitar case, unless it housed a machine gun or bazooka.

"Lot of folks tell me that. You got anything to drink or not?"

I went inside and dug out a couple beer cans from the fridge, thought about BeBe's words that she liked him, trusted him, believed him. She was probably just attracted to him.

Back on the porch I tossed his can at him and he caught it without blinking.

"So what do you want here?" I asked, assuming my usual place on the swing.

"I told you. Got business with my father. Need to settle some things before I move on with my life, make a fresh go of it."

"What kind of business?"

"You wouldn't understand. Hell, he probably won't understand. . . . What's he like, Bounty?" His voice fell in pitch, lost some of its calm, steely edge, and a kind of neediness shone through.

"He's a jerk. If you're waitin' around to see what he's really

170

like, I can save you some time. He drinks too much, goes ballistic over everything I do, picks fights with my mom, thinks he can do no wrong. He's a used car salesman, not the big race car driver you knew." My beer tasted bitter. "He wants me to work at his car lot forever, stay here and go to community college, if at all. He wishes I were more like him."

"Why do you say that?" Jake asked.

"Isn't that what every father wants for his son? He wants me to be just like him and my mother wants just the opposite and I'm locked somewhere in between."

"I don't imagine he's gonna think I'm like him."

"I wouldn't be surprised if he doesn't talk to you."

"He has to. He owes me that, at least." He downed the last of his beer and crushed the can.

"Want another?" I asked, surprising us both.

"Yeah, that'd be nice."

When I came back I brought the rest of the twelve-pack and decided that I wanted to smoke. Jake's Camels rested beside his boots. "Trade you," I said and pointed.

He handed them over and grinned this big-toothed grin. "Don't get me arrested for contributin' to the delinquency of a minor."

"I'm eighteen, funny man. I guess that's what got you arrested in the first place."

"Nope. Armed robbery, attempted murder, assault, resisting arrest, illegal possession of a firearm, whatever else they could tack on. I was just eighteen when it happened." He leaned out across the porch railing like we were on a cruise ship.

"So what'd you rob?" I lit up, took a deep drag without inhaling. I was starting to enjoy myself, a late night talk-show host.

"Convenience store, a little market called EasyGo on the corner of Havana and Ocean Boulevard in Daytona Beach. It was about two in the mornin' and me and some buddies were high and needed cash. One of 'em handed me a gun and a ski mask, and three of us went in to do the deed. But the clerk was

171

this old man, a real fighter, managed to press his joy buzzer and set off the silent alarm. He kept stallin' and then he tried to jump me for the gun. It went off, he took it in the back, and the cops pulled up. My two buddies were long gone."

His report reminded me of how he told Mom and me about who he was, his relationship to Daddy, just the facts, a dutiful reporter maintaining the needed objectivity. It was funny then, because for all the details of his story, I trusted him more, not less. He looked off into the night, through the trees down to the water, which, when neither of us moved, we could hear gurgling its silvery chimes.

"So you served your time, and now you're a free man," I announced.

"Yeah, I like to think so. But it's not quite that easy. You get used to somethin' and it starts to feel like home, even if you didn't choose to be there to start with. Funny, ain't it?" He stood up and came over to sit in the swing with me.

I bummed another cigarette and lit it off his. The stars seemed brighter, and it suddenly felt very late. I didn't like letting down my guard, something bad would happen, it always did.

"So you and the old man don't get along, huh?" he asked.

"Not exactly. We help each other." I was starting to feel lightheaded and hot from the beer.

"Help each other?"

"Yeah, you know, use each other. He gets me to work at the car lot, do whatever he says, or at least I used to." Sweat trickled furiously beneath my shirt, under my arms and down my sides.

"And what do you get? How do you use him?"

I laughed. "I blame everythin' bad in my life on him."

"That's a pretty neat trick," Jake said.

"Yeah, you should try it sometime." I waited for him to join in, cement our tentative bond with a little daddy-bashing. But he kept silent, and when I looked over at him, his eyes were already fixed on me, looking for something. It made me nervous.

After a few minutes passed and neither of us said anything, I asked, "You hungry? I want a pizza."

"Yeah, I could eat somethin'."

It was only ten, even though the night seemed to have lasted a couple of days. On the way to Terry's I thought about Jake visiting our grandfather in the nursing home, wondered how he found out about him, wondered why he'd go visit an old man who could never know him. We rolled the windows down and the rush of air felt good. An Eagles song came on the radio and Jake turned it up, smiled to himself in the dark, some secret memory that still brought him pleasure.

Terry's stayed open till midnight, but inside things were winding down, actually slow for a Friday night. It smelled of tomatoes and onions, garlic and beer. We took a booth in the back with red vinyl seats, the kind you loved to slide on as a kid. Our waitress, Dixie, a girl whose sister I'd graduated with, came over to take our order—a large deluxe with extra cheese, hold the anchovies.

He lit another cigarette and said, "I got out just in time. All the joints are goin' cold turkey, new law or somethin'."

I nodded and wiped the mouth of my bottled import beer. Jake drank iced tea.

"So what happened to your momma?" I concentrated on the words but realized I had slurred them.

"She was a good woman, fragile. Drank some, for her nerves, she said. When McGraw left we moved back to Florida, in with her folks—I was four, I think. She got a job workin' for her daddy's mattress factory, hated it." He stirred more sugar into his tea.

"When I was about ten," he continued, "she had a breakdown. Grandpa found her curled up in a corner of the warehouse. He took her straight from work to the hospital. She spent the night there—had tried to kill herself, pills. She never came home again. They put her in a care hospital, tried to track down my daddy, but couldn't find him."

Our pizza arrived then, hot and steaming. Dixie whipped out a cutter from her apron pocket and wielded it across the thick crust like a Ginsu blade before serving on to our white plates. I ordered another import.

"Slow down, chief," Jake cautioned after the waitress walked away.

"I can take care of myself." I bit into the zesty pie, dribbled cheese down my chin onto my shirt.

"I'm sure you can, but you're the one with the car keys."

"That's right."

Dixie returned and sat a cold, green bottle down in front of me. I savored a long draw and watched the foam rise out the top.

Jake ate in silence for a few minutes, and then I asked him to finish his story.

"Not much left to tell. I never saw her again after I got busted . . . she was never well enough to come visit me and my requests to visit her were turned down, too risky. She died in the institution five years ago." He started on his third piece.

"Uh-huh," I nodded as if I were the warden and agreed that he was too risky indeed. "So your momma's parents raised you?"

"Yup. They made the best of a bad situation, being stuck with a kid they didn't want. Fed and clothed me, tried to keep me out of trouble. They loved me as much as they could, I guess."

"Are they still alive?" I had been eating too fast, on top of the beer, and I felt queasy.

"My grandma's still alive in a nursin' home in Miami. Grandpa died right after I was sentenced." He looked off toward the kitchen to avoid my eyes, and I imagined him sitting in the back of a church, handcuffed to a security guard during the funeral. I tried to help him by changing the subject.

"Yeah, we all got our troubles. Gran Mac's had Alzheimer's for almost two years now." I didn't know where to go with this, didn't want to feel the weight of my worries compounded by another person's sorrow. "Hey, let's play pool, cowboy. I'll bet you twenty bucks I kick your butt."

He looked me in the eye and laughed. We got up and headed for the back of the restaurant where two dilapidated pool tables leaned toward one another, the focal point of a waiting area that included video games and pay phones. I ordered a pitcher of whatever was on tap and noticed that the place was picking up, a lot of kids my age and a few older couples. The jukebox, a Wurlitzer with neon piping in green and purple, crooned Tanya Tucker. She was down to her last tear drop and wasn't gonna take it anymore.

"Take it easy on the brew," Jake warned as he selected a cue stick. "Somebody's got to drive home. Besides, I don't want you accusin' me of takin' advantage of you after your twenty's in my pocket." He chalked his selection with one hand, held a cigarette with the other.

Jake looked right at home, muscles twitching beneath his T-shirt as he buffed the blue cube back and forth. He looked like he ought to have a Harley waiting outside and a girl somewhere who never wore a bra. I felt dangerous by association.

We decided on solids and stripes instead of straight eight ball, and I broke the triangle with a sharp clack, watching the green three ball spin into a corner pocket. "Stripes," I yelled. I hadn't deliberately set out to get drunk, but I was feeling so good that intentions didn't matter anymore.

I missed a perfect setup with the seven ball as Jake flicked his Camel into a large plastic bucket of sand next to the table. He made two shots in a row, hard shots that he made look easy, before the chalk-bruised cue ball followed his third strike into the pocket.

"Scratch," I whooped.

"Not so loud," Jake said.

He sounded louder than I did, but smiled as he said it, letting me enjoy myself. I felt warm and fraternal then, proud to be seen with this man who shared my blood source. I had an urge to take his face in my hands and affectionately shake it, pinch his cheeks like a spinster aunt. And maybe I would have if it hadn't been my turn.

Even though I got to set the cue ball after his scratch, I missed an easy shot. After rolling a few inches the cue ball spun in place, and I watched hypnotically as it reflected the low billiard lights. My pitcher was empty.

"We're brothers," I suddenly cried out. "Brothers. I've got a brother."

I started laughing then, and Jake helped me sit on the slatted bench alongside the wall. I downed the last of my glass, feeling drunk and not caring.

"We better wrap this game up and get you home," Jake said in my ear.

"Did you know we're brothers?" I whispered, still laughing. I flagged a waitress for another pitcher, but Jake shook his head.

"Yeah, I heard that rumor, but I like you anyway. Come on, let's go home."

"Did we finish our game? Did I win?"

Jake guided me through the maze of smoke and tables toward the door. I stopped along the way at the men's room for the third time that night. There was a line and all the men in it seemed like old friends. A man in a denim shirt behind me propped me against the wall, smiled like a native of the country I was now exploring.

On the way out I chugged a half-empty glass from an abandoned table.

"Got to get you out of here," Jake grunted.

"Naw, the fun's just startin', Jakey. Let's hang around."

I suddenly realized I had a lit cigarette in my hand. A magician, that's what I was. For my next trick I would make my parents disappear. No, they'd already disappeared; the trick was to bring them back. Somewhere they waited for my cue before they crawled back through the secret panel. Ta-da! I'd pull back the curtain and they'd step out, smiling, holding hands in midair like a draw bridge.

Next thing I knew, the cigarette was between my lips, inhaling itself down my throat. The Amazing Bounty amazed even himself. I tried to blow a smoke ring but ended up blowing smoke in Jake's face. He coughed and shook his head.

"We're brothers, we're brothers," I chanted the magic words into some strange woman's face as we passed. She looked too old to wear spangled tights and be my assistant.

"You're a wild man, Bounty."

By this time we were in the parking lot, dark because the streetlight was busted. Two guys were fighting beside the building and I wanted to get involved, but Jake kept his hand on my neck and guided me to the passenger's side of the Merc. I liked how secure it felt leaning up against him, could feel how strong he was despite how drunk I was. My mood dropped, sharp all of a sudden, demons from all my worries descending en masse, bats around the moon.

"Do you know how to drive?" I asked as we reached the Mercury.

"It's been a while, but it'll come back. You're sure in no shape to drive. Give me the keys."

"Hell, no," I said, changing my mind for spite. "It's my car, and I'm gonna drive it myself."

I resented whatever momentary warmness I'd had for this stranger. He caused all this. If he hadn't sent that stupid picture in the first place, things might still be normal this summer. Sure, my father might still be drunk, but at least he'd be at home and I'd know what to expect.

I swung at Jake and missed. He grabbed my hand and I twisted free.

"Come on, cowboy," I coaxed.

I looked around for the previous fight, hoped the four of us could just consolidate into one big brawl, but they were nowhere to be seen. Jake backed away as I lunged and connected with his jaw. My knuckles hurt. He stood dazed for a second and then wrapped himself around my shoulders, pinned me to the car. He reached inside my pocket for the keys and scraped them against my leg until they were in his hand.

I didn't say anything, felt hot and confined, as if a wool muffler were over my head. Inside the car I dozed with my head bobbing against the plush velour, rolled the window down. The night air felt so cool after the sweat from my fight. I kept asking Jake what time it was, and he answered me repeatedly, patiently, like a parent with a child learning to tell time.

When we got back to the house, I half-expected my parents to be there, home again as if nothing had happened. They'd make Jake leave and send me to my room. But they weren't. The house sat quietly in the dark of our dead-end street, our beer cans and Jake's belongings still on the porch.

Then I was in bed and so sleepy. Jake had helped me with my shoes and socks and was pulling a sheet over me when I tried to speak. He interrupted, "It's okay, Bounty. You just had too much beer tonight. You'll be okay."

After the lights were out throughout the house, I turned Jake over and over in my mind. Part of me hoped he was a serial killer—I thought of Grandma and the Misfit in "A Good Man Is Hard to Find"—and that even as I lay there drunkenly fighting sleep he was loading a gun, polishing the barrel. I'd be off the hook. My parents would come home; they'd be the ones to find my body, bloated and purple-red from the heat. My mother would scream and my father would go catatonic, never recover. People would talk around town and say, "Poor Bounty, such a good boy. Gunned down by a lunatic ex-con. Who'd have thought it?"

The other part of me recognized my father in Jake, the way they both put people at ease, could make you instantly like them. Why, you'd known them all your life. The like turned into trust, the trust into hope. The ephemeral chit-chat and concern, the flow and art of the superficial, drawing strangers to them with the magnetic grace of a storyteller. Charm, maybe, or charisma. You could only hate a man like my father and Jake for trusting them too much, for never abandoning hope in them. But I'd long ago turned off the spigot of hope my father poured. He was left to channel it into strangers sitting next to him at ball games, mechanics at service stations, customers at the car lot.

Maybe Jake would murder me in my sleep, slit my throat with one of Daddy's straight-edged razors from the medicine cabinet, steal every appliance and scrap of jewelry he could find. Or maybe he'd save me from drowning, pull me back from the edge of the river that gushed with the torrent my summer had become. In my mind on the edge of sleep, there was nothing in between.

The phone rang. I thought it was a smoke alarm until I remembered that we didn't have one. My eyes hurt, my head hurt, but somehow I managed to make it stop. I don't remember walking over to the wall phone and placing the receiver to my ear; I only recall hearing my mother's voice, a child lost in the grocery store following the familiar sound of his name.

"Bounty? It's Momma." She sounded close, just over the hill at the neighbor's or at her metal industrial desk at Imperial Insurance.

I thought I would throw up. Leftover beer and fresh adrenaline coursed through me, and I thought my gut would burst like our sink pipes sometimes did in winter.

"Momma? Where are you? You okay?" I managed.

"Fine, sweetie. I'm at the beach, tiny place called Seabluff in Carolina. Your daddy's here. He's been in the hospital. But he's gonna be okay. Gonna be fine." She delivered her message staccato-like, a telegraph operator reading a Western Union.

My tonsils felt as if they were crawling around in my throat, trying to push the right button to make the sound come back.

"That's good," I squeaked.

"You okay? How are things there? I'm sorry I left the way I did. Sorry I haven't called sooner, but it took me a few days to find your father, and then I've visited him every day at

Lighthouse, that's the hospital." Her voice shook, whether from the connection or her message, I didn't know. She continued, "Are you eatin' enough? Did you find the casseroles? Do you need any money? Did I sign enough blank checks?"

My head spun around the room, the table, ladder-back chairs, the morning glare through the window across the room above the kitchen sink. "When are y'all comin' home?" I forced the room to bring its dizziness to a halt, tried to settle Dorothy's spinning farmhouse back on the Kansas prairie where it belonged. *Just a few minutes longer, hold on to my voice for just a few minutes longer*, I thought.

"I'm not sure yet. Probably end of the week. We've still got a lot of talkin' to do."

"Did you tell him? About Jake?" I asked.

"Not yet. That's one of the things we still need to discuss."

Silence and finally some static.

My mother finally said, "You sure you're okay? You sound a little congested. You haven't caught a summer cold, have you?"

"No, no, I'm still a little sleepy's all." My voice surged to life again. If I could just coast another minute or two.

"Well, I guess I better let you go. Your father asked about you. He's really sorry, too, Bounty. He asked if you'd pray for us."

Afraid to wait for my response she said, "Well, bye-bye," and hung up. From her hotel room or lobby, or from a pay phone in the restaurant where she'd eaten a big breakfast, she hung up. And I did the same on my end, placed the receiver carefully on its cradle as if I were hanging a piece of art.

I hadn't realized it before but Jake was sitting at the table munching Cap'n Crunch.

"Your mom?" he asked.

"Uh-huh," I nodded.

"She find her husband?"

"Yeah, they should be back end of the week." The thought of their return sent me into the bathroom. When I came out, Jake stood at the counter with a tall glass of liquid, reddish-orange.

"Drink this. It'll help, I promise."

I choked it down, trying not to gag, tasted tomato juice, egg, pepper, some other mystery flavor, fruity and spicy, cloves maybe.

Looking at him suspiciously, I tried to remember the night before, why Jake was standing there before me and why it was okay. He wore a pair of prison-issue gym shorts, no shirt, hard lines stenciled below his chest, a trail of hair winding like dark twine down his abdomen. He looked part Indian, a shaman conjured from some ancient time, come to work his magic.

"Part Cherokee?" I asked and licked the last tomato juice from my lips.

"Seminole, a quarter," he said.

And that afternoon he fished like an Indian. Graceful and strong, the power of his lure, not the earthworms we'd dug from in front of the barn, but the very charm I'd contemplated the night before. We sat creekside at the widest and deepest part, down below the hill where our house sat watching us like a proud parent.

I kicked off my tennis shoes. Jake had remained barefoot the entire day, despite my warning against copperheads in the tall grasses edging down the hill. Dipping my toes in the water's edge brought little relief to the throb behind my eyes. My head didn't feel like a head at all, more like a sprained ankle above the neck. Jake had assured me the sun and shade would help.

"That's what fishin's for in the first place," he explained. "Not the catch, the fattest or longest, but the art of slowin' down, losin' yourself in the river, hearin' the water tell you its tale, catchin' a glimpse of yourself in the cool clearness as you bend over to retrieve a fish or unsnare a line."

Except for my hangover, it was a perfect day for doing just that, August-hot and shimmery, made for fishing or swimming, locusts cussing somewhere in the field behind us. The summer

181

rains had made everything greener and more lush than most Southern summers and it looked tropical, overgrown; Daddy never had gotten around to having it bush-hogged down here. You could smell honeysuckle and wild rose, oleander, crepe myrtle, all mingled together in a sweet musky perfume traveling with the heat. The water whispered a language of murmurs and gurgles, its story already begun, and like a parent deciphering baby talk, Jake cocked his head toward the stream. A grasshopper lighted on his brown-haired leg.

"I've dreamed about this," he said, breathing in.

"Fishin'?"

"No, freedom. Not just the freedom of spirit, but the physical. The smell, taste, feel, sound of it. I'm out, Bounty. Debt paid and jail term served. It's over. There's nobody to make me go back."

He adjusted the bill of one of my father's old NASCAR caps and turned his head toward me.

"What was it like?" I asked.

"Jail? Hmmm . . . like a routine you're locked into and can't break out of. The bars aren't so bad, it's the routine, the drudgery of every meal at the same time, every rec period, every chapel service, every free period. That's what takes the life out of you. And that's what makes it so appealin', why some folks never make it out for very long. The routine." He looked skyward, one lone cloud meandering on the horizon above us.

"So how'd you keep from goin' crazy?" I snapped a piece of saw grass and ran it smooth across my tongue until it cut.

"I read a lot. Learned to keep inside myself. Counted the days till I got out. Then there was Ben, too. He kept me sane."

"Another inmate?"

Jake wedged his cane pole into the soft, mossy creekbank and braced it with a rock. He leaned back on his elbows and took his time replying.

"Nope," he finally said. "Just a friend."

"I thought you didn't have any friends. Just the goons you robbed the store with, the ones who left you to take the rap."

"Yeah, well, I had one friend. Came to see me 'bout every day. Talked to me about things that matter. Wanted to help me get my life straight. Introduced me to Sartre, Camus, Freud . . . the Bible."

"Don't tell me. This is leadin' to some dramatic conversion experience." I felt bad for spoiling his story, but was suddenly afraid he'd whip out a little pamphlet and quote Bible verses, the dread you feel opening the door and finding a Mormon and his bike on the other side.

"Was he a televangelist?" I added.

"Go to hell," Jake snapped. "He was the man I shot in the convenience store."

-12-

"Go to hell," Jake repeated. "I should've let you drive yourself home last night." He meant it. Standing up, he brushed the dirt and grass from his legs and seat and walked off toward the row of apple trees to our left.

I stood up, too, discovered my left foot asleep and cussed Jake Carnes under my breath. Pins and needles then. I staggered in a small circle until I could put all my weight on it. I didn't know what to do, didn't want to go chasing after him like a schoolgirl.

Jake's cane pole twitched, bobbed hard, and I grabbed the tan base just as it was about to come loose from its rock prop. A seven-inch bream wriggled on the line's end, a dark little fish with a light silver streak running down its backside. I wet my hands and unhooked him, set him free into the Styrofoam cooler we'd brought for our catch.

I started to yell for Jake but caught myself. His footfalls, twigs snapping and weeds parting, were no longer audible. He must have wandered down to the other side of the creek, where it bent and turned back on itself to flow south into the Duck

River. The spot was supposedly the mouth of the springs, and my father had once threatened to dam it up unless the city laid more water lines. They complied.

I found myself walking in the opposite direction, away from our fishing spot, away from the small bream swimming hopelessly in circles in his Styrofoam home. I followed the creek across to the edge of our property line, where it borders with the Ridleys' farm, down the canopy of oak and apple trees. At the property line was a kind of natural bridge that had been supplanted by stones and cement from the Ridleys. There I waded in up to my knees and let the cool current soothe me.

It was a primeval place, like an altar, peaceful and dappled with shade from the overhanging branches woven above it. I hadn't been there all summer, had forgotten how peaceful it was.

<hr>

The last time had been last fall. A sweltering Indian summer, it was an election year and the local races were especially heated, for mayor, city council, sheriff.

Daddy was tight with the challenging candidate for sheriff, Doug McCullen, and had me campaigning for him all that summer. When election day came, Daddy paid me three dollars an hour to stand outside the Clear Creek Elementary Gym and hand incoming voters pencils and matchbooks with old Doug's name on them. It was one of the hottest days of the year, and by ten o'clock in the morning I looked like I'd been swimming. But I stuck with it. Part of me even enjoyed it, the excitement, the hope that I could somehow influence people, as if they were voting for me instead of Doug McCullen.

My father was supposed to bring me some lunch, but he never came. I snacked out of a vending machine and stayed anyway. Lunchtime brought out a lot of voters. When my mom came to vote after work, she said that I should go home, that I looked dehydrated.

So I left and went home and ate supper, even though the

polls didn't close until eight that night. Daddy came home about seven-thirty, drunk and mad as a Spanish bull. "I thought I told you to stay there until the polls closed! What am I payin' you for?" he went on and on and refused to pay me for the eight hours I had worked. He and my mom went round and round with her telling him that she was the one who told me to leave and that he was nothing but a drunk who forgot to bring his only child some lunch (as if I were a three-year-old) and who had better pay him what he owed him.

But I couldn't stand it. I left and headed for the creek and came here, to the cool dark and shelter the bridge offered. I talked out loud to myself, carved into the cement grooves of the bridge with my penknife.

He never apologized, but he did hand me the money at breakfast the next day. Doug McCullen won, and Daddy got first choice to bid on impounded vehicles that the sheriff's department brought in.

I found my initials etched into a smooth cement groove and wondered how long it would be before they wore away. How long it would be before my parents wore away.

Would I ever escape, ever leave this place behind, or would I always feel like my parents' voices were inside my head like a bad song on the radio, the first one you hear in the morning that stays with you all day? They hummed inside a jar and refused to leave. And yet still I felt guilty for even wanting that, for even thinking I needed to escape.

What would happen if I opened the Pandora's box of my head and let their voices float away? Who would I be then, who would love me, where would I go?

＊

I saw Jake walking toward me then with his shirt off. He looked like an actor, an Indian guide from *Last of the Mohicans*. I watched him carefully and tried to decide if I should apologize. Maybe he was coming to tell me that he was leaving.

"Nice bridge," he said casually. He sat down beside me and dropped his feet into the water. I could feel the heat radiating from his bare shoulder next to mine. It was a good feeling.

"You build it?" He splashed his feet against the current.

"Nope. Neighbors did. Marks the property line."

"Look, I'm sorry. I don't wish nothin' bad on you. I'm glad I was there to drive you home last night."

His ponytail was tucked up under his cap; for a minute I thought he'd cut it off. Jake would look good with short hair. It made his ears stick out, endearing and boyish, a small flaw on an otherwise perfect masculine bust.

The water rolled below us like crystal marbles with swirls of green and blue and brown every now and then. I liked throwing twigs and moss over my shoulder and then watching them as they floated under the bridge, between our feet.

Jake braced himself on the stone arch like a gymnast, palms down, forearms taut. His hands were wide and not as tan as the rest of him, big veined, brushed with dark hairs on top like brown tinsel. His fingers were long, and I wanted to touch them.

"You don't need to apologize. I was a jerk."

He didn't say anything in return, just nodded and looked me in the eye. He didn't look away, and I couldn't, even though I wanted to, a deer paralyzed by headlights in the dark. In his gaze I could see this tiny room in the center of his pupil, this dark hole where he'd spent most of his life. There was a light in it now.

When the silence seemed unbearable, Jake smiled big, half-laughed, clasped my neck, and shook me into his shoulder, a playful kind of hug.

I didn't resist. I pushed him forward into the stream, but he was too quick. Just as he toppled over, yelling and laughing, he grabbed my foot and I followed behind him, a live instant replay. Only about ten feet deep, the water felt refreshing and colder than the tepid flow beside our fishing spot. Jake came up sputtering, still laughing, determined to dunk me.

As he bobbed above me and forced my head under, I

realized how glorious it felt, then burst free, left the dark pressure of murky sounds and no air for the surface of deep breaths and sunlight.

We wrestled in the water awhile longer before calling a truce and walking back to our fishing hole. I had a second bream waiting miraculously on my pole, still embedded firmly in the bank. We baited again, napped in the late afternoon sun, and ended up with five little fish by the time we headed back up to the house.

T he next day, Sunday afternoon, Clark Heraldson pulled up in his big Mercedes. I was inside finishing the funnies when the knock came at the door. Jake was down at the creek, fishing by himself.

"Bounty, is your father back?" he said. He looked worse than I'd ever seen him, eyes inflated to the edge of his face, unusually rumpled in his khaki shorts and madras shirt. He smelled of whiskey.

"No, sir. Afraid he's not. I'll tell him you came by." I started to shut the door but his hand caught it, pushed it back against me, a tug-of-war. He stepped inside, and I backed up next to the bar.

"So where in hell is he? Where's your momma? Her office said she's on vacation."

I nodded and regretted it, wished Jake would walk through the door.

"Well, if your folks aren't here, you and I got some business of our own to discuss. I signed your loan papers yesterday, Bounty. Once you got 'em in your hand, one of our nice tellers be glad to cut you a check, send it on up to school, waitin' on you." He swayed in place, and I stepped around the bar toward the gun rack.

"They're locked in my desk, all safe and sound. If you want out of this two-bit town all you gotta do is treat me right. Treat me right, I treat you right." He laughed and the smell of whiskey was potent. His blond hair hadn't been combed.

"My wife's still out of town, son. Gets mighty lonesome for a man." He stepped forward. "With your mommy and daddy gone I'll bet you're lonesome too." Another empty laugh.

I'd waited too long, should've already grabbed the gun, called for Jake.

He came closer, touched himself. "We got some business to do," he snickered.

"Go to hell and take your loan with you," I yelled and lunged for the shotgun.

He grabbed my arm, and I fought him off with one hand and tried to grab the barrel with the other. His weight and height were too much for me as he pinned me against the wall and squeezed the shotgun out of my hand. It rattled to the floor.

He pressed his body on mine, and I closed my eyes and tried to knee him. His hand was on my fly.

"What—?" Jake walked in, dropped a string of fish, and pounced on Heraldson. My half-brother punched him squarely, connected with a nose or eye, I couldn't tell. Heraldson swung wildly until Jake struck again and sent him staggering backward toward the door.

Jake grabbed the collar of the banker's plaid shirt and shoved him outside, against the hood of the big sedan. The hood ornament broke off with a metal snap.

Heraldson's nose was bleeding. "You must be the bastard son." He wiped his nose on his sleeve, got in the car, and sped over the hill.

I picked up the broken hood ornament and threw it after him with the speed of my best fastball.

I sat on the porch steps then and just looked at Jake. Tears formed behind my eyes but couldn't break through.

"You okay? Who the hell was that?" He came to sit next to me.

My head was shaking back and forth.

"Heraldson. My boss. Bank VP." That's all I could manage for a long time, but I didn't allow myself to cry. I scanned the

189

pasture below, the suddenly hot afternoon, the tree tops, the weeping willow out behind the machine shed next to the garage. Jake lit a cigarette and handed it to me, and I welcomed it, inhaled the tobacco deeply.

He went inside and returned with the fish, knelt on the lowest step, the one not covered with green outdoor carpet, and began gutting and scaling. I watched, mesmerized by the way the blade moved across the translucent film of scales, the way the lifeless eyes stared up at me. His hands worked patiently, gently scraping and slicing until only a dozen triangles of fillet remained. The bones were too delicate, too intricately embedded in the flesh to remove. You just had to be careful and eat around them.

We had them for supper, and I realized I still hadn't said anything. Jake had taken a nap in the porch swing and just let me be. I'd sat on the same porch step until he brought out plates of battered fish, fried potatoes.

"You wanna talk about it?" he asked.

I nodded and spit out a tiny bone, like a needle. "But what's to talk about . . . ?" I couldn't express it.

"Yeah." He dipped a French fry into a ketchup bath on the side of his plate.

"He's blackmailin' Daddy, I think. He was holdin' my student loan over my head, tryin' to get me . . ."

"It's over. He won't mess with you again. I promise."

We just sat there for a long time then. Silent and full, each with our own thoughts. The six o'clock freighter whistled by, later than usual, on the tracks on the other side of the big pasture hill, about a mile away.

I slapped at mosquitoes on my neck and tried to remember if we had any repellent.

Finally, I said, "When I was about eight or nine I went fishin' with Daddy and Gran Mac and a bunch of their buddies. I don't know where we were, out in the country somewhere, and we were all along this rickety plank bridge, fishin' in the river. I was havin' a good time and everything, maybe even caught a fish, but then my line got tangled. I leaned over the edge of the bridge and kept pullin' and tugging. And then I fell in.

"I didn't yell or scream or nothin', just fell in, a clean nose-dive. Nobody saw me at first. They were on the other side or down on the riverbank. I thought I was going to drown. I went up and under three times. I'd heard that you didn't come back after that third time. The water felt wild and torrential, like the dam had burst." I looked at Jake to see if he understood.

"So your line's still tangled and you're still drownin'?"

"Yeah, I feel that way most times. I'm still this little boy goin' under for the last time, and I need somebody to reach in and pull me out."

"So what happened? Who saved you?" he asked.

"No one. I started swimmin' with the current and made it to the riverbank. My father had to have a drink on the way home, he was shakin' so bad." Maybe part of me had been lost that day, snagged on the river bottom. Perhaps I'd traded souls with a river-spirit, some Cherokee brave or Crow maiden who'd drowned long ago. That would explain why I'd felt so displaced all my life, why I'd gotten by on such luck or whatever it was that kept me alive.

"You're lucky," Jake concluded as if reading my thoughts.

The sun had set somewhere in the middle of my story and dusk was spreading itself out. Orange melted along the big hillside, and I could hear cicadas warming up the band. I wondered what he thought of me.

"You got a girlfriend?" Jake leaned back in the swing and blew a smoke ring. It floated in front of me, expanding, wafting into a larger and larger circle until it faded into the dusk. I wanted to try myself, although I'd never succeeded before, so I snagged a smoke and lit it off Jake's.

"Not really. There's a girl I'm friends with at work. I care about her, but we're just friends." I flashed back to Heraldson's kitchen and his similar question, his remarks about BeBe and

191

how blind I was at the time.

"What's her name?"

"BeBe. She's a year older than me. She's black." I leaned back and tried my own smoke ring. It looked more like a smoke horseshoe, and I inhaled too much and started coughing.

"No, like this," Jake said and demonstrated. The way he formed his mouth looked like a fish, or someone caricaturing a kiss. I tried again.

"Better," he said. "You'll get the hang of it. BeBe's the girl was with you at the nursin' home? Your parents know about her?"

"Are you kiddin'? My father still thinks the Confederacy exists. He'd burn a cross in her yard if he even saw me lookin' at her. We're just friends." I kept trying until a smoky dough-nut hovered above me and disintegrated into the breeze. Momma's wind chimes clanged softly.

"You got it, chief," Jake said proudly.

I decided to ask him the question I'd been avoiding all afternoon.

"Jake, that business with Heraldson today—is there some-thin' wrong with me? Do I look queer or somethin'?" I averted my eyes, hopeful that he couldn't see into me, into my fears that I got what I deserved for my fleeting desires for Clark Heraldson.

"Is that what you're worried about?" He sat up and looked at me until I forced myself to look back. I nodded.

"Do you ever feel normal, like you're a man, not just a boy caged inside a man's body?" I blurted.

He looked at me a long time. "I think you're okay, brother," said Jake Carnes.

"But there was somethin' about Heraldson I thought I liked. . . . I even wanted to be like him." A shiver whipped across my back.

Jake lowered his voice. I didn't know if he was talking to me or to himself. "When I was a child, I used to speak as a child, think as a child, reason as a child; when I became a man, I did away with childish things."

"That's in the Bible, isn't it?" I looked at him blankly, working to interpret the words in light of my sexuality. He nodded and his eyes said that I'd have to figure it out for myself, which I resented. But it did set my mind in motion.

"Paul's first letter to the folks in Corinth."

"You know, I always think of God as this absent-minded professor who's incredibly brilliant and wise but who can't remember our names from day to day. He created this world, his laboratory, and the experiment got out of hand. Now he can only study us from the other side of a two-way mirror. Every now and then he taps on the glass to remind us that he's there. But I'm afraid he really can't do anything."

"What would you want God to do if he could?" Jake wondered.

"You have to ask?"

"No, but tell me. If he were your personal genie, what would you wish for?" he asked.

"But he's not a genie," I countered. "Who says I believe in God in the first place?"

"You just said you imagined him as an absent-minded professor."

"Exactly. I said I *imagined* him. How do I know he's real?" I enjoyed getting a rise out of Jake, a skeptic at his séance.

"I'm not gonna preach you a sermon on why I think God's real. And I don't think that's the question you really want to ask."

Jake stopped the swing and stood up to lean against the column beside the steps. His words hung in the air sober and serious, more substantial than our smoke rings.

"And what's the question I really want to ask?" I finally shot back.

"I can't answer that, Bounty McGraw." He took a last drag and flicked the butt into the dark yard. "Only you can."

His words annoyed me all the next day at work, but they also haunted me. I didn't like wrestling for a deeper meaning behind the surface of my life, trying to assess events like crossword clues. It didn't work because there were too many possibilities, too many words with the correct number of letters. But somehow Jake was right, and I resented him for it. I didn't doubt so much that there was God, but I was disturbed because I didn't know what question I did want to ask.

I tried to dismiss Jake's faith as that of a simpleton ex-con who had to have something to sustain him throughout his prison term. But like Jake himself, whatever he believed and why he believed it seemed more complex and substantial than the gossamer faith of the churchgoers I'd known.

I thought about going to Catholic school in first through sixth grades, the incongruity of it with the rest of my life, with the rest of the area for that matter. But the strong Irish Catholic community in the county was well established and when they opened a private school in Crescent, Mom fought tenaciously. "Bounty's smarter than us," she told my father and paid for it herself.

How intrigued I was with the priests and nuns, the statues and prayers, rosaries and crucifixes. Grandma Epperson worried about them brainwashing me, converting me from the good Baptist I should be over to a system that "prayed to Mary."

For the first couple of years there, every time I visited Granny Epp, she asked what I was learning and what I believed. She asked if I participated in mass, if I took communion, if I prayed to anyone other than Jesus. The first time she asked that last one, I said yes. When she asked, "Who?" trying to hide her horror, I hesitated before saying, "God."

"That's okay, sweet boy. Jesus is God, you see." I never told her that I occasionally prayed to Joseph as my patron saint or that I had bought a tiny Saint Christopher medal on a silver chain at the church bazaar.

Even though I never converted to the Catholic church, I did fall in love with the ceremony and traditions. The beautiful chapel with its gold tapestries and bleeding Christ upon the cross, the statues and candles, the incense and velvet robes on holy days were exotic and sensual—closer to art than anything we called worship at First Baptist.

But I remained a fine Protestant. At age ten, I was cornered by a vacation Bible school worker who asked, "You don't want to go to hell, do you? You'd do anything to escape the eternal lake of fire, wouldn't you?" So I followed him down the aisle, nodded in the appropriate places, purchased my fire insurance, so to speak. I was even baptized and had a handkerchief tucked away somewhere in a drawer that the pastor held over my mouth when he dunked me. Granny Epp embroidered my initials on it, the date, and John 3:16.

Nothing really changed then. It's funny. I still went to school, prayed when I needed help on a test or had to go to the blackboard with an erection. Still prayed when Daddy drank and Momma cried. *That could be a country western song*, I thought and laughed aloud.

But Jake raised all kinds of memories and thoughts in my head. It felt like I had once thought of God as some kind of cosmic Santa Claus, and when I found out the good elf only existed in my imagination and my parents' wallets, then I abandoned him to the same mythic realm.

But something about Jake made me curious about what he believed in, made me feel like there was more there than my wise-cracking cynicism could dismiss. And that bothered me.

I wanted to believe then, to know as earnestly and simply as you can possibly know. But I couldn't do it; it felt strained and immovable, like trying to force yourself to go to the bathroom or recalling a foreign language you've never known.

BeBe came by my teller cage in a sleeveless swath of dark green, a living forest, and updated my desk calendar by tearing off the weekend. "Wake up, baby," she said and nudged me.

The middle of August. A month in all of my eighteen years that always seemed full of possibilities, bittersweet, a paradox. Maybe my Augusts blocked the way, kept me from believing. I don't know what it was about the month, but in my streak of bad summers, August was always the worst. And the best. It was the worst because whatever had been brewing all summer long—Daddy's drinking, Mom's depression, my conformity—usually peaked. Of course, this summer broke all the records, and August wasn't even over.

But normally, once August was over, it became the best month because school started again. Like most students, I complained and lamented the loss of summer with my friends. But inside I relished the relief, the eight-to-three world of maps, dissected frogs, math equations, grammar, and poetry. I liked the way the school buildings smelled those first weeks of September, clean and inviting, a bit stuffy from the summer, but safe as a pine forest.

And that was the grief I already felt, the relief that would never come now. With things the way they were with Heraldson, I'd be forced to attend community college right there in town, at best.

Somehow I should have expected all that had happened. My hope for a summer of change, of breaking free and running wild, becoming my own man, seemed foolish and naive. The month obviously had a personality and mind of its own, an annual visitor who continually kept me guessing about what his stay would bring.

It was funny, but I envisioned August then as this person. In much the same way, I thought of the days of the week as being different colors. The August who visited me each year of my life was aging, with crow's feet and smile lines when he tipped his hat. He wears a dark suit—maybe some years seersucker (after all, he is summer)—but this year definitely a dark suit, black or navy. He wears a hat to match, the kind with a dipped brim in front and a grosgrain band. He carries a valise, an overstuffed briefcase, like a traveling salesman or a bachelor uncle. He never knocks but just comes in and stays for a month.

He laughs at me, I think. He brings all kinds of hard stuff for me to deal with and then redeems himself by taking me out of it with school starting. I don't like him, but I feel I'm at his mercy, afraid of what worse things he could pull out of that black leather case of his.

"Are you listenin' to me?" BeBe stood behind me with her hands on her hips.

"I'm sorry. What'd you say?" I turned.

"I said, 'Do you want to go to the drive-in with me tonight?'"

"Let me think about it." I felt very silly then for personifying something as bland as a calendar month, as if I'd been caught making a wish list for Santa or placing my baby teeth under a pillow. I wished my troubles were that simple, that time could be personified—that I could hit him or lock him away so I could jump from July to September. But even thinking that, I knew August would still laugh at me, giving away months of my life because I'm afraid. Mr. August never let me figure him out.

"I need to bring you up to speed," I told BeBe. She was pretending to pout at my lack of attention.

"On what?" she said, her lips pursed angrily but I found it sexy.

"What d'ya think? On my life. . . . Jake's stayin' at the house. He was waitin' on the front porch when I got home Friday night."

"And you let him stay? What changed your mind?" Her eyes got big.

"I don't know. I ended up gettin' drunk. He took care of me, we just sorta drifted into him stayin'. My mom called too. She found my dad."

Mrs. Sherman looked up from her desk, and I lowered my voice to tell BeBe the rest of the story. She was still speculating on what would happen next as we counted up and put our cash drawers in the vault.

Instead of the movie BeBe offered to come over and cook supper for us, spaghetti, her specialty. I teased that she just wanted to see Jake again, and she batted her lashes at me. "I can only handle one white boy at a time," she sassed.

Driving home that afternoon, I felt light inside, a small pocket of helium inside my lead balloon. BeBe was coming over as soon as she'd gone home, then to the store. Jake seemed excited about the possibility of a home-cooked meal. "I haven't had many in a long time," he explained when BeBe showed up and began peeling onions and chopping garlic.

He'd borrowed a red polo shirt from me for the occasion. It didn't take long for Jake to win her over, and vice versa.

She made a few wisecracks at first—"Bounty tells me you just passed the bar"—but soon resumed her flirtatious self.

Jake played it cool, asked lots of polite questions. He teased me about being interested in BeBe and neither of us seemed to mind.

"If this was a date, you wouldn't be here," I told him.

He laughed and said, "You just want me here in case you have questions, Cyrano de Bergerac style." BeBe giggled like a young girl.

The table conversation was lively. BeBe had brought flowers from her mother's garden, black-eyed Susans, daisies, and purple coneflowers. I used my mother's best china, the set that had been her mother's with little roses around a blue border. The sauce smelled and tasted like rich Italian artwork, full of basil and garlic, tomatoes and parmesan.

"Your secret recipe?" I asked.

"My grandmomma's," BeBe said with a full mouth.

Just then a long noodle dangled down Jake's chin and he slurped it in like a reptile. We started laughing and had a contest to see who could slurp the longest piece. BeBe won, which meant Jake and I had to do the dishes. We would've anyway since she'd done all the cooking.

"Let's have dessert outside. Strawberry shortcake," BeBe said and began assembling the parts. "And let's play a game. What kinda games you white people play? You ever heard of a game called *Mon-op-o-ly*? I kick butt at that. Pay up the rent— it's your landlord from hell!"

Loading the dishwasher, I splashed her from the faucet and

she screamed in laughter. Jake just smiled.

We sat on the porch cross-legged with the ragged Monopoly game I'd found in my bedroom closet. Jake chose the race car while BeBe and I argued over the shoe. I reluctantly conceded and placed the top hat on Go beside the others.

It was strangely unsettling to be having such a good time at my own house. The berries and whipped cream slid down as cool and easy as our mood. BeBe, our banker—"Because Bounty can't count, and Jake's been in jail"—landed on St. Charles Place, completing her first monopoly.

"I'm not out of this yet, Ms. Devereaux," Jake said and rolled the dice. He landed on Chance.

By dark, lightning bugs twinkled in the yard, but I'd turned on the porch light two monopolies ago. BeBe had brought out beers for all of us to fuel our capitalism. And it worked—Jake had Park Place, BeBe had Boardwalk, and I had all the railroads. We each had our neighborhoods with green and red houses and hotels.

BeBe backed her talk with a solid strategy, saving a regular percentage and building conservatively. My brother and I favored a more reckless, hit-or-miss approach.

"Pay the rent!" she shrieked as I counted out my roll to Marvin Gardens. I doled out my pastel colored dollars as a pair of headlights cut right through me. My mother's Olds.

My parents were out of the car before any of us could say a word.

-13-

"What the hell's goin' on?" my father exploded. He walked to the edge of the porch with my mother behind him.

I stood up, but Jake and BeBe just sat there. After a minute had passed, BeBe rolled the dice, moved her little silver shoe the matching number of spaces.

"We're playin' Monopoly," I said sheepishly, looking to my mother for help.

"Who are these people?" he ordered. My mother came to his side and took his arm; she would be no help to me.

"This is BeBe Devereaux, who works at the bank with me." She looked up and smiled, "Pleased to meet ya."

"And this," I paused dramatically, "is Jake Carnes. Your son."

My father caught the edge in my voice but didn't acknowledge either introduction.

"I didn't expect you back so soon," I said.

"Obviously not," my mother spoke for the first time.

"So this is what you do when I'm away?" Daddy started in.

"Invite hippies and nigger girls over to drink beer on my front porch?" He was sober but his voice flared the way it did when he drank. "Get them the hell out of here," he ordered.

Jake began putting the game away, matching the money to its corresponding tray, collecting the property deeds. BeBe sat with her back straight and rigid, like an angry cat. I looked down at them, mumbled, "Guess we better call it a night." Then I remembered Jake was staying. BeBe could get in her VW Rabbit and shift up the hill and out of sight, but my half-brother was staying.

Jake got up and stretched, lit a cigarette, and leaned against the porch rail.

I walked BeBe to her car, down the front steps and across the yard to avoid my parents. "He didn't mean what he said," I whispered. "I'm really sorry."

"Oh, he means it all right. People like him always do," she replied, seething in the dark.

I threw caution aside and kissed her cheek. "Thanks for supper."

Back on the porch Jake sat alone in the swing. The door stood open, yellow light pouring out in a wounded stream. The trunk of the Cutlass had been popped. The red suitcase stood below it on the asphalt along with several paper bags and a floral makeup case I'd never seen before. My mother came out and shut the door behind her as I grasped the suitcase handle. I could see the orange tip of Jake's cigarette shining faintly. Then he must've inhaled because the small glow flared brighter.

"Have you lost your mind?" Momma slammed the trunk and picked up the grocery bags and makeup case.

"I told you, I didn't think y'all would be back this soon. They're friends. I live here, too. At least for a few more days, for as long as I can stand it."

She put the bags down again, frozen in place. She chose

her words carefully: "I need your help, son. Your father's sick. He's been in a hospital for over two weeks now and is still on medication for his nerves. We need to help him as much as we can. And that means not upsettin' him."

"No, Momma, not this time. I been fallin' for that line over and over again all my life." As I spoke I imagined a huge carp biting the same hook at the bottom of a pond over and over, breaking free, and then taking the bait again. "When you left here you were gettin' a divorce. Now you're back and I'm supposed to walk around on tiptoes to keep our happy family together? I won't do it."

My mother looked shocked, a contingency she hadn't counted on, a speed bump on her preconceived road to recovery. I anticipated her next words.

"Bounty, please don't do this to me. I can't take it right now. It's been a long week, and I'm worn out. Please." She reached for my shoulder with her right hand as I backed away.

"No," I said. "I'm not some child you can manipulate into bein' your good little boy."

"Don't raise your voice. Your father might hear." She looked over my shoulder. "Why's he still here? Can't he see this ain't the time for a family reunion?"

"He's been stayin' here the past few days. Ran out of money for the motor lodge, so I been lettin' him stay here."

My mother dropped her arm and clasped her hands nervously. "Well, he can't stay here now. Your father's already upset. I told him about this supposed son of his, that he was in town, but we didn't expect to find him here waitin' on us. You'll have to tell him to leave."

"You tell him," I said. "As far as I'm concerned he can stay." My mother hugged herself as if she were cold.

"You and I are gonna have to talk. But not tonight." She picked up the bags and marched inside again, the storm door accidentally slamming behind her.

I walked over and joined Jake on the swing. "I need a cigarette." He lit one off his own and handed it to me. "Did you hear all that?"

"Not really. I could tell you weren't cooperatin'. Where am I gonna sleep tonight? Somehow I don't think that sofa bed's the best place anymore." He leaned forward, stopped the swing, rested his elbows on his knees like a man about to pray.

My mother came out then, stepped cautiously onto the porch, and came toward us like a soldier through a minefield. I noticed Jake had disposed of all the beer cans.

"Mr. Carnes . . ." she began softly, "can I talk to you?" She looked over at me, but I wasn't budging.

"Yes, ma'am," Jake offered and put out his smoke. He stood up and bridged the distance between them by a couple of steps.

"I don't know how to say this . . . any nicer, but . . . well, you can't stay here, I'm afraid." Her breathing was heavy.

"I'd like to talk to your husband 'bout that," Jake said with kindness in his voice.

"You can't do that either, I'm afraid. He's restin', on medication and all. Maybe you can talk to him later in the week."

Jake crossed his arms before speaking. "I'd like to honor your wishes, Mrs. McGraw, but I plan on settlin' my business with him as soon as possible. I've been waitin' a long time." My mother was shaking her head, and I hoped she wasn't starting to cry, and I hoped Jake didn't fall for it if she did.

"I'll sleep in the barn tonight, if that's all right," he offered. "And I'll talk to your husband tomorrow."

My mother nodded, then raised her head, and sure enough, tears squeezed out the corners. She turned to go in.

"I'll stay with you," I announced. "Solidarity and all that."

"Don't upset your folks, Bounty. You better stay in tonight. They need you."

I chortled. "They may need me, but I don't need them. I'm tired of it all. No, I'm stayin' with you whether you like it or not. I'll be right back."

Inside the house all was quiet, as calm as if my parents had never returned. Then I heard my mother in the bathroom, water running, the odd sounds of her bedtime rituals. My father must've already been in bed.

The contents of one of the sacks had been emptied on the counter—peanut butter crackers, pretzels, a banana peel, a bottle of aspirin, sunscreen SPF25 for my mother's freckled complexion.

Then I noticed, set out in rows, half a dozen medicine bottles, amber-colored plastic and one white one. "Take as needed every six to eight hours." Most were from Walgreen, Seabluff, South Carolina, and a couple from Lighthouse Hospital Pharmacy. They looked like tranquilizers, maybe. Some he should take only once a day. I chuckled out of meanness at the thought of my father off alcohol and on drugs.

I collected sleeping bags and pillows, a flashlight, arranged ice around four beers in a Styrofoam cooler, grabbed my parents' pretzels on the way out. Jake was waiting for me at the corner of the house.

The barn loomed majestically in the dark; a few chickens startled as we passed by. We headed for the loft silently by the guide of my flashlight and found a pair of yellow eyes staring back at us from the top of the stairs.

"The Allisons' cat," I explained. The gray and white striped tom disappeared over the edge of hay bales into the night.

"How 'bout here?" I motioned to a corner where the light wouldn't shine in as soon as the sun rose.

"Fine," Jake nodded and began unrolling his bag. "You don't have to do this."

"Maybe I want to, okay?" I untied my sleeping bag and positioned it a few feet from his, put the cooler between us.

Jake unhitched his boots, yanked the white socks off his feet, stretched out on his bed for the night. I did the same and got us each a beer from the cooler, unfolded the bag of pretzels. We sipped for a few minutes, listened to the quiet, which wasn't so quiet with the old barn settling and shifting, the cicadas, a bullfrog from the creek.

"Why'd you come here?" I asked finally.

"I thought I told you." He sounded surprised, turned to face me by reclining on his side, propped his head on his elbow.

"Yeah, but what's this business you got to settle with Daddy? If you want money, he's not gonna give it. You saw tonight what a jerk he can be."

"No, some money'd be nice, but that's not what I'm after. I came to talk."

"He's not a talkin' kind of man. That's why he and I are so different. He talks a lot, about the car lot, about what the Braves are doin' wrong, what the President should be doin', but he isn't saying anything. You're gonna be disappointed," I warned.

"That's better than nothin' at all," he said, and I turned this over. "He ever tell you he loves you? Ever tell your momma?"

I considered his question analytically, scanned the concordance of scenes in my life where the word *love* and my father appeared in the same room. There were many times, but none of them carried any weight.

"Yeah, he says it a lot. Mostly when he's drunk and I'm takin' care of him. He gets all sappy and tells me how much he loves me, how he'd die in the street for me. Funny, but I don't think I've ever heard him say it to Momma. . . . I can't remember."

"So you don't believe him when he says it to you?" He slurped the remains of his beer. Mine tasted too warm so I took an ice cube from the cooler and wedged it into my can.

"Guess I don't. Why should I? If he don't say it when he's sober, why should I believe it when he's drunk? If he loved me, he wouldn't do the things he does."

"You know the old story about the snake charmer and the cobra?"

"What? No, I don't think so. What's it got to do with anything?"

"There's this snake charmer in India, see, and he's walkin' down the jungle path one day when he sees this cobra all coiled up in a ball. He's about to go 'round the snake when the cobra says, 'Master, I've been wounded by a mongoose. I'd be ever so grateful if you'd nurse me back to health. I could perform for you.' So the charmer says, 'How do I know you won't strike me?' And the cobra says, 'You have my word.' So the snake charmer picks up the cobra and takes him home and feeds him milk and honey till the snake is well. Then the cobra says, 'I am ever grateful to you. As I promised I will perform for you now.' The snake charmer took his fife, or whatever they play in India, and a woven basket and headed to the marketplace. He put the cobra in the basket and began to play. The cobra rose up hooded from the basket and swayed to the music. The charmer made much money from passersby who threw coins out of their amazement and admiration. At the end of the day the snake charmer took the cobra home and the snake bit him." Jake wet his throat with a second beer.

"So what happened?" I asked, waiting for him to continue.

"That's it. That's the story." He took another drink.

"What's that got to do with me and my father?" I asked, exasperated.

"The snake kept his word, probably even loved the charmer for saving his life. But he did what he had to do." He ignored my frustration, but I kept trying.

"So Daddy's the snake and I'm the charmer, big deal." I puzzled for a moment. "Or am I the snake and he's the charmer?"

"I imagine we're all both at some time or other."

But I wasn't satisfied. "So is drinking what my father has to do, or is leaving what I have to do?" I didn't like the story but felt drawn to it, oddly encouraged.

"I don't know. Just somethin' to think about." He paused for a moment. "Maybe I like the story because there're things we all have to do."

"Everything's fated? Predestined? We have no choice or control? I thought you believed in God and stuff?"

"I think we have lots of choices, Bounty. I believe we can choose to be part of a bigger plan or not. I think we choose whether or not we forgive the snakes that bite us."

"Right. The guy's dyin' from cobra venom and says, 'Thank you, Mr. Cobra, I forgive you. I know it's somethin' you had to do.' That's not the way it works, Jake. You of all people should know that."

"Because I've been to prison?" He sounded defensive.

"Well, yeah. I mean, you've been dealt a hard hand. Yet you seem pretty calm about it all. Aren't you angry? Don't you want to make Daddy pay for runnin' out on you? Don't you blame him for your mother's breakdown? Don't you blame him for not bein' there to keep you from gettin' in with the wrong crowd and goin' to jail?"

"I used to. . . . Maybe sometimes I still do."

"And what changed? You meet Jesus on the side of a deep-freeze or somethin'?" I looked him in the eye, my vision well-adjusted to the dark, and saw he was smiling.

"You could say that. One day the guard comes to get me, says, 'You got a visitor.' I laughed, figurin' there'd been some mistake. But he takes me into the visitation room, and there's this old man in a wheelchair. It was the clerk from the store I'd robbed, the man I'd shot wrestlin' for my gun."

He lit a Camel, offered me one, and I shook my head. He blew smoke into the night air, and it wafted up and out the square-cut open window that I'd thrown many a hay bale through.

"I thought he came to cuss me out so I immediately turned to go. But he smiled and told me to wait, that he had to talk to me, at least once. I listened and he talked a lot. . . . He came to forgive me."

"Did you want to be forgiven?" I asked.

"Yeah. I don't think I knew it till then. But it made a big difference. Ben started comin' every week. Loaned me books and told me stories. Brought me his wife's fruitcake every Christmas."

"You seen him since you got out?"

"He died last year. But he knew I was gettin' out this summer. He knows I'm free." Jake took a last puff and carefully snubbed the filter into the Styrofoam cooler. It hissed and choked out.

I lay there for a long time thinking through all this and kept coming back to the cobra and the snake charmer. Jake took my silence for sleepiness and said good night. He rolled over and began to breathe evenly, little percolating sounds. I counted stars until they were inside my head, spinning me farther and farther away from a life with fangs and a forked tongue.

I showed up at work the next morning and got some bad news. "I'm afraid we're going to have to let you go," Mrs. Sherman tilted her head and smiled sympathetically. "It seems Mr. Heraldson performed a spot audit on our branch yesterday after we closed. He found you out of balance by over a thousand dollars."

"What?" I was confused. "But I balanced yesterday, to the penny. I didn't even use the change in the cigar box. There's some mistake."

She patted my hand. We sat across from each other at the green-specked Formica table in the kitchenette. "I thought so, too, Bounty. I even called the Proof Department this morning and double-checked your figures. But what Proof has for your machine tapes is very different than what you recorded on your report sheet yesterday. I'm sorry, Bounty." She leaned forward and whispered, "I pleaded with Mr. Heraldson, but he said to just be glad the bank's not pressing charges. I'm sure when Mr. Rosenstein gets back from vacation he'll want to talk with him." Her perfume permeated the small room, sickly sweet, cloying. I couldn't breathe.

I shook my head and tears of rage formed behind my eyes.

"No one else knows, Bounty. And I won't tell them. I believe you're a good boy and maybe this will be straightened out. But for now, I don't know what else to do but ask you to leave."

"Fine. I'll clean out my window and go."

"I'm really sorry," she echoed.

"I don't blame you, Mrs. Sherman. There's somethin' else

goin' on here, I promise you that." I stormed out of the room and began dumping my drawer contents into an empty Safe-T pop box.

"What's wrong?" BeBe asked, touching my blue oxford sleeve.

"Heraldson. He framed me, made it look like I stole a thousand dollars yesterday. I'm fired."

"Oh, baby, I'm sorry. He can't do that." She moved closer to me. Sarah Anne turned from her glass cage at the drive-thru to listen.

"He did it. But somethin's gotta give, if I have to go see him myself. He's gone too far." I was finished and couldn't decide whether to go home or straight to his plush office off the square in downtown Crescent.

"Take Jake with you," she said. "Call me as soon as you can. I'll go straight home after work." I turned to go and she pulled me back. "You'll be cleared, Bounty."

I sat in the parking lot for a long time. The morning sun had already turned the interior of the big Merc into a dry sauna. Home first, I decided. Maybe Jake would want to go with me.

<hr>

And he did. But after I'd told him the whole story, about the wire-transfer account, the huge cash flow in and out during the past six months, about Heraldson hounding me about Daddy's return, Jake had a better idea. "Let's go see your father first. Find out what's goin' on between him and Heraldson, and maybe you'll have somethin' to negotiate with."

It made sense to me. I loosened my tie and agreed. Jake finished getting dressed—my mother had gone in to work so there was no one in the house—and we sped down Highway 27 to the blue-plastered J & R Motors office that had once been a Phillips 66.

I hadn't seen either of my parents that morning and had only surmised that my father would be there. My mother had

209

left a note, telling me to call her at work later and that my father needed my help at the car lot that evening. As we pulled into the parking lot, I noticed the red, white, and blue bunting from the Fourth of July sale still wrapped around the miniature stadium lights planted like trees along the perimeter of the lot. Although only six weeks had passed since the fourth, it felt like it would take volumes to document the history since then.

My father sat behind his desk going through the mound of mail covering his blotter. He was back in his clean T-shirt and overalls and had a tan that made him look older than I'd ever seen before, the gray at his temples sprinkled white, the lines around his eyes junctioned into bloodshot threads in the eyes themselves, an interstate exchange on a road map.

He looked up and took in both of us. "You're in a lot of trouble, buddy boy," he snarled. "Clark Heraldson called me this morning. I guess you and your ex-con brother split the money."

Stunned, I looked at Jake, but he didn't take his eyes off our father. I let loose.

"I didn't take any money. Heraldson's lyin' and you know it. If I were gonna embezzle, I'd take more than a thousand dollars. I want to know what you and Heraldson got goin'. I know about the account."

It was my father's turn to be surprised. "What account? I don't know what you're talkin' about."

"The wire-transfer account. The one you originally set up to pay for the hospital in Florida where Jake's mother was. I know about the $300,000 laundered through that account in the last few months. I wanna know if you're in some kinda trouble." The blood rose in my face and drained from my father's, some kind of bizarre power transfusion taking place.

"Less you know, the better. I'd like to think you didn't steal no money from the bank, and maybe you didn't. I don't know what to believe anymore. You've changed."

"This isn't about me changin', Daddy," I countered his attempt to derail the conversation.

"What do you want?" He looked at Jake and stood behind his desk.

"I want to talk to you. But this may not be the best time."

"No, this is the only time I've got for you. Bounty, wait outside," he ordered, about to succeed in his diversion.

"I want to know what's goin' on. And I'm not leavin' till you tell me."

"Oh, you're leavin' all right. You don't talk to me that way, buddy. You'll respect me as long as you're under my roof." He was back in control, back to his old self. I noticed his hands were shaking.

I looked at Jake as he nodded to be left alone with this strange man whose blood coursed through both our bodies. I took his lighter and pack of Camels and sat on the bench out in front of the office, could hear Ricky clanging a wrench around in the garage. With a cigarette between my lips I leaned my head toward the glass front to hear the voices inside. Jake's cobra story was still in my mind, but it didn't take the edge off my anger.

"So how much money's it gonna take to sweep trash like you out of town?" my father began.

"I don't want money." Jake stayed in control.

"Why'd you come here then?" Daddy asked.

"To talk to you," Jake replied. I imagined him cool and calmer than ever before, a smooth current waiting to pull my father into the rip current below.

"Well, you've ruined my life in the process. Hope it makes you happy. . . . What's there to talk about?" My father's voice sounded fainter, as if it were drifting out of range.

"Why'd you leave? Why'd you ignore my letters?" Jake's voice rose, and I stubbed out my cigarette even though I'd smoked only half. I flicked it across the pavement and began rehearsing what I'd say to Clark Heraldson.

"That's none of your damn business," Daddy's tone roared with volume. Jake replied with something low I couldn't make out. Then my father retorted, "You came here just to ask me that?"

211

"Why didn't you ever divorce her? Is that why you paid for the hospital? Or did you feel too guilty? She tried to kill herself over you. You need to know that." Jake sounded more excited than he'd been the whole time. It frightened me, and I envisioned him pulling a pistol out of his pocket or a knife out of his boot and paying back Jimmy McGraw. Maybe Jake was the cobra in the story.

"Shut up," my father said.

"I'm your son, whether you like it or not. And trust me, I hate it. But I'm your son."

"You expect me to welcome you back with open arms? The progidal returnin' for the fattened calf?" My father's biblical allusion would've surprised me if not for his mispronunciation. I imagined his eyes even redder than before, expanded to cover the top half of his face.

"I don't expect nothin' from you. That's all I've ever had except for the breath I'm breathin'. I didn't come here to fight. I came to forgive you. I came to forgive you and get on with my life."

There was silence for the longest time. I stood up and fidgeted with my tie, lit another cigarette. All I heard was a metal ping from the garage. Maybe they were embracing. Or maybe now was when Jake slid the knife in his chest, some pagan forgiveness ritual with Jimmy McGraw sacrificed on the altar of his own desk.

My father spoke: "You self-righteous bastard. You're just like your mother, thinkin' you're better than ever'body else. Like I need your forgiveness. Get out. Get the hell out of my life, and don't ever come back. As far as I'm concerned, I only have one son."

"Whether you admit it or not, you've done me wrong. You killed my mother, and you're partly responsible for me landin' in jail. You're a pathetic man. And whether you accept it or not, I forgive you anyway. At least today I do."

"Who made you God? Go to hell with your forgiveness. Get out, I said!" The office door slammed and the glass rattled in the front windows. Suddenly Jake and my father were standing beside me, propelled by the force of their own voices.

"Bounty, take this punk to the bus station in Pikeville and buy him a ticket for as far away as they're goin' today." Daddy thrust a handful of bills in my shirt pocket. "Make sure he leaves." He turned and was around the corner in the garage before I could protest.

There was nothing either of us could say, so Jake and I got in the Mercury and burned rubber out of the parking lot. I wasn't thinking about where we were going, and before I knew it we pulled up in front of the bank.

"Come on," Jake said, "I'll go with you." We waded through the lobby, past customers to Judy Tate's desk in the corner.

"I need to see Mr. Heraldson," I demanded as confidently as possible.

"I'm sorry, Bounty, he's already left for the day. He wasn't feeling well. Can I help you, or would you like to leave a message?"

"Thanks," I mumbled and turned to go. *Not feeling well, my butt*, I thought to myself. He was probably raping and pillaging poolside.

Jake and I walked outside but didn't stop at the car, kept going up the sidewalk around the square. Sunlight bounced off the mirrored facade at the end of the courthouse. We crossed the street and Jake stopped to read the plaque below the statue of Wilfred T. Haynes, leader of our local movement during the War Between the States. I sat on the park bench beside the memorial.

"I'm sorry, Jake," I offered, looking up at him.

"I know. You told me so—right?" He sat beside me.

"No, I'm just sorry, that's all. Maybe you comin' and sayin' what you said will mean somethin' to him someday. You gonna try to talk to him again?"

"No. I said what I came to say, now I can go. I got a job waitin' on me west of here. Branson, Missouri, playin' backup for the brother of a guy I knew in stir."

213

"So you're leavin'? Just like that?"

"You heard the old man. He wants me out of town anyway. I can catch the bus and be there by Friday."

"Take me with you, Jake," I said.

He looked at me and smiled into a laugh before he realized I was serious.

"Take me with you," I repeated. "We can leave right now."

-14-

"Y ou know I can't do that," Jake replied. "Your parents would have me arrested for kidnapin'."

"I'm eighteen, not a kid anymore. I can leave and they can't do anything about it."

"I'm sorry, Bounty. If I had a secure future somewhere, could take care of you, I'd invite you along. But the only thing worse than one broke drifter is two."

I hung my head and felt the sun beating down on me. I hated my parents. I'd been blackmailed and framed by a pervert who everybody in the county respected and awed. I'd lost my job and my student loan. I'd gained and lost a brother—all in the matter of a few short weeks. Looking down, the grass blades between my feet looked sharp and pointy, Kentucky bluegrass mixed with clover. I popped a handful of stems and began tying them together to make a chain.

"It ain't the end of the world, ya know," Jake said.

"Easy for you to say. You're leavin'. You're free as a bird, no cares and no commitments. You can do anything you wanna do." I tossed the rope of clover into the street.

"If you want, I can stay until tomorrow."

Nodding my head, I mumbled, "Okay."

If nothing else, it would spite my father. We stood up at the same time and headed toward the car. I checked the bank parking lot again, but no Mercedes in the reserved space up front. Clark Heraldson's grinning, naked body flashed behind my eyes and I shuddered just as the clock at the top of the courthouse chimed noon.

We drove most of the way home in silence. Jake rolled down the window to smoke his last Camel and crushed the empty pack into a ball. I pulled into Ray's to fill up.

"How ya been, stranger?" Ray smiled and pushed his teeth back.

"Okay, I guess. How 'bout you, Ray?" I unhitched the metal head and maneuvered the hose into the tank.

Jake got out and went inside the cluttered office for a pack of cigarettes from the machine.

"Been busy. Lots of tourists in town—folks from Nashville, Birmin'ham, Atlanta, even out of state. Hubert Odell's takin' peoples' pi'tures now, chargin' a dollar apiece for 'em." Ray chuckled and wiped his brow with a greasy rag from his hip pocket.

"What's all this about?" Jake asked from behind.

"Your friend a stranger? I thought ever'body knew 'bout deep-freeze Jesus. Hey, ya know what I got? Look here." Ray shuffled inside and returned with a magazine in his hand.

"*Advance* copy. They sent 'em from New York City to Jessie Odell and some of the county stores. Tammy down at the Qwik-n-Grab gave it to me. Won't go on sale in the rest of the country till next week." He handed it to me and Jake looked over my shoulder.

Princess Di smiled at us from her millionth-odd cover appearance, but the little blurb across the top read, "Give Me That Thawed-Out Religion." And sure enough, there on page 74 was Hubert and Jessie Odell, standing proudly on their porch in the dark next to a murky blob on the white freezer.

"If you hold the pi'ture across from ya like this," Ray took the magazine from my hand and backed up a few feet, "it's almost like seein' the real thing."

I squinted like a nearsighted person and could make out a profile, bearded and weepy, similar to what I'd seen before.

"I'm not sure I see it," Jake said. "Bounty, you should've told me 'bout this."

The article itself was short—only about three hundred words, with quotes from the mayor, the police chief, the pastor of First Holiness Church, and the Odells, of course. Miss Jessie came off sounding like Granny Clampett, which I guess was unavoidable, with statements like, "The Lord's turned my freezer into a divine TV set. It's tuning in to Jesus. He has a message for all those who'll listen."

I stood there thinking, *Great, so now there's audio to go with the visual.* References were also made to the Shroud of Turin, to the Mother Cabrini shrine in Colorado, and to a Mexico City billboard in which a plate of spaghetti hid the icon of Christ on the cross. I thought an allusion to "Where's Waldo?" would also have been appropriate.

"Got another copy at home if you want that one," Ray offered as I paid him for the gas.

"Show it to your daddy. What's he think of all this anyway? Ain't seen him in a while."

My father and Ray might pass for brothers now, both tanned and weary looking.

"He's been to the beach with Momma, but they're back now. I don't think he puts much stock in this," and I thanked him for the magazine as we drove off.

"So have you seen it?" Jake asked, all excited.

"Yeah, I saw it back when it first started happenin'. No big deal—a bunch of dents in the side of an upright freezer reflectin' porch light. It looks like some kind of bearded profile. Could be Jesus. Could be Willie Nelson, for that matter."

"Can we go see it tonight?"

"You really want to see it? It's a farce, Jake. Like everythin' else in this town," I said bitterly.

He didn't say anything, looked out the window as we neared the very subject of conversation. I softened, "We can go. Might as well end your stay with a bang. I'd hate for you to be so close and miss out. Especially now that everybody in the U.S. will think our whole town, probably our whole state, is populated with inbred Odell clones, runnin' around barefoot, dippin' snuff, handlin' snakes, and tunin' in God on the nearest appliance."

Jake laughed and ruffled the back of my head. It felt natural.

***

We spent the rest of the afternoon down at the creek, fishing, also according to his wishes. My philosophic ex-con brother was unusually quiet, and I wondered what he would take away with him from Clearfield, Tennessee. We weren't interested in fishing, at least I wasn't, so I finally broke the silence.

"So, you're really leavin' tomorrow?"

"I'm afraid so, Bounty. It's time. Time to start over where nobody knows I'm an ex-con, where it doesn't matter where I've been or what I've done. What about you? You gonna stick around?"

"What choice have I got? Heraldson's made sure I won't get my student loan. It's too late to apply anywhere else. I'm stuck here."

"You're only stuck here as long as you let yourself be." He yanked on his line and whisked it above us before recasting. Mine was wedged in the bank beside me, and I didn't care if some big fish, like old Max the wonder carp, snapped it in two.

"Then take me with you. I won't be any trouble, I swear. I can take care of myself," I pleaded.

"I'm sure you can and that's why I'm not worried about leavin' you here. But right now, I can't take anybody with me. Make sense? Besides, you got some unfinished business of your own here to take care of. How much peace would you have if you just up and left your folks right now? For me it's easy. I don't know them, haven't lived my life with them. For me, comin' here was a token, a symbol for myself of somethin' I needed to do. But you got ties here, Bounty. Whether you like it or not."

"Ties like a hangman's noose. I'm not sure how much more I can take. . . ." I looked off into the heat, the green expanse of pasture surrounding us, like a giant reclining, the curving hillsides like his chest and hips.

I thought about what Jake said, not just his words then, but the sum of all his words in the five days I'd known him. Like a cryptographer reversing syllables and comparing vowels, I wanted to break his code, discover all that he communicated beneath the words, unspoken artifacts buried behind his eyes. I felt like my father was right, that somehow Jake mailing the photograph had set everything in motion, that we were all converged in an intersection, crash-jammed into one another.

Mr. August came to mind, the little caricature of doom I'd imagined at the bank last week. I could almost hear him laugh, snickering at my plight. He was dressed out of character: instead of the dark suit, he wore a Hawaiian shirt and Bermuda shorts, a big Panama hat, and sunglasses. He sipped a drink with a little pink paper umbrella in it.

"You ever comin' back?" I asked.

"You want me to?" He sounded surprised.

I imagined him then in some country western bar, twanging his heart out for tourists older than my parents who'd just come from the *Hee Haw* extravaganza at the Johnny Cash Theater. Maybe in his spare time, he could go to college, study philosophy or religion, find a good little church, a good little woman. He'd be a happy man.

"Sure, if you want to," I said halfheartedly.

"Are you sorry I came?"

"I don't know," I said, and it was the truth.

⁓

That night after a burger-run to the diner, we parked just inside the gate of our pasture and came up behind the trailers, all crowded into a row like Monopoly houses. Darkness had just set in, and I knew it would be a busy night with all the advance copies of *People* floating around. Cars already lined the narrow median separating the highway and the steep ditches on either side. By the time we got there, probably a hundred or so pilgrims milled around.

The shrine had, indeed, become commercial: Hubert Odell charged people a dollar to have their picture made with the freezer, two dollars if you used his Polaroid camera. What he didn't tell folks is that the flash negated whatever shadowy image there was to be seen on the appliance in the first place. So you ended up with a dimly lit snapshot of you beside an upright freezer.

I know because Jake and I waited in line to have our picture made—his idea. He loved the place like I knew he would. Couldn't believe he hadn't noticed the crowds before this, or that I hadn't told him about it sooner.

He loved the carnival atmosphere, the shoddy little aluminum trailer with the cement block steps up to the porch, the way the Odells had chained off the front yard with clothesline. Jake insisted that we have a picture, a souvenir for him if not for me (he offered to pay for two) even after I explained that the flash would never capture Jesus' profile. "Of course it won't, then it wouldn't be a mystery, now would it?" And he laughed this laugh that was so rich and free-flowing I had to laugh too.

I had the same feeling as we shared knowing looks while overhearing bits of conversations. "Looks just like what I dreamed it would." "Have you seen *People* yet?" ". . . all the way from Louisiana, yessir, drove all day." "I brought a quart of still whiskey to leave. Figure if that don't please the Lord, nothin' will," the latter cackled by Booger Odell, Hubert's older brother, renowned for the quality of his homemade liquor and for urinating behind city hall on a regular basis.

Finally we took our turn, stood on either side of the image, a peculiar trinity if there ever was one. We cut through the picture line again and headed over to the small yard between the trailers. While we leaned against a five-hundred-gallon silver propane tank, I unrolled the pack of cigarettes from Jake's T-shirt sleeve while he waved the Polaroid film back and forth to speed up development time. The picture gradually faded in like an old TV set, the two of us standing awkwardly like red-eyed animals trapped next to a blur of bright white; we finally allowed ourselves to laugh out loud.

Over our shoulders the crowd expanded, the voices grew louder, and Hubert opened a new roll of film from the case he'd bought at Wal-Mart.

"Are people as stupid as I think they are sometimes, Jake?" I leaned next to him to see the photo again.

"Don't be so sure people are stupid. Who are we to say? Some people here tonight know more 'bout God than you and me probably ever will."

"Come on, Jake. You don't believe that, do you? I mean, what were you laughin' for if you think it's for real?"

"Just because I can laugh don't mean I know everythin', or think those people are fools. If you asked me, Do I think Jesus is really on the side of that deep-freeze? I'd say no. But at the same time, maybe there's somethin' there. Maybe it doesn't matter whether that's him on the freezer, but what matters is what the image reminds people of." He paused thoughtfully before continuing.

"Somehow that deep-freeze is funnier if I allow the possibility that there is somethin' holy about it. Does this make any sense?" He unfolded his arms and lit a smoke off mine.

"Yeah, sort of. I know what you're sayin', even felt it once. Back when Daddy first left in July, I came down here one night real late. Nobody was here. I wanted to believe it was real, just like I sometimes want to believe that my life makes sense but can't. I wanted to leave something, so I tossed a penny like it was a wishin' well."

"There may be hope for you after all."

The crowd was peaking now; the line for pictures snaked all the way out to the road. All the mingling feet sent puffs of auburn dust around in circles. Children ran and shrieked behind trees and other trailers, playing kick the can with an old Coke bottle. People surrounded our silver tank and one man jumped up on it with his own camera, a Nikon.

Suddenly I saw my mother edging her way through the crowd toward us. Before she reached us I could see her lips moving, inaudible words drifting into the din of the herd surrounding her. Just as she made a final lunge beside us, a shot rang out and the crowd fell silent except for a handful of screams.

Another shot and glass breaking. Someone was shooting out windshields somewhere along the roadside. Then I heard my father's voice.

"Damn trespassers. Don't mess with me, by God. I'll make you think Jesus is on that damn deep-freeze and send you to meet him if you don't get your cars off my land." Funny enough, he didn't sound drunk, only mad.

I jumped up on the propane tank and could see him, positioned behind a tree with his shotgun in hand. My mother was next to Jake down below me by this time. "Do somethin'," she begged. "It's his medication. He's all strung out. Do somethin'."

The crowd remained quiet, then suddenly Hubert Odell was on his porch with a shotgun of his own.

"Daddy," I yelled and waved my hand like a windmill.

He weaved into the edge of the crowd and tried to move toward us. People didn't know what to do. "I called the police," Miss Jessie stated matter-of-factly for all to hear.

"Let me through here," my father demanded. He pointed the barrel straight up and fired; it made his shoulders shake. But like Moses parting the Red Sea, everybody made a path for him.

My mother was in tears. "Jimmy, stop this foolishness. Let's go home before you get arrested or somebody gets hurt."

"Thought I told you to leave town." Daddy pointed the shotgun at his oldest son.

"You did. I leave tomorrow. You'll never have to see me again. . . . Put the gun down." Jake spoke in short, even sen-

222

tences as if experienced in crisis management.

"Bounty, thought I told you to take him to the bus stop. Did you disobey me?" I stood fixed on top of the tank, as silver as it could be in the moonlight.

"Leave him alone," Jake interrupted.

"I could blow your sorry brains out if I wanted to," my father whispered like a wild man. He sounded like a lunatic but not a drunk, a supplicant of the moon destroying the temple of idolaters. Maybe he'd lost it once and for all.

"Jimmy, Jimmy McGraw, listen here to me." It was Miss Jessie coming down the porch stairs with Hubert and his gun behind her. "This is a place of worship, Jimmy McGraw, and you ain't got no right to come out here shootin' and scarin' people half to death. If you got business with your family then go on home. We're all here to see the Lord."

She was a feisty one, I'd give her that.

"Like hell, you say. Place of worship?" he snorted. "You and Hubert worshipin' the almighty dollar. Pack a fools is what you all are. . . ." He spun around and got in Miss Jessie's face.

"Jimmy, don't," my mother whimpered.

"Shut up," he ordered.

"You're embarrassin' us. Stop it right now!" Momma came back with more courage than I thought she possessed, but it sounded tinny, a mother trying to curb a bratty child.

"Jimmy, listen to Eileen, don't do this, not in front of your children," Miss Jessie coaxed. "Go on home now and sleep this off and I won't press charges."

"Stop usin' my pasture for a damn parkin' lot, or it'll be me who's pressin' charges."

"I'll see what I can do. Now, go home and sleep it off."

"You think I'm drunk, you old biddy? Well, I'm not. I been sober for almost three weeks now, and it's been hell. If I were drunk do you think I'd be out here? I want them cars out of that field now." He aimed skyward and fired for the fourth time.

Miss Jessie began to pray, "Please Lord, help this wicked man see the light, and protect all these innocent men, women, and children from the devil who would destroy our sacred place of worship—"

My father pushed past both Odells and bounded up to the porch. He cradled the shotgun upright in a cupped palm with one hand and pressed his other shoulder against the freezer. It rocked once and then toppled over and skidded down the cement steps, face down on the sacred side.

The crowd let out a little gasp, and Miss Jessie cried, "Oh, dear Lord!"

Jimmy McGraw lost his balance in the process and fell on top of the deep-freeze spread-eagle, the shotgun thudding to the ground, fortunately without going off.

Hubert and Jake grabbed him, but he was spent, a rag doll with no remorse. We heard sirens then and both a sheriff's car and a Clearfield police car pulled up in blue and red swirls of light. They handcuffed my father and led him away.

I couldn't bear it any longer. I leaped over the head of a woman wearing a flouncy straw hat and took off through the field. My mother called out behind me, but I would not turn back.

I felt like an animal—no thoughts, no consciousness, just running faster and smoother than I'd ever managed before. When my foot caught in a gopher hole, I slowed and stopped at the barn, leaned against the wagon bed next to the gate. It was settled now in my mind; I would go with Jake, whether he liked it or not. I was half-surprised he hadn't followed me. Heat lightning crackled in the distance.

I took the long way around the house, out behind the chicken coops, hen house, smokehouse, around the rows of apple trees. The sky shimmered light again above the line of trees, a hairline crack threatening to shatter.

The path I followed was visible even in the dark, even with the moon hiding itself behind thunder clouds. I followed it, could see from the dim glow of lights on in the bathroom and kitchen, until it turned into a ditch row beside the gate that led down to the creek. In the still night air the cicadas and whip-poorwills had been replaced with the conversations of water, the springs gurgling music, urging the impending rain to join in. But only thunder replied, the faroff kind, faint and deep, like a bell pealing from miles away.

I jumped the gate and followed the overgrown gravel road down the hill. I headed on down till the land flattened out and wandered over toward the Ridley bridge. The wind inhaled and let out a swirl of warm air and rustling leaves overhead. I'd have to hurry to beat the rain.

Only, what did I need to hurry back to? To bail my father out of jail? Listen to my mother cry? I really was in no mood to hurry. I felt slow and at ease, comfortable with rain or no rain, even a lightning bolt. Let it come and let me be part of whatever it was.

Under the dark canopy of elms and baby oaks next to the banks, the bridge seemed like a dark room floating above the water. I sat down Indian style on the cool stone and felt removed from it all, distant as the jags of light that continued to cut through the cloudy sky. If I had a saving grace, I decided then, it was this very distancing—not detachment where you're cut off, but just a pulling back, a director heading to the balcony to check the scenery and props, the painter checking for depth and effect.

How long I sat there, like some kind of yoga instructor or Zen master, I don't know, but eventually I felt eyes on my back and heard a low breath like a soft growl. Slowly I turned my head and found the biggest chestnut eyes I'd ever seen. One of the Ridleys' horses, a big ebony mare marked up white, star-burst nose and anklets. She whinnied again and stuck her nose as far over the barbed-wire fence as she comfortably could.

"Hey, ol' gal, what you doin' out here spyin' on me?" I said.

I stood up, went over to the creekbank and up to the fence. She came over to me. I figured she'd be disappointed when I had no sugar or apples to offer, but she stayed and let me stroke her head and mane. Her horse smell so pungent, leather and earth, manure and saddle wax, a perfume all her own.

Before I knew it, I had pulled the wire fence apart and squeezed through, pulled myself up by her mane and was riding bareback across the Ridleys' land. This had always been forbidden growing up. When I was about ten I climbed the fence and rode one of Pete Ridley's ponies without asking him or my parents. Daddy gave me a harder time than Pete ever did. Daddy threatened me with all kinds of punishments, but instead made me muck out the Ridleys' stalls for a month.

Didn't seem like such a big deal to me when I'd done it. That's what horses were for, to ride. But like so many parts of my life, it scared my father, something uncontrollable perhaps, something that didn't belong to him. Looking back I wondered if Daddy was afraid that I'd like Mr. Ridley better than him, if he'd become the evil tyrant while our neighbor became the kindly surrogate father I'd always wanted.

The mare felt smooth and playful. She wanted to be ridden, wanted to do more than the canter I was keeping her at. But I couldn't see so well in the dark and didn't want to run her or me into the low branches. Finally, at the narrowest part of the creek, about three feet, she jumped of her own accord. I bounced so high and pulled so hard on her mane that I was afraid she'd buck me when we came down together on the other side. But then she took off.

Clouds and trees, water and rocks whirred by while my trusty mount took me for a ride, two shadows melded together into the night. It felt good to go so fast, something reckless and yet grounded, not like going fast in a car, which seemed artificial by comparison.

I could see the faroff lights from the Ridleys' farmhouse and prayed no one was looking out the window. Horses neighed and whinnied from the stables on the other side of their barn. I wondered how this one had escaped without the rest. But it didn't matter. All I cared about was hanging on, my head at eye level with hers, my back and butt parallel to hers.

I wanted to keep going, a Pony Express rider jumping fences and fording rivers, going and going, farther and farther away. We'd head west, through the flatness of West Tennessee, the bumpy Ozarks of Arkansas, down through the prairie lands of Kansas and Nebraska, over into Colorado, Utah, finally the coast, running on nothing but sheer adrenaline now into the sands, beyond the surf and white-capped waves to a depth we could no longer ford, going down together, one ship. But like some alien force-field, I felt bounded by the knowledge of my parents. I could not go.

When we'd tired of each other, the feisty mare properly returned to the stable under the cover of darkness. The first fat plops of rain were beginning to fall. I still had a ways to go to make it home, if that's where I was going, but I couldn't run. The rain picked up, fell more evenly and rounded as I looked up, felt warm and refreshing, bath water. I took cover under the roof of trees that sheltered the bridge. I wished I'd held on to Jake's new pack of Camels.

The horse ride and the rain seemed like gifts, something to keep me holding on. Twigs snapped in the dark to the side of me and I jumped.

"Been lookin' for you," Jake said out of breath as I almost lost my balance. The thundershower had dwindled to a soft sprinkle. "You okay? You look like a drowned rat." He looked more human and mortal than I'd seen him look before. It was funny, but he reminded me of the horse I'd just ridden, brown and strong, now tired and relaxed.

I smiled. "Nope, I'm fine. Just enjoyin' the rain."

"You've had one helluva day," he said. The rain stopped except for an occasional drop from the wet branches overhead. We both sat down and I took off my Nikes. The stream was warm from the rainwater.

"What's that smell? Man, you stink."

"Took a little horse ride."

"Horse ride? Where'd you find the horse?" Jake took his cigarettes out of his pocket. Most were crushed or broken, but I didn't care.

"Ridleys next door got horses. Haven't you heard 'em before?"

He shook his head, took a deep drag, and appraised the situation.

"Your momma's gone to check your daddy into the hospital. I drove her over to post his bail. He'll be all right."

"That's good," I said and felt uncomfortable, awkward with him and whatever sympathy he came to offer. They were my parents now, my father. Jake was the lucky one to be disowned and on his way out of town.

"I'm goin' with you in the mornin'," I announced.

"No," he said firmly. "We've already discussed this."

"Well, then, I'm goin' somewhere, as far as I can. There's not much else worse that can happen."

"What do you want to happen, Bounty? What good's runnin' away?"

"You tell me. You're doin' the same thing."

He waited a long time, and I thought I had him until he spoke. "No, if I were runnin', I never would've come here in the first place. I've tried to face up to my past, done everything I can do. Now I'm free to go on."

"So am I," I argued.

"Look up there," Jake pointed through the tree tops to a patch of sky. The clouds had parted and a handful of stars burned through. "What do you see?"

"Stars, some clouds," I said.

"You see the stars up there, Bounty? You see 'em, don't you? You fight so hard to see the stars and not the light. But for whatever reason, you do see light behind 'em. You see more than stars.

"Remember how you told me about your idea of an absent-minded professor who created us and now has to sit back behind

228

his two-way mirror and observe, helpless to intervene? You said he can only tap on the glass occasionally to remind us that he's there. Well, what if you're right? What if he taps on the glass all the time, reminds us night and day that he's there, just not the way we want him to."

I inhaled my last drag and snuffed the butt in the dirt beside me. My smoking abilities were definitely increasing, no coughing at all now. Maybe I better quit before I got too good at it. My thoughts turned back to what Jake had said.

"My point's still that he can't do anything but tap on the glass, though. I want somebody who'll break through the glass, who'll reach into the water and pull me out."

"Maybe he does and you just don't see it. You're standin' here, aren't you? You could've drowned that day you told me about, but you didn't. I could've died in prison half a dozen times . . . but I didn't. There's a lot of could've-beens in life, Bounty. How many's it take before we sit up and notice? I don't know 'bout you, but I've had too many. I think we all have, it just don't go our way all the time. He breaks through that mirror all right, but sometimes we forget that glass will fall, that we get cut even though ultimately he's rescuing us. I don't think his business is about coming out of the genie's bottle every time we rub and givin' us three wishes. I think he cares more 'bout us than solvin' anybody's problems."

"You're a crazy man, Jake. You don't have proof there's a God any more than I do. I can't figure you out. . . ."

"Maybe you're not supposed to. Thing is, I think he has to be crazier than us. You've heard there's a thin line between love and hate? Well, I think looking, really looking for him means admitting you're in love—and that's why we're mysteries to ourselves if we're honest. It's like walkin' that tightrope of a line every day of your life. Some days it cuts, and you bleed, sometimes it feels as good as sex. . . ."

"What about tonight? Today, for that matter? Where's the justice in somebody like Heraldson gettin' away with what he does? What's right about Daddy drinkin' my life away? What about him makin' a fool out of himself and our whole family tonight? That all points to God somehow?"

"You're a smart man, brother. Don't waste your life asking the wrong questions."

My anger burned in the darkness. We were back to me not knowing the right questions again, excluded, stumbling around somewhere on back roads while everybody else knew the password and found the main gate. I lit another cigarette even after I'd just decided to quit smoking.

"—And before you ask me what the right questions are . . . I can't tell you. Even if I wanted to. Your questions and my questions and the Odells' questions and the readers of *People* magazine's questions are likely all the same, but we'll never take 'em seriously until we ask 'em for ourselves. Me tellin' you what to ask won't do any good."

I tried to imagine a giant cosmic hand tearing through the fabric of night sky just then, plucking Jake and me like flowers, taking us on an Aladdin's carpet ride of tangible, verifiable proof. But how disappointing. The thought surprised me with its intrusion, and I wondered if I'd feel any different even if the giant hand did reach out and break the glass. Hell, maybe he already had.

"Mr. August," I whispered.

"August? What?" Jake sounded like an old man, hard of hearing.

"Summers have always been hard for me, Jake. I started thinkin' last week how August is always the cruelest month. Whatever crisis or drinkin' spell my daddy's on usually peaks then, but I also get to go back to school, back to the comfort of routine. And this year there's nothin' to go back to. I'm stuck here.

"I imagine August as this man who shows up like an IRS inspector, an accountant who juggles time, keeps me guessing. Just when I think I can't take any more, he'll give me a break. . . . You showin' up, for instance."

Jake nodded as I concluded, "August is a no-win situation."

"You willin' to forgive all the Augusts in your life, Bounty?"

I just looked at him, with a slice of moon suddenly outlining both our faces.

"What do you mean?"

"Let go of all those musty calendars you're hanging on to in your memory. Let August go back to being a month of the year. Instead of a scapegoat for your absent-minded professor."

I sighed and thought, *Here we go again*. Actually I liked the image of me clinging to all these old pages of calendar, squirreling them away like proof for my acquittal. But then Jake had to bring it back to God. I suddenly felt drained, the "weak trembles" my momma called them, like when I'd play basketball and my blood sugar dipped and I had to eat a couple candy bars before I'd feel like finishing the game.

I wondered what it would mean for me to let Mr. August go, if I even could. Hadn't I tried to banish him on my own, asked him politely to leave? When that didn't work, I'd kicked him out, only to have him beat me back inside. It felt more like he should ask me to forgive him. But somehow that seemed impossible, as impossible as him existing outside my imagination. For me to forgive him, well, I wasn't sure what that would look like.

"Every month is August, if we let it be. . . ." Jake seemed to speak without moving his lips.

"But it still comes 'round at least once a year," I added.

A whippoorwill competed with the husky cicadas. The line of elm trees that topped the steep ridge overlooking the creek shook like a dark clothesline in a strong breeze. As they recomposed themselves, it blew across us. Jake unfastened his ponytail and let the wind comb his damp hair. He looked handsome, an Indian greeting the evening spirits.

As much as I resented his sermon, I couldn't bear to think about him leaving.

-15-

"**B**et you never had prison pancakes," Jake said the
next morning.
"My mother makes good pancakes," I said as I
poured out juice.

He placed a steaming tower of even cakes before me. They
did, indeed, look different from my mother's, darker and flat-
ter, crisper. Light burst through the kitchen window then, as if
to accentuate the difference, as if the clouds had shifted and
yawned themselves away.

"So what's the secret? A little of the warden's blood?" I
poured what looked like half the bottle of Aunt Jemima over
my tower. The thin cakes soaked it up like sponges, expanded
to cover another quarter-inch of the plate. "Neat," I said.

"Nope—can't tell my secret." Jake sat across from me, and
we watched his pancakes inflate with syrup.

My mother had called already from the hospital. "He's doin'
real well, Bounty. But the doctor wants to keep him for obser-
vation for a couple more days. Is Jake still there? Thank him
for me, for last night."

232

"He's leavin' this mornin'," I said, not letting on that I was still inclined to go myself.

So I dawdled over my breakfast, had seconds, took my time in the bathroom while Jake packed his duffel bag. I found him sitting on the porch, all ready to go.

"You play that thing?" I pointed to the guitar case.

He smiled in reply and took out the golden Harmony guitar from its black case. "Got a request?" he asked.

"Whatever," I said. "Nothin' sappy."

He strummed across the six strings a few times, adjusted the heads at the top of the neck, tried a few chords until he corrected the pitch.

He lit into a fast one, lots of fancy frets and chord shifts. It reminded me of the jazz I'd heard on my mother's radio stations that summer, the upbeat dixieland stuff. Only this had more of a rock edge to it, Clapton maybe. I was pretty sure I'd never heard it before. His fingers blurred, and I picked out a recurring melody, subtle beneath all the fancy overlay. When he stopped I applauded.

"What's it called?" I asked.

"The Bountiful Blues," he said and grinned up at me.

"Come on—what's it really called?"

"Like I said. I wrote it in prison, and it ain't had a name till now."

I was flattered and wished I had a gift for him. But this meant it was really time to go. I couldn't keep the water behind my eyes any longer.

"What's wrong, man? You okay?" He seemed too close, too far away. Jake stood up and leaned his guitar against the porch column, put his arm around my shoulder. I shrugged him off.

"Go ahead and leave. I don't give a damn. You're no different than anybody else. You're probably worse because you pretend to care. Lousy ex-con." He pulled me to him then, tight and strong, like being bound with wire, and I hugged back.

"It's okay, little brother, it's okay. I understand. We've never had a brother before, and now we do." He swallowed hard and

233

his Adam's apple bobbed up and down his neck. "I do care about you, I swear I do . . . I got what I came for—the best parts of our old man are in you. If I never see him, I've seen enough of what's good in you. I'm leavin', Bounty, but I won't run out on you. . . ."

His words were the right ones, not that I wanted to hear them, but they came from somewhere else, from an eclipse of the moon or an apparition on the side of a deep-freeze. I'd never had a brother before, and as hard as I tried, I couldn't deny that I had one now. I couldn't deny that it made a difference.

I don't know how long Jake hugged me, but finally the phone rang and I broke away. It could only be my mother since it wasn't yet nine o'clock. I watched my brother put his guitar back in the case, lock it shut, while the phone rang two more times.

"Hello," I said and tried to hide the emotion in my voice.

"Bounty?" a familiar voice rang in my ear. "Bounty, this is Doug Rosenstein down at the bank. I need to talk to you ASAP. Can you come in right now?"

"Uh, I guess so. I thought you were on vacation. Is this about why I got fired? I swear I didn't take that money, Mr. Rosenstein." I tried to regain my bearings.

"I know you didn't, son. Just come down here as soon as you can, and I'll explain everything. Thanks." He hung up.

I started to laugh, thinking about him explaining everything. He'd invite me into his office, pour me a cup of coffee, and then begin explaining my mother and father to me, the dynamics behind Clark Heraldson's particular brand of evil, the theosophy behind summers like mine.

"Who was that? We better leave for the bus station pretty soon. I called and mine leaves in an hour," Jake said. "What's so funny?"

"That was my branch manager down at the bank. Said he wants me to come down right now. Maybe I'm gonna get arrested. Maybe they'll have a father-son discount on my bail."

Jake shook his ponytail out of his collar. "Let me call the bus station back and see if there's a later one I can catch."

"Thanks." I went to change shirts.

⬤━━━

We loaded Jake's stuff in the old Mercury and headed down to the bank. When I saw the police car and people waiting in front of the bank, it only confirmed my fears. I was going to be arrested for a crime I never committed. I turned off the ignition. Through my rear-view mirror I could see Mrs. Sherman, BeBe, and Sarah Anne talking to a state patrol officer, a heavy-set man with a puffy face and droopy eyes. It was hard to believe he needed to interview all of them if he came just to arrest me. Maybe they'd been robbed during the night.

"I'll wait here. Holler if you need me," Jake said and rolled down his window.

As I paced over to the group, trying to look as concerned as possible, I realized that Rosenstein was missing. No wonder he didn't fit in—he was the counterfeiter. He'd called me down here to take his rap. Maybe he and Heraldson were in cahoots.

"Bounty, we're so glad you're here," Mrs. Sherman said as if she were hosting an open house.

"What's going on? Am I in trouble? We get robbed?"

BeBe and Sarah Anne both looked more excited than when the *People* magazine reporter came to town.

"You'll never believe what happened! Clark Heraldson's skipped town. He's been embezzling money from the bank. Can you believe it?" Sarah Anne squealed with delight. BeBe tried not to smile.

"What's she talkin' about, Mrs. Sherman? Has the bank gone under?" Mrs. Sherman took my arm and leaned on me as if she might faint. The patrolman had gone back to his car to take a call from the beeping, static radio on the dash. The morning sun seemed brighter than it had a right to be.

"There are state and federal agents in the bank right now,

Bounty, confiscating documents. They've already been to the main bank in Crescent, and other agents are at the two branches in Pikeville as we speak." Mrs. Sherman, with her name tag, Idabelle, pinned to her pansy-print dress, regained her composure. "I've even been subpoenaed," she whispered.

"Can you tell me what happened, Mrs. Sherman?" BeBe came up behind me and took my other arm while Sarah Anne tried to pump more information out of the cop.

"Mr. Rosenstein called me this morning about six, Bounty. Asked me to meet him here about an hour ago. He took me inside and sat me down in his office. He showed me a badge and ID. Seems he works for the FBI—or is it the TBI—one of those bureaus of investigation, I forget which."

BeBe squeezed my arm in suspense even tighter than she had the night we sat on the porch swing.

Mrs. Sherman continued: "It seems Mr. Heraldson, our bank vice-president, you know, is in some trouble. He's been embezzling, diverting funds into dormant accounts then transferring those to a California wire account in his own name. Been doing it for months, maybe years, Mr. Rosenstein said. Clark's always been such a good boy. I was shocked at first, said there must be some mistake. . . . The bank will be closed today, but should reopen tomorrow. As soon as the agents inside have finished you can talk to Rosenstein yourself. Maybe you'll get your job back." She smiled.

"And get your name cleared, baby," BeBe echoed.

Just then the front door opened and a tall, neat man in a dark suit ushered us inside. It took a few minutes for my eyes to adjust from the morning glare, but I could hear the door being locked behind us. The large patrolman stayed out front.

Rosenstein came out of his office with two other dark suits.

"I'm sorry to put all of you through this, I really am. But it can't be helped. Now, if I could just see each of you, one at a time, we can get finished and let you go home."

Mrs. Sherman sat in a lobby chair and fanned herself with a brochure on home loans.

"Jenkins," Rosenstein barked, "get this lady some water. Miss Devereaux, I'll begin with you.

"Jenkins, get these other people some coffee." A blond, Nordic-featured agent bounded up with water and the stained coffee maker pot from our tiny kitchen. BeBe sashayed behind Rosenstein as if she were about to take the witness stand.

No one talked while we waited, and it didn't take long. BeBe returned after fifteen minutes and Sarah Anne was called in. BeBe came over and whispered details to me at the coffee machine.

"Get ready."

"For what? I haven't done anything."

"Your daddy's involved somehow. He asked me if I knew anything 'bout the account. Mentioned James B. McGraw, Sr. Mentioned a couple other accounts and names, too." BeBe looked up at the blond agent standing erect with his hands at his sides. No one had said we couldn't talk, but BeBe and I continued to whisper.

"This is all I need. It's not like my father's not in enough trouble after last night."

"Is that hunk of a brother still in town?" BeBe added another packet of artificial creamer to her personalized mug.

"He's leavin' today; he's out in the car now. Got a job waitin' on him in Missouri. Here comes Sarah Anne. . . ."

Rosenstein motioned for me next, and Sarah Anne giggled like she'd just been asked on a date. Inside his office, Rosenstein seemed more powerful than I'd ever seen him before as he sat behind his desk.

"Try to relax, Bounty. Just a few questions we're required to ask all the tellers."

"Yessir," I swallowed hard.

"Do you know Clark Heraldson well? He hired you, right?"

"That's right. No, I wouldn't say I know him well. I mean, he invited me to his church, over to his house for a swim, but that's about it."

"Did you know he was embezzling funds through dormant

accounts and computer wire transfers? Did he ever give you any indication about these activities at the bank?"

"No, sir. I'm as shocked as everyone else."

Rosenstein nodded his head as if to say, "Right."

He continued: "Are you familiar with any of these accounts? Recall waiting on anyone who used these accounts? Listen closely. Thomas C. Harrison, account number 093438721, Ellen Solomon, account number . . ." and he rattled off half a dozen more.

I shook my head at all of them.

"What about this account, Bounty—James B. McGraw, Sr., account number 430329883?"

"That's my father's name, Mr. Rosenstein, you probably already know that. But he has lots of accounts, and I don't know anythin' about that one, or which one it is. Is my father in trouble?"

"I . . . we don't know yet. I don't think so, son. But this dormant account in his name has been used frequently, especially in the last few months. We'll need to talk to your father, of course."

I don't know why I didn't say anything. It sure wasn't to protect Heraldson. Only if I told part of what I knew I'd have to tell it all, including the feel of Heraldson pressed against me, the smell of his breath, the hate behind the blueness of his eyes. . . . Maybe it had been my fault, maybe I'd led Heraldson into thinking I wanted what he offered.

"Is there something you're not telling me, son?"

I began talking then, poured out the story about Jake, about me and BeBe discovering my father's dormant account and how I feared that someone was blackmailing him. Then I took a deep breath and told him about my student loan, about Heraldson's advances and threats, about being framed and fired earlier that week.

"Why didn't you tell anyone? Go to the police?"

I paused, wondering how to explain it to someone like Rosenstein. "I was embarrassed, I guess. Didn't want Heraldson spreadin' lies about me or anythin' . . . afraid folks might think I was . . . *different*."

He nodded. "I'm sorry that had to happen, Bounty. Anything else you think of that might be helpful?"

"No, sir, can't think of anything."

"If you do, give me a call." He leaned across the desk and handed me a card just as his phone rang. He pressed the phone to his ear, didn't say a word, then slammed it down like a hot iron. We both jumped up. "Jenkins," he yelled, rising to his feet, "get Bruszenski on line one. They picked up our man in Atlanta International on a flight to the Caymans."

I felt giddy telling Jake all the news, and he insisted we stop for a cup of coffee to celebrate. Stopping at the Qwik-n-Grab, I bought a single can of beer instead.

Jake popped the top and said, "To better times ahead." We sat there for a few minutes in silence, next to the Dumpster in a parking lot in a small town that used to be mine, trading sips back and forth even though it was barely ten o'clock in the morning.

At the bus station in Pikeville, big Greyhounds lined the parking lot and side streets. His bus hadn't left yet, had been running late out of Chattanooga, and so we waited a few minutes in the lounge area. An old black lady watched *Donahue* on the screen elevated in the corner while two little boys fought over a matchbox Corvette.

Sitting on the edges of orange vinyl seats, Jake took out a worn leather wallet and said, "Look." He took out dog-eared pictures of his mother, of our father standing next to an old race car, a picture of his grandparents, of the man named Ben. In the last clear plastic square was a trimmed-down Polaroid of two brothers standing next to a white blob on a trailer porch. I regretted not getting my own picture made, but I felt hopeful, something was changing, as I heard Mr. August whispering in my ear.

"You remember the question you asked me yesterday?" I said as a big silver bus roared into the loading zone.

"Which one?" Jake looked at me, replaced the billfold in his hip pocket.

"About whether I was sorry you came or not."

"Yeah, I remember."

"Well, I'm not." Neither of us wanted to repeat the good-bye we'd already said that morning on the porch. We both started laughing then, and it buoyed my hopeful feeling even more.

"I want to hear from you. To visit you. For you to come visit me." I wanted to be sure it would really happen.

"I will. I promise." He hugged me again, then pulled back.

"You're some piece of work, Bounty McGraw. I've got one helluva brother." He smacked my face, gently, with his open palm, laughed again, and shook his head.

As he was pulling away in the big gray bus displaying "St. Louis" in the destination window up front, my eyes brimmed with water again, but I let him go and promised myself that we'd continue to be brothers.

By the time my parents came home from the hospital on Friday, Clark Heraldson was being held in Nashville on a string of white-collar charges. The *Crescent Courier* had gone to press a day early to provide the latest coverage. It seemed Heraldson was a bigger rat than even I originally suspected. He was alone when they picked him up in Atlanta. His wife and daughters were found at her parents' home outside Lexington. Carole seemed oblivious to the entire affair. Clark had hired Stan Howard as local counsel—he gave no comment to the press— as well as some Washington big shot who'd been an assistant to the assistant DA in the Watergate hearings.

I couldn't get over it. As much as I hated the man and thought he was getting what he deserved I still felt sorry for him. "Goes to show," Mrs. Sherman opined in one of her newspaper quotes, "you just don't ever really know what goes on in someone's head."

Heraldson's name made the Nashville and Huntsville six o'clock news, CNN, and the lower right corner of *The Wall Street Journal*. The list grew to include embezzlement, forgery, wire fraud, mail fraud, and several other terms I'd never seen before. I thought back to us standing in the doorway of his bedroom, his hand on my chest. What if I'd agreed? What then? Would he have let me in on his scheme, asked me to forge names and fake wire transfers at my oak-veneer teller's window? And what struck me most was, I might have done it.

My father was almost feeble as my mother helped him from the car. It was awkward, of course. I came out and stood shyly on the porch until they made it to the door. Then I shuffled up and received a loose hug from each of them. My father smelled of lotion and citrus aftershave.

He'd been subpoenaed that morning before he left the hospital. If he agreed to work with the state and testify against Heraldson, all charges of conspiracy—because of his knowledge of what had been going on—would be dropped.

After my father had been nestled into the dentist's chair with extra pillows, he looked over at me, leaning against the bar, and asked, "Your brother gone?"

I nodded in reply.

He breathed deeply and shut his eyes. My mother stood in the door, and I motioned for her to come in.

"I have something I need to tell you both." I knew if I didn't tell them first thing, I never would.

My mother looked at me, saying, "Can it wait?" and communicated with her eyes that it better wait.

My father roused up. "Let him talk."

"Judy Tate called from the bank today. When they were

cleanin' out Clark Heraldson's office they found a lot of unprocessed loan forms locked in his desk. She said that the bank decided to go ahead and process all documents previously signed and dated unless there was suspicion of criminal activity. What I'm sayin' is, they found my student loan application, and it had been approved. They cut a check today and mailed it to Knoxville."

I'd spent all day brooding over it. Despite everything that had happened that summer, despite the events that very week, my father's excess and my brother's exit, the hardest punch came when I hung up the phone and heard Judy Tate's voice buzz in my head. "You'll be all set when school starts in a couple of weeks. Good luck, Bounty," she'd wished.

I couldn't believe the tug-of-war in my gut—this was exactly what I'd wanted, what I'd longed for, not just this summer, but for most of my life, to put them behind me, to forget Clearfield was even on the map, and move on to a new role, a new setting with different props and happy actors.

Down by the fishing spot, and later by the stone bridge, I'd wandered around inside the only life I'd ever known, sorting through the snapshots of my upbringing. There could be no other life than this one. It was all I knew.

I could not go, my parents needed me. My father needed something, if nothing else a guardian. And my mother—how could she cope with her delusions of affairs that never happened, with marriage to a man who squeezed her heart back and forth like an accordion? No matter now much weight she lost, how much she cut her hair, how many jazz pieces she mastered, it would never be enough to take my place.

Then I remembered Jake's words the night after my parents returned unexpectedly from the beach, coupled them with the words he spoke after Daddy busted up deep-freeze Jesus.

No matter how long I stayed, I could never forgive them without some distance, without some letting go of the steering wheel that had come off in my hands. And as much as that would hurt them, they could never get on with their lives as long as I hung around trying to patch things along for them.

As much as the knots in my stomach evolved into some kind of living being, turning painfully inside me, as much as I felt wrenched and knew they would feel wrenched, I would go away. Away to college in a city several hundred times bigger than the town that would always live on inside me. That's why I had to tell my parents first thing.

After my news, neither one of them moved from their sad tableau for several moments until my father clasped my mother's hand. I didn't know what else to say, how to make it any easier on them. Daddy shut his eyes again, and Momma finally sat on the couch. I was braced for a fight, for the hard words that would have to be said to ensure my hard freedom, for my mother's weepy manipulation, my father's fierce and angry control.

Instead, the room itself sighed with a kind of relief. In fact, I was disappointed that they didn't put up a fight, was caught off guard by their silent resignation. We were all strangely comforted by the passing of the beast that had bound us together for so long. Maybe now something else could grow in its place.

⸺⸺

I can't recall in detail the other conversations I had with my parents before I returned to school. I know there were several, but only two come to mind. The first was with my mother on the following Sunday afternoon as we drove to Nashville for back-to-school sales. It was funny; my mother seemed to accept my going away to college with a calm resolve, but panicked over the new clothes I'd need, how I'd furnish my dorm room.

Once we hit the interstate, she turned down the radio and glanced over at me. "It's been a long summer, hasn't it?" she said.

"Yes, ma'am, you could say that." I meant no disrespect but didn't want to chit-chat.

"I'm sorry. We never meant to hurt you. Your father feels really bad about what happened at the Odells. I think he even feels bad over how he treated Jake."

"Too late now," I said.

"Yes, it is, Bounty, but you're about to begin a whole new life of your own." I hoped she wouldn't get weepy on me. "And I hope you won't make some of the same mistakes that your father and I have made."

"Me, too," I chimed in and wondered where she was going with the conversation, if she was working up to talking me into staying home.

"We all do things when we're young, Bounty, that haunt us. That's why I've always cautioned you about who you date and what you do." She paused and old anger flared up in me. I silently dared her to bring up BeBe, then wondered if she even had ideas about what BeBe meant to me. I turned my head and watched a big Deere tractor plow under an empty-eared corn-field.

"Your father was married before. When he was young, he got a girl pregnant—in Alabama or somewhere. She was unstable, drank too much; they had a baby and your father was racin' cars to make a livin'." She poured out details in random order, whatever came to mind, verifying what I'd already accepted from Jake. "He left after she had a breakdown and went back to Florida to her people. He came to Tennessee and started workin' for TVA. They never officially got divorced, but after so many years had passed and they hadn't heard from each other, well, he figured it was the same as legal."

"I know." The Olds seemed to take off, faster over the stretch of I-24 between us and Hickory Hollow Mall. Green belts and rocky hills whizzed by. My mother's knuckles glowed pale through her tan hands gripping the steering wheel.

"Jake's a good man, isn't he? Like you." She looked over at me, and it was the first adult look she'd respected me with my whole life. I glanced at the speedometer to see if we were going faster or if it just felt that way.

By this time we'd reached the mall exit and my mother seemed afraid to speak again.

"How's Daddy mixed up with Heraldson?" I asked.

She pulled into the mammoth parking lot, past the fast-food places and little strip malls on either side, and found a parking place where a minivan was just pulling out.

"Last spring your father went to close an old account, one he'd used to pay for his first wife's mental hospital. After she died he'd forgot about the account until the bank changed computer systems and updated. When he went to close it, he found a huge sum of money in it—over a hundred thousand dollars. He told them it had to be a mistake. He made an appointment with Heraldson the next day, but when he checked the account it was back down to nothin'. Heraldson tried to explain it away."

I reached across and turned the ignition so that my electric window would roll down.

She touched her hand to her face and continued: "When your father wouldn't let it drop, Heraldson blackmailed him. He traced the mental hospital, found out that Jimmy'd never divorced his first wife, that she had been crazy, and that there was a son in the Florida State Prison. Your daddy agreed to keep his mouth shut and let Heraldson use the old account. It's that simple. Your father did the only thing he could've done to protect us. . . . He didn't want us hurt."

I was sweating by this time. Afternoon shoppers trickled back and forth with baby strollers and shopping bags, on-sale grills, and withered perennials. It made sense and fit most of the pieces together. My mother got out of the car then, eager to lose herself in the cool, cavernous retail expanse of new jeans, khakis, and undershirts to be purchased for me.

The rest of the day I thought like a film director, imagined scene after alternative scene between Clark—the villain who'd sold his soul for the good life—and Jimmy, the lovable alcoholic protagonist torn between two families. I couldn't get it right no matter how many times I replayed it or how many versions I imagined. I think what surprised me was that my father didn't ask for a cut of Heraldson's take. Or maybe he did and Clark laughed in his face. Maybe my father really was trying to protect us.

⸻

I wanted to ask my dad about it the next day as he sat on the porch swing and watched me wash the Mercury. By the time I'd taken my shirt off and was waxing the hood and front fenders, he'd come out to stand in the driveway and supervise.

"Need some help?" he offered.

"No, sir, I think I've about got it." Since he'd come home from the hospital this second time, he was docile, like a kitten, quiet. His medication had been cut in half, but he still slept a lot. He didn't even look like himself in a pair of green golf pants and a yellow polo, hair slicked down. His sideburns now looked totally white and I wondered why he hadn't borrowed Mom's Miss Clairol for his usual touch up. My father now embodied the new South, the past desperately disguising itself as the present.

"What's he like?" He couldn't hide the lilt in his voice, the sound of a man realizing he'd missed an opportunity, something irretrievable.

"He's . . . well, you'd like him if you gave him a chance. He's a good man. He was sincere about what he said to you, what he offered." My throat was dry from inhaling the greasy smell of car wax. I laid the chamois buffer on the gray fender and stood up straight. My father's eyes watered in the noon heat.

"Maybe so," he said, and I wondered if he could even recall what Jake had offered.

He leaned forward, took a step, then pivoted in new-white tennis shoes I'd never seen before.

"You still set on leavin'?" His voice was flat and stoic.

This is it, I thought. *He'll try to talk me out of going.*

"Yessir, I am. Something I have to do."

"I understand. Time for things to change. For all of us."
And he turned and went inside.

As I told BeBe about these conversations a few days later, she
shook her head in disbelief. We were at the new Taco Bell, after
work, in the orange and white motif no-smoking section.

She sat across from me and nibbled a chicken burrito. I had
a steak fajita in front of me, but I couldn't quit thinking about
missing her after I left. Guacamole oozed through the side of
my tortilla on to my chin as I made a futile attempt to lean over
my orange tray. BeBe laughed as she handed me her napkin.

"Didn't this girl tell you? Didn't I say you'd be goin' off to
college this fall? . . . There was a dark time in there when you
couldn't see it, but I never lost faith." Her tone reminded me
of our conversation the night my mother left, her story about
her uncle's revival when she was a girl.

"This time," I said, "maybe things have turned themselves
around."

"Heard from Jake?" She finished her burrito and moved
on to nachos.

"Yeah, he called last night. He's doin' okay, likes his job. He
was real excited that my loan came through and everything." I
reached across to share her nachos.

"So what now, white boy? You're off to the big city, and I'll
still be here."

"I'll write you. You can come visit me." I was serious.

BeBe stirred her last nacho in a drop of coagulated cheese.
"You mean it? I'm not too good at writin' letters."

"BeBe, I wouldn't have made it through this summer without you. But I'd care about you anyway. Of course I mean it."

She adjusted her leopard spot headband as if it was too
tight.

"I'm a sad sister, Bounty McGraw. I'll be missin' you. We
may still have us a romance before it's all over with." She smiled

that all-teeth smile, and I decided to work on getting her to join me at college in Knoxville.

—————

When I got home from lunch, I was surprised to find both my parents home and wondered if Daddy'd had another setback. But they assured me everything was okay. "We've just come from town, son," my father said from the porch. "Sit down here with us."

"We've been to the lawyer's office and the realtor's. Your daddy and I are gonna try a trial separation," my mother said matter-of-factly.

"Just for six months," Daddy chipped in, "until we get some things back in order."

Like they'd been in order before this summer, I thought.

I looked at them strangely, tilted my head like an owl and tried to see through to the bottomline, estimate the potential for future heartache from this. Mine seemed minimal at this point, and theirs . . . well, they were two adults, I figured. Let them try it. I wouldn't have to be there to watch.

They'd found my father an apartment in the old Jeffries Hotel in Crescent. A family-owned furniture store now occupied the lower floor. It would be convenient for him to have the Chuck Wagon on the square just a few blocks away.

"You'll come visit me when you come home, won't you?" he asked. I couldn't believe this was the same man I had feared, loathed, and longed for most of my life.

"Yes, I will."

—————

On the Saturday morning at the end of August when I pulled out of our driveway over the hill, nothing felt like I'd expected it to. Here was the day I'd anticipated for half my life—emancipation and all that—and I felt . . . well, sad in a giddy way, like sweet and sour sauce, the one my mother marinated chicken in sometimes, full of vinegar, full of honey. I felt like a traitor, betraying them, leaving them to fend for themselves, or like a woman I read about who pulled into a service station off the interstate and left her kids in the rest room. But I left anyway.

My mother cried and my father wiped sweat off his brow with a red kerchief. "Call us when you get there," my mother said. I promised I would. "Drive careful," my father warned. I promised I would. Then just as I was about to get in the car, I went over to them, standing there close together, my father's arm around my mother's waist, and said, "I love you both."

I drove away and part of me never came back; a part of me buried itself beneath the house, down in the cellar, under the foundation, encased in memory.

I slowed and honked for the fun of it as I passed the Odells' trailer even though no one was up or out yet. After my father toppled the deep-freeze, the profile of Jesus was badly scarred and scratched beyond its previous glory. Personally, I thought it looked more authentic, like Christ might have actually looked after dying and rising again. But crowds slacked off when the scandal with Heraldson broke and siphoned both public and media attention away from the divine.

Miss Jessie had told the paper last week, I read, that they were going to take the deep-freeze off the porch and set it up down in the old school gym, which now functioned as a senior citizens community center. They would hire a "lighting expert" to duplicate the porch light effect and try to recreate the holy image of our Lord and Savior. I think everyone felt the same as I did, though—it would never be the same. Its time had passed, like the summer itself, and trying to prolong it seemed futilely disconnected from what it had originally been.

As I drove through Crescent, down Patsy Cline Boulevard, around the square with the courthouse still clashing against itself with old stone and new mirrors, past the Crescent County National Bank, which looked small and pitiful in light of all that had happened, I couldn't help but remember my adult glasses, the way I saw things at the beginning of the summer, my snapshots of old men at gas stations and creekbeds that ran for miles in sheets of green. Now they didn't feel so much like glasses as permanent lenses, undeveloped parts of consciousness and sight suddenly sprung to life, triggered not so much by events but by some internal sense of timing or some mysterious hormone.

By the time I hit the interstate, with its eighty mile stretch between me and Chattanooga, I lowered my sun visor and discovered something remarkable. Clipped to the underside of the visor was a Polaroid of me and Jake standing next to the Odells' deep-freeze. On the side of the freezer was an image of Jesus like I'd never seen before.

Epilogue

I endured the fall like a visitor from another planet, each experience new, even the mundane—lines in the cafeteria, chemicals in the biology lab—strangely exciting. Autumn brought a warmth of color to East Tennessee, red maples, yellow to burnt orange elms, all melting together.

I enjoyed the classes, the purchasing of books, weekend ballgames where the Volunteers clashed against some other collegiate rival, the intramural games I joined in with other boys from small towns in Tennessee and elsewhere, some, like me, already men.

That fall I walked around campus late at night occasionally, up beyond fraternity row and the athletic fields, around Circle Park and the beacon of The Torchbearer, to the library and back again.

I would imagine what was happening at home, my old home, with high school football games and harvest festivals, old men in overalls at the barbershop discussing this week's game, drinking colas with peanuts in them. The air there would have taken on a twinge of something cool and crisp, just catching up to

251

the Smoky Mountain air where I was. I would imagine my parents sitting together on the front porch swing enjoying the night, all the golden-orange beech leaves piled in the dark beyond them.

I did not return home until Christmastime that year. By then BeBe had visited twice, I had four letters from Jake, and my parents and I had settled into a routine of weekly phone calls. I had a full semester under my belt by then, had finally learned my way around campus, had made friends in the dorm and in classes. When I went home for the holiday break, it was for the last time.

My parents had decided not to get a divorce, but to sell the house and move into a new development outside of Crescent, a split-level with guest rooms and walk-in closets, built-in appliances, and an entertainment center. There was a community pool, tennis courts, jogging path, and hot tub.

My mother quit her job and started keeping books at the car lot—despite her innocence, Janet had been fired.

My father got older and richer looking thanks to the E-Z Sun Tanning Salon that opened right after I left. He continued to dress like a golfer, even on into the fall, and I never got used to seeing him in cardigans and trousers during the holidays.

They seemed different, happy. They had endured the separation like penance, a couple of love-struck teenagers hindered by feuding families. My father started appreciating my mother and not just what she did for him (even if she did agree to do his laundry after the first month of their separation crawled by). They dated, whisked away to the Opryland Hotel or the Chattanooga Choo-Choo for clandestine weekends.

My mother kept her hair short.

So they sold the house to Barry Purcell who works for his daddy's construction company out of Pikeville. He has a wife

252

and four kids to enjoy the barns, pastures, and creek. I sorted through my room and kept little of it, a few pictures and books, some high school awards, and a poster or two. My parents kept less than I did, and I helped them pack up what they considered worth saving.

I invited Jake for Christmas, but he had met a woman he thought he loved and they were spending it together with her family. He promised that we would see each other by summer, even if he had to hitch back. I spent New Year's Eve with BeBe at one of her tonks with others of her friends and family. She had quit work at the bank, completed her beauty school courses, and would be transferring to the University of Tennessee that spring semester. She rode back with me and as we crossed the Crescent County line, it felt more permanent than before, perhaps because the house was sold, the land passed on to another family with their own secrets and anger and the veiled love between them.

"Whatcha thinkin' so hard on? How're you gonna juggle all your other girlfriends around me?" BeBe teased.

"It's funny, BeBe, when I think of last summer now, it's not because of any souvenir I've kept, or any pictures that I replay in my mind. It's more like lookin' at a part of myself, like stretchin' out my arm or foot, an old scar that's softened into a beauty mark."

"You're some kind of poet, Bounty," she complimented.

And I could've told her more. When I think of that summer now, words and images float through my mind like helium balloons or birds set free from cages. I can't encompass it all. "Is that really the question you want to ask?" Jake challenging with that sardonic smile of his. "What would it be like for you to forgive all the Augusts in your life?" I couldn't answer his questions then, and maybe now I'm just starting to, just beginning to listen to my own voice, to the real echo that resonates like a skipped stone across deep water.

That means shutting out other voices, putting my parents not to rest in the bitterness of the past, but in proper perspective. Not condemning them to a faceless, changeless future, but just letting them be. Forgiving them. Realizing that I need their forgiveness as well, need to let all of us open up the present for ourselves, to marvel at change. Every day I must choose to release them from the amber fossil of my exaggerated memory, bring them by lightspeed to whatever I have to offer, whatever love and pain I bear for them, accepting whatever they bear for me.

I'm not sure how or even why, but something in me turned last summer, a clock reset to a different rhythm of time and music, chimes that no longer go unheard. Everything does have meaning and not everything's worth the meaning I assign it.

Sometimes I catch myself enjoying the rush of the wind or a sunset so beautiful that it could never be sentimentalized if I tried. I listen to my own scratchy music filtered through whatever man I've become, am becoming.

Like my parents and myself, Jake, BeBe, all of us, Mr. August has changed as well. He no longer shows up at my front door in a dark suit and fedora with valise in hand. I see him now wearing cutoffs and Hawaiian shirts all the time, winking at me from behind trees and clouds. He's still a terrorist, an unwelcome guest at times, but he does whatever it takes to bring us back to ourselves, to something bigger than ourselves and the pitiful plinks of hopeless coins we toss in dry fountains.

He visits us all in some form or another and whether or not we let him in and ultimately forgive him is much more than a matter of personifying a calendar. It's how we handle images of Jesus on porch freezers, the age lines around our mother's eyes, fathers who polish love and violence from a bottle, brothers we didn't know we had, cobras that we nurse back to health only to have them bite us.

"You'd look good with a moustache, Bounty," BeBe interrupted my thoughts.

"I was thinkin' the same thing," I said and smiled.

There are times in our lives that cling to us like scales, but finally have to be unhooked, cleaned and examined, cooked, and eaten in a meal of great celebration, tears, and laughter.